The
TEMPLE

also by Stephen Spender

Poetry
20 POEMS
POEMS
VIENNA
THE STILL CENTRE
RUINS AND VISIONS
POEMS OF DEDICATION
THE EDGE OF BEING
COLLECTED POEMS 1928–53
SELECTED POEMS
THE GENEROUS DAYS
COLLECTED POEMS 1928–85

Plays
TRIAL OF A JUDGE
MARY STUART
THE OEDIPUS TRILOGY

Fiction
THE BACKWARD SON
THE BURNING CACTUS
ENGAGED IN WRITING

Prose
THE DESTRUCTIVE ELEMENT
FORWARD FROM LIBERALISM
LIFE AND THE POET
CITIZENS IN WAR – AND AFTER
EUROPEAN WITNESS
WORLD WITHIN WORLD
LEARNING LAUGHTER
THE CREATIVE ELEMENT
THE MAKING OF A POEM
THE STRUGGLE OF THE MODERN
THE YEAR OF THE YOUNG REBELS
LOVE–HATE RELATIONS
T. S. ELIOT
THE THIRTIES AND AFTER
JOURNALS 1939–1983

Stephen Spender

___The___
TEMPLE

GROVE PRESS
New York

Published by Grove Press
a division of Wheatland Corporation
920 Broadway
New York, N.Y. 10010

Library of Congress Cataloging-in-Publication Data

Spender, Stephen, 1909-
    The temple/Stephen Spender.—1st ed.
        p.   cm.
    ISBN 0-8021-1057-6
    I. Title
PR6037.P47T4 1988   87-35055
823'.912—dc19   CIP

Acknowledgement
The quotation from W. H. Auden on page v is from *The
English Auden* edited by Edward Mendelson, reprinted
by permission of Faber and Faber Ltd

Manufactured in the United States of America

First Edition 1988

10 9 8 7 6 5 4 3 2 1

The original manuscript was dedicated in 1930 to W. H. Auden and Christopher Isherwood. Now I add: 'With memories of Herbert List.'

Came summer like a flood, did never greediest gardener
      Make blossoms flusher:
Sunday meant lakes for many, a browner body,
      Beauty from burning:
Far out in the water two heads discussed the position,
Out of the reeds like a fowl jumped the undressed German,
And Stephen signalled from the sand dunes like a wooden madman
      'Destroy this temple.'

It did fall. The quick hare died to the hounds' hot breathing,
      The Jewess fled Southwards

          W. H. Auden, from the first of Six Odes (January 1931)

CONTENTS

Introduction   ix
English Prelude   1

PART ONE   THE CHILDREN OF
                  THE SUN   23
1 *The Stockmann House*   25
2 *The Weekend on the Baltic*   83
3 *The Alerichs' House*   103
4 *The Walk Along the Rhine*   109

PART TWO   TOWARDS THE DARK 133

Epilogue 'In 1929'   207

Two years ago, John Fuller (whom I now thank) told me that during a visit he had made to the United States he had read in the Rare Books section of the Humanities Center of the University of Texas the manuscript of a novel by me. It was called *The Temple*, and was dated 1929. I wrote at once to the Librarian for a xerox of this. A few weeks later, a young lady appeared at my London house with a bundle under her arm, which contained a copy of the novel. I had completely forgotten that in 1962, during some financial crisis of the kind to which poets are liable, I had sold the manuscript to the university.

There were 287 pages of what was more draft than novel. It was written in the form of a journal in the first person and was autobiographical. It was about the narrator (called 'S') going to Hamburg to stay with the family of a young German called Ernst Stockmann in the summer of 1929. In the first section, the narrator describes various characters he met in Hamburg that summer. Another section is about a walking tour along the Rhine on which he went with a friend called 'Joachim' whom he had met in Hamburg. Other sections are experimental. They were attempts at 'interior monologue', laying bare the innermost thoughts of Ernst and Joachim. There was also some account of 'S''s trip with Ernst to a Baltic resort. In the last section 'S' returns to Hamburg, but in the autumn of 1929, not as I have made him now do, in November 1932.

I have drawn extensively on the manuscript in rewriting the opening section and also that about the journey along the

Rhine. But I scarcely glanced at the rest because my own memory, combined with the exigencies of narrative and the perspectives of hindsight, wrote or rewrote most of the book for me.

I remember typing out several copies of a slightly later version of *The Temple* which I sent to friends, among them Auden, Isherwood, William Plomer certainly – to get their views about it – and a copy to Geoffrey Faber, my publisher. Faber pointed out that there could be no question of publishing a novel which, besides being libellous, was pornographic according to the law at that time.

In the late Twenties young English writers were more concerned with censorship than with politics. The Wall Street crash which was to spread shock waves of economic collapse and unemployment throughout the world and which would soon make Germany the scene of struggle between Communist and Fascist, did not happen until 1929. 1929 was the last year of that strange Indian Summer – the Weimar Republic. For many of my friends and for myself, Germany seemed a paradise where there was no censorship and young Germans enjoyed extraordinary freedom in their lives. By contrast England was the country where James Joyce's *Ulysses* was banned, as was also Radclyffe Hall's *The Well of Loneliness* – a novel about a lesbian relationship. England was where the police, at the order of Mr Mead, a London magistrate, took down from the walls of the Warren Gallery pictures from an exhibition of D. H. Lawrence's paintings.

Censorship, more than anything else, created in the minds of young English writers an image of their country as one to get away from: much as, in the early Twenties, Prohibition resulted in young Americans like Hemingway and Scott Fitzgerald leaving America and going to France or Spain. For them, drink; for us, sex.

Another result of censorship was to make us wish to write precisely about those subjects which were most likely to result in our books being banned. There was almost an obsession among young English writers at this time to write about things which were, as subjects of literature that could be published, forbidden by law.

All this explains, I think, a good deal about *The Temple*. This is an autobiographical novel in which the author tries to report truthfully on his experiences in the summer of 1929. In writing it I had the sense of sending home to friends and colleagues dispatches from a front line in our joint war against censorship.

That I really felt like this is shown, I think, in some lines I wrote in a letter to John Lehmann – sent a bit later than 1929 from Berlin – and quoted by him in his posthumously published *Christopher Isherwood – A Personal Memoir*:

> There are four or five friends who work together, although they are not all known to each other. They are W. H. Auden, Christopher Isherwood, Edward Upward and I . . . Whatever one of us does in writing or travelling or taking jobs, is a kind of exploration which may be taken up by the others.

Writing *The Temple*, I felt that I was very much one of my generation, exploring new territory of living identified with a new literature. This was the time when the title of almost every anthology or literary magazine incorporated the epithet 'new'.

The series of Odes in Auden's *The Orators*, each one dedicated to a friend, and with the reference to 'Stephen' and 'the temple' in the first Ode, stresses this sense of the shared adventure.

This was 1929 – just before the Thirties when everything became politics – Fascism and anti-Fascism. In the first part of *The Temple* Paul believes that he is sharing a 'new life' with German friends – a happiness to be found in Weimar Germany. There is bitter irony then in the fact that he should do so in that country which within four years was to be taken over by the Nazis who imposed on it, through their tyranny, the most rigid censorship.

There is, however, in the first half of the novel some sense of terrible events to come which cast their shadows over my young German characters.

Re-writing, I have heightened the contrast between summer

sunlight and winter darkness by advancing the date of Part Two of the novel to 1932 (originally both parts took place in 1929). The encroaching atmosphere of dark politics covering the whole landscape is the night into which my German characters are seen moving. To have advanced Part Two to 1933 would have been effectively to have transformed them by extinguishing them. The political interpretation of everything preceding 1933 by everything succeeding it would have made them and German youth during the period of the Weimar Republic seem irrelevant to the post-1914 violent and war-torn twentieth century. *The Temple* is pre-thirties and pre-political.

In this novel several pages about Hamburg overlap with my memoirs *World Within World*. When I was writing the parts of that book about my stay in that city, I raided the manuscript of *The Temple* and in reworking *The Temple* I have drawn occasionally on *World Within World*. I found that I could not invent purely fictitious characters to fit into an autobiographical novel. I could draw only on memories of people I knew, developing their characters according to the requirements of the fiction and of hindsight. Thus 'Simon Wilmot' is a caricature of the youthful W. H. Auden as is 'William Bradshaw' of the slightly less youthful Christopher Isherwood. Both are much changed here, fantasized in one passage when, on the Baltic, Paul imagines them walking into the hotel dining-room where he is sitting, bored to distraction by Ernst.

In Hamburg I became a friend of Herbert List who is the 'original' on which I draw the portrait of Joachim Lenz. List was then a young coffee merchant. He later became famous as a photographer. Between 1929 and the early 1950s I did not see List. The later passages about Joachim are invention.

The Temple is then a complex of memory, fiction and hindsight. Hindsight is certainly the most decisive of these, for it made me realize while I was reading the manuscript how it referred back to 1918 and the First World War, and was in turn looked back on from the standpoints of 1933 and 1939. 1929 was the turning point of the *entre deux guerres*, something of which I seemed prophetically conscious in the poem 'In 1929' which I wrote that year. This poem forms the central point of *The Temple* in a discussion of it between Joachim and Paul. 1929 can be looked on as the last pre-war, because pre-Hitler, summer, bearing the same relation to February 1933 as July 1914 does to August 1918.

The geography of Hamburg and the Rhine is left vague here, because this Germany is really a country of Paul's autobiographical fictionalizing. There are distortions of history to suit the author's youthful mood throughout *The Temple*.

London, 20 April 1987

What Paul loved about Marston was his self-evident (so he passionately believed) innocence. He had noticed this quality the moment he first saw him, early in their first term together at Oxford.

Marston was standing in the college quad one late afternoon, a few yards away from his fellow members of the college football team. These were engaged in one of their post-prandial orgies, running frenziedly round in circles, passing from hand to hand a loaf of bread stolen from the college kitchens to serve as a football. With a shout of 'Get him!' occasionally two or three would combine to dive together and grab another's balls. Marston seemed not to know whether he belonged or did not belong to this exercise. He stood at its edge looking on, a very slight smile on his lips. The top of his head was round, with close-cut hair, helmeting his quiet features. He had the slightly puzzled look of one who feels lost among companions, blaming himself perhaps because he does not fit in.

Paul, who was witnessing this scene from the college lodge, broke through barriers of his own shyness, and invited Marston to a drink in his rooms. Over beer he asked him questions about himself. Marston answered straightforwardly. He told Paul that his father was a Harley Street surgeon with a liver complaint; thus he frequently got angry with his son. Paul could not imagine anyone in any circumstances getting angry with Marston. Dr Marston had wanted his son to join the University Boxing Club. So, out of sweet docility (Paul thought), to please his father he became a University Boxing Blue. But, as he almost jauntily told Paul, having to fight in a match terrified him. 'I get sick before it and turn pale green all through, old son.' Paul asked him what he thought of Hell Trigger, as he was known to

1

his friends, Captain of the college rowing eight. Hell Trigger's voice could be heard yelling obscenities from the quad. 'He seems a very decent sort of chap, but I'm not sure whether I'd want to see or be seen with him twenty-four hours after I go down from the University, old son.'

Paul became a rather over-concerned confidant of Marston. He asked him questions and got truthful answers. He never felt certain that Marston liked telling so much.

One day, Marston said that what he most enjoyed was going on a sail-boat alone; but perhaps even more than this, solo flying. He belonged to the University Flying Club and his ambition was to become a pilot. He also liked going on long solitary walks in the English countryside, which he thought the most beautiful in the world (he had been once to Yugoslavia and once, for skiing, to the Alps). He loved the West of England. Hesitantly, Paul suggested that during the Easter vacation they go together on a walking tour. Marston jumped at this. He said he had always wanted to walk along the river Wye. He produced maps. They fixed a date – 26 March – when they planned to take a bus from London to Ross-on-Wye.

The walk, lasting five days, was a total failure. Paul, thinking that Marston must be bored by poetry, had spent the week before they left swotting up books on sailing, aircraft and boxing. After a cup of coffee in Ross-on-Wye, they found their way to a towpath along the river bank. As soon as they had started off Paul began talking about new types of aircraft. Marston, though polite, seemed bored: and when Paul changed the subject to sailing boats, he seemed scarcely more interested. While walking on the morning of the second day, through a countryside where leaves showed on tips of boughs like jets of flame, Marston said he had a stomach ache. It seemed to Paul that for Marston to admit that he had a pain could only mean that he was in torment. For the next hour, he watched him without saying anything for fear that the effort of answering might be too much. At last, he asked anxiously: 'Are you still in pain? Should we go to a village and try to find a doctor?' 'Oh, do shut up,' said Marston. 'You fuss over me like an old hen!' Then he added, 'I think I'll do a shit under those trees,' and walked away.

2

On the third day a diversion was provided by a dog which attached itself to them, following them all day through fields sprouting green until dusk, when its owner, a farmer, caught up with them, shouting that they had stolen his dog and that he would sue them for theft. He took down their names and addresses. This was an excitement that for two hours relieved their boredom.

That night they stayed at a bed-and-breakfast boarding house where they had to share a bed. Neither of them slept. Next morning, Marston got up saying: 'Sharing that bed gave me a pretty grim idea of marriage, old son.' They ate breakfast in silence.

Later Paul, who had brought his Brownie box camera with him, took a photograph of Marston seated on the river bank and poring over a map spread out across his knees.

When they returned to London, Marston was the first to jump out of the coach on to the pavement. Without turning his head to say goodbye he walked briskly away. Paul was looking at Marston's back as he heard him whistle a tune from the American musical comedy hit, *Good News*.

The photograph was pale: greyish fields, whiplash leaf-tipped boughs of willow trees seen black against the gleaming river tiger-striped with wavelets. A nineteen-year-old boy in old grey flannel jacket and trousers sat on a grassy river bank, leaning over a map which should have been their happiness. He looked like an English Great War pilot in France studying a map of the Western Front. Beyond the helmet-shaped back of his head, only the edge of his cheek and one side of his nose showed. He seemed strangely alone. For Paul the photograph was a lens concentrating the unforgettableness of one English spring morning. It was a very ordinary snapshot, so modest in its three or four elements that at any moment afterwards he could assemble the pieces together in memory.

During the summer term following this walk, at Oxford, Paul made a friend very different in character from Marston. This was the poet, Simon Wilmot, son of a doctor who was also a psychoanalyst. Where Marston seemed entirely innocent, Wilmot knew all about the complexes of Freudian guilt in himself and others – guilt to be surmounted, he insisted, by the removal of inhibitions. One must not be repressed. Repression led to cancer.

Wilmot was at Christ Church, college of Bloods, the Rich and Aristocrats whom he only saw in chapel or at meals. Outside his own college, he had a reputation as an eccentric 'genius'. Fellow poets from all over the University were his friends. They visited him in his rooms, each separately by appointment. Wilmot, terribly untidy in appearance, arrangement of his books and papers, eating his meals, nevertheless took care of every instant of his time.

Paul met Wilmot at a New College garden party. Wilmot, who had heard rumours of Paul's notoriety as mad, gave him, through eyes which seemed a bit too close together, a clinical squint and invited Paul to his rooms on Peck Quad at 3.30 the following afternoon.

Next day, Paul knocked at Wilmot's door at 3.40. Opening it, Wilmot said: 'Oh, you. You're ten minutes late. Well, come in.'

Although it was mid-afternoon, the curtains of Wilmot's sitting-room were drawn close. Wilmot was in an armchair with a standard lamp behind it. He signed to Paul to take the chair opposite him. Paul sat watching Wilmot. Light shone on his sand-coloured hair above the forehead which had skin smooth as parchment as yet unwritten on. With those close-together pink-rimmed eyes, he was almost albino. Whenever Paul said anything which could be interpreted as neurotic, Simon glanced down at the floor as though registering it on the carpet.

Wilmot fired off questions at Paul who tried to give answers that hinted at mysteries. He wanted to seem an interesting case. 'Oh really!' said Wilmot when Paul told him that his mother had died when he was eleven, his father when he was sixteen, and that he and his brother and sister had been brought up largely by Kate, the cook, and her sister Frieda, the housemaid, and had lived with their grandmother at her house in Kensington. Symptomatic.

Simon looked at the floor and asked: 'What will you do when you leave Oxford?'

Paul said he wanted to be a poet. Simon asked him what

4

modern poets he admired. Paul was at a loss. Then he said wildly that he loved the war poems of Siegfried Sassoon.

'Siggy's No Use. His war poems Simply Won't Do.'

Wilmot made pronouncements with almost absurd emphasis on certain words as though they were Holy Writ.

'Don't Sassoon's poems count as modern poetry?' asked Paul.

'Siggy Makes Statements. He Holds Opinions. He ended a poem about the fighting on the Western Front with the line: "O Jesus, make it stop!" A poet Can't Say That.'

'What should he have written then?'

'All a Poet can do is Seize on the Opportunity offered by the Situation in order that he may make a Verbal Artefact. War is simply material offered for his art. A Poet can't Make War Stop. He can only make a poem out of Material it gives him. Wilfred wrote: "All a poet can do today is warn."'

'Wilfred?'

'Wilfred Owen, the only poet who made His Own Idiom of the Western Front. Wilfred didn't say "O Jesus, make it stop!"'

In an icy, utterly dispassionate voice, separating each word from its neighbour as though he were detaching it from the poem and holding it up for inspection, he recited:

> Smiling they wrote his lie; aged nineteen years.
> Germans he scarcely thought of; all their guilt,
> And Austria's, did not move him. And no fears
> Of Fear came yet. He thought of jewelled hilts
> For daggers in plaid socks; of smart salutes;
> And care of arms; and leave; and pay arrears;
> *Esprit de corps*; and hints for young recruits.
> And soon, he was drafted out with drums and cheers.

Wilmot said the lines as though they were drained of emotion, of meaning even; words exposed, Paul thought, like rocks when the tide has gone out, bare in dry sunlight on the brassy sands. If Wilmot's voice betrayed any expression it was one of detached clinical interest in this list of military attributes – Daggers in Plaid Socks, Pay Arrears, Smart Salutes.

Abruptly Wilmot said: 'Show me your poems.' Paul, who carried his poems around with him as a traveller in a foreign country carries his identification papers, pulled out of his pocket

5

twelve foolscap pages, execrably typewritten. Wilmot took them from him with a gesture of slight dismay, murmuring, 'What energy!' He started leafing through them with extreme rapidity, occasionally grunting what seemed approval or, more often, disapproval. Once he gave a guffaw and exclaimed: 'But you CAN'T!'

After five minutes he had read through the twelve pages. Paul picked them up, page by page from the floor, where Simon had let them fall.

'What did you think of them?'

'You must drop that Shelley Stunt.'

'You don't like them?'

'We Need you for Poetry.'

Paul felt he was of the Chosen Few.

'Now you must go. I have to work,' said Wilmot abruptly, jutting out his underlip.

Paul invited Wilmot to a return visit, to his rooms at Univ. Wilmot peered, frowning myopically, into his diary, and said that he could manage that day week. He showed Paul to the door and shut it firmly after him.

A week later, they were eating sandwiches and drinking beer in Paul's rooms. Simon ate nine of the dozen sandwiches provided and then said in a mock-indignant voice: 'Aren't there any more sandwiches? I like the roast beef ones.'

Paul ran down to the college kitchen where he managed to procure only two diminutive pork pies. Returning to his rooms, he found Wilmot seated at his desk, reading Paul's Notebook. He looked round, not in the least embarrassed by Paul's arrival and merely asked, 'Who's Marston?'

Paul realized that there was no question of protesting at Wilmot's behaviour. One either accepted it without demur or walked out of his life for ever. Paul said: 'Marston is a friend of mine.'

'That is obvious. What else?'

Paul described their walking tour.

Simon looked down at the floor, grunted, and said, quoting from Paul's description in the Notebook he had just read of the scene of Marston sitting by the river.

'"The map of happiness we never shared."' He recited the

line as though the words were spoken on the moon. They sounded to Paul as though they were not by him but by Wilmot. 'That is poetry,' then: 'Perhaps you should always write journals,' he said, consideringly. He went on – 'What is there in any way remarkable about that young man?'

'Nothing.'

Wilmot shouted with laughter: 'Don't be absurd, Schoner! There can't be nothing remarkable about him! Why did you prefer him to the others in the first place? Why did you choose him? Is he a Terrific Looker?'

'The other Hearties pretend to be ordinary and decent. But really they're loud and vulgar and self-advertising. Marston, without his realizing it, is utterly different from them. He is gentle and unassuming and he loves the English countryside. He is like someone who wherever he goes creates around him an island on which he is alone. He is innocent.'

'Oh, you think he is perfect?' Wilmot squinted down at the carpet.

'I suppose I do.'

'No one is perfect,' said Wilmot, jerking up his head and looking straight at Paul. 'All you mean is that he is a Loner.'

'He is an airman – a pilot.'

'An airman?' Wilmot became interested. 'Well, that could be Symptomatic. Airmen want to be Angels.'

Paul had a sense of triumph. He had made Marston sound neurotic. He had produced symptoms for him. Simon asked: 'By the way, are you a Verger?'

'A what?'

'A virgin?'

Paul blushed furiously: 'I suppose so.'

'Well, you must know whether you are or you aren't.'

'I am then. Are you?'

'I could hardly have gone to Berlin (where through some extraordinary aberration – they must have been quite dotty – my parents sent me when I was seventeen) and still be a virgin. Germany's the Only Place for Sex. England's No Good.'

Paul could think of nothing to say. He asked: 'Shall we go to Blackwell's bookshop? I want to buy a copy of *The Sacred Wood*.' Simon had told him that the only book of criticism published

7

since the war worth Touching with a Barge Pole, was T. S. Eliot's *The Sacred Wood*.

Leaving Blackwell's an hour later they ran into Marston in Broad Street. Paul introduced Marston to Simon who stared at the boy with unconcealed curiosity. 'Paul has told me about you,' he said. Marston looked dazed and exclaimed: 'Oh!' 'See you next week, Paul,' said Wilmot and walked away.

When Paul next called on Simon, he asked him what he thought of Marston. Squinting down his nose, Wilmot said: 'The Helmeted Airman.'

'Did you like him?'

'He seemed Very Nice,' said Wilmot icily. 'Of course, it's obvious why you are attracted to him.'

'Why?'

'Because you realize he's only happy 10,000 feet above the earth. You and he are very alike,' he added mysteriously.

'Why? I always feel that we're completely different.'

'You're both Heaven Reachers. That is why you are so tall. You want to get away from your Balls. You like him because he is indifferent to you. For you, Indifference Never Fails to Attract. It's Irresistible. You are afraid of physical contact so you fall in love with people with whom you feel Safe.'

'You mean Marston doesn't like me?'

'I think he might love you for finding him Interesting. After all, not many of us would.'

'Well, what should I do?'

'You have to tell him how you feel, you can't escape that.' Wilmot squinted down at the carpet with the air of a scientist examining a specimen.

With a feeling that this was for the last time, Paul invited Marston for a walk in the Oxford park. Marston hesitated, looking distrustfully at him, and then said, with resolute cheerfulness: 'All right, old son.'

They walked down to the little river Cherwell, where they sat on a bench. 'Why did you ask me to go for a walk? Is there something you wanted to ask me?' said Marston, turning round and looking very straight at Paul. Since they went on their walking tour he had never once referred to it.

8

'I think that perhaps we should give up meeting.'

'Why?' Marston looked disconcerted, but waited patiently as though it was up to Paul to decide their relationship.

'Well, our walk was a complete failure, wasn't it?'

'I suppose so.' He looked into the distance. Then he smiled enchantingly and said in his jaunty voice: 'Yes, I think it was.'

'I bored you utterly for five days on end.'

'Yes, I suppose you did, old son. But –'

'But what?'

'Perhaps you wouldn't have bored me so much if you hadn't made such desperate efforts to entertain me.'

'How?'

'By mugging up what you think to be my subjects and never for one moment in five days jawing about anything else. You didn't, really, did you, old son?' he asked, turning his head and looking at Paul very directly.

'Well, what else should I have talked about?'

'You could have talked about things that interested you and not me.'

'Poetry! That would have bored you to tears.'

'Yes,' he laughed. His eyes suddenly caught Paul's. He broke into laughter again, then he put his hand to his mouth and stifled a consciously parodied yawn. 'But perhaps we would have found some subject that interested us both.'

This brought Paul up against the truth. He thought, what do we have in common except my liking him? I should have talked about him. I should have asked him clinical questions – are you a Verger – like Wilmot asks me. He saw that very clearly – it might have worked. But thinking so, his heart sank. He saw that the only basis of a real relationship must be their interest in each other. Basis. Abyss. They had no interests in common, apart from themselves. Marston – who really was innocent, truthful, unvulgar, brave and beautiful – everything that in his publicizing way Paul had told Wilmot he was – would bore him. And he, of course, already bored Marston. He said: 'I think we should decide not to see each other.'

'Whatever you like.' Marston looked away towards a very green field: background to athletes playing on it. Then he said: 'But isn't that rather difficult since we are both at the same quite small college?'

9

'Well, we'll see each other, but we won't talk.'

'All right, old son, if that is what you want.' He lingered, as though waiting for Paul to say more.

'Goodbye then,' Marston said, as he got up from the bench and started walking towards the athletes. But then he turned round and said, 'By the way, did your friend Wilmot suggest that you stop meeting me?'

'No, he didn't suggest anything of the sort – quite the opposite, in fact.'

'Oh well, I just wondered. Sorry.' Then he added: 'To be perfectly candid, that's the first conversation we've ever had that didn't bore me. This afternoon you didn't bore me at all.'

Returned to the college, Paul put on his gown and went to the Dean's rooms to ask permission not to have meals in Hall. Dean Close was only twenty-five. He had the air of having been 'got' by the college because he was so young and hail-fellow-well-met, in contrast to the other dons with their air of dusty remoteness. Dean Close wore grey flannels that seemed even shabbier than the 'Oxford bags' of most undergraduates. Paul could not help regarding him as a spy sent by the old into the enemy territory of the young. Perversely, this made Paul rather want to confide in him, to confess things.

He knocked at the door which was immediately opened by the Dean who, putting his head round it, said heartily: 'Come in, my dear fellow! What can I do for you?' Very red in the face, Paul explained in a few hesitant sentences that he wanted the Dean's permission not to eat in Hall for the rest of that term. Dean Close laughed and asked him why he was making this eccentric request. 'Because I do not want to see Marston.' 'How can that be?' asked the Dean. 'I do not know much about the matter, but it has always struck me that you and Marston were pals. I often wondered what interests you two chaps have in common.' 'I am in love with him and I have arranged that he and I should not meet for the rest of the term, at the end of which will be the summer, when we shall not meet anyway,' Paul said. Dean Close blushed furiously, hesitated, then said heartily, 'Well, we are in a pickle. I'll have to tell my colleagues about your request, but I assume that since it is so near the end of term there won't be any objection to your not eating in Hall. I don't have to give them a reason.' Then with a burst of boisterous candour: 'Between ourselves, old chap, are you perfectly sure that this is the right decision? Hadn't you better stick it out?' 'Perfectly sure,' said Paul, and reaching into his jacket pocket, he pulled out a poem as confession of his feelings about Marston. Dean Close took it and read intently:

> Lying awake at night
> Shows again the difference
> Between my guilt, his innocence.
> I vow he was born of light
> And that dark gradually
> Closed each eye,
> He woke, he sleeps, so naturally.
>
> So, born of nature, amongst humans divine
> He copied, and was, our sun.
> His mood was thunder
> In anger,
> But mostly a calm English one.

Dean Close read the poem through twice and said, 'May I hang on to this, old man? Do you have another copy?' And he pocketed it.

Now that Paul had stopped eating in Hall, for his meals he boiled an egg or cooked sausages over a gas ring provided in his room by the college, or went out, often with Wilmot. They took long walks through the countryside near Oxford, taking the sandwiches Wilmot so liked with them, and eating in the fields. Paul came to see Wilmot as trying out scenes in a play in which he would have a leading role on a stage of writers. Wilmot did not think much of those at present performing. If all this was absurd, the speeches he had written for his part – his poems – had a gravity of tone, a strange impersonality, almost remoteness, wholly serious. After reciting one of his poems – he knew all his work by heart – 'they are waiting for Someone,' he said. He was the Someone. But above him he placed a former school friend, William Bradshaw, The Novelist of Tomorrow. 'I send

11

everything I write to Bradshaw, I accept his judgement Absolutely. If he approves of a poem I keep it, if he dislikes one, I scrap it instantly. Bradshaw is Incapable of Error. He is the Novelist of the Future.'

'What is he doing now?'

'He is a medical student at University College Hospital in London. He thinks that today the Novelist has to know the physiology as well as the psychology of characters. His interest in Behaviour is Clinical.'

Simon thought that letter-writing was self-indulgent since all letters were written by the writer not to his correspondent, but to himself. Accordingly he cut down his communications to the absolute minimum. The last week of term, he sent, by college messenger, a two-line note to Paul. Written in microscopic handwriting it occupied a space the size and shape of a postage stamp at the centre of a page. It ran:

Dear P, Obliged cancel all arrangements with my Oxford friends this week. Bradshaw here. Simon.

An hour later this was followed by a second note:

Dearest P, Please come tomorrow at 3. Bradshaw wants to meet you. Love, Simon.

Paul arrived at 2.55. An indignant Wilmot opened the door and said, 'You're early. We're still working,' without seeming to look at him. Bradshaw, who was seated at a table on which typescripts were spread, looked up and, glowingly, smiled. He was small and neat with a very large head in which there were shining eyes which looked across the table with an expression that seemed to say: Don't take any notice of Simon. Wilmot passed a page of typescript to Bradshaw. Bradshaw read it through, taking what seemed at least three minutes of ticking silence to do so. 'Well, what do you think?' asked Wilmot, a bit impatient. 'Simon, how can I concentrate, when you sit there firing revolvers at me?' Simon blushed.

Bradshaw looked up from the typescript and said in a voice incredibly like Wilmot's own:

After love, we saw
Wings dark on the skyline.
'Buzzards,' I heard you say.

Bradshaw raised his hands from the table, looked up at the ceiling and howled with laughter.

'But, Simon, you CAN'T,' he said, in Simon's own voice. 'Don't I just see it! There they are in the valley, the two of them, lying in the grass and then one of them looks up to the skyline and says, "Buzzards." "What did you say?" asks the other. "BUZZARDS!" "Well, what the hell do the buzzards think WE are?"'

Simon laughed, a bit embarrassed, Paul thought. 'Well, that goes out,' he said, taking up a pencil and crossing out three lines.

'Hadn't we better stop now, Simon?' said William Bradshaw, looking across the room at Paul. 'I don't know whether you've noticed, Simon, but you appear to have a guest. Perhaps you would be so kind as to introduce us.'

'Mr Schoner – Mr Bradshaw,' said Wilmot, sulkily.

Wilmot left the room. Bradshaw looked at Paul and said; 'I am very glad to meet you. I asked Simon to arrange for us to meet. He showed me some of your work. I must say it struck me as among the most interesting writing I have seen by a young writer.' He spoke as if he was infinitely old and mature. 'That story you wrote about your friend Marston was unforgettable. So sad and yet so wildly funny, the scene with the dog.'

Some days after this, just before lunch, Paul was standing in University College Lodge and wondering whether Marston would pass through it on his way to eat in Hall. He liked just to look at him every day as he liked to look every day at a certain drawing by Leonardo in the Ashmolean. As Paul lingered there, pretending to read college notices, Dean Close appeared from the quadrangle and stopped, saying, 'Paul Schoner! Just the chap I was looking for. What luck that I should have run into you! I want you to meet my young German friend, Dr Ernst Stockmann. Let me introduce you! Paul – Ernst, Ernst – Paul!'

Dr Stockmann, who looked slightly older than most undergraduates and slightly younger than Dean Close, was wearing the blazer of Downing College, Cambridge.

Dean Close vanished, leaving Paul with Dr Stockmann, who started talking in quiet precise tones about the college Chapel across the quadrangle as seen from where they were standing. Dr Stockmann said its architecture reminded him of the religious sonnets of John Donne, and of certain German mystical poets whose work had affinities with Donne. He told Paul that he himself had studied at Cambridge but he would far rather have gone to Oxford, in fact to Univ, so that he could contemplate its architecture, which, although not exceptional, had a quiet assurance – a kind of handed-down innocence – which struck him as exquisitely English. He gave an allusive smile when he said 'English', as he added: 'It reminds me of your poem about a friend of yours – called Marston. I hope you won't mind that my friend Hugh Close showed it to me.'

Paul was flattered. He never thought Dean Close would show his poem to a stranger. He said warmly that he too wished Dr Stockmann had been at Univ, for then he would have had a friend with whom he could talk about poetry. 'Which my fellow undergraduates at this college – the Univ "hearties" – despise.'

Dr Stockmann smiled discreetly and suggested that Paul join him at a luncheon he was having with some friends at the Mitre Hotel, just across the High. 'I think you will find, well, just one or two sympathetic to you.'

There were several smartly groomed young men at the table, the kind Paul told himself he could not stand but by whom, secretly, he was impressed. He felt incapable of taking part in their conversation. His income at Oxford was only £350 a year, whereas his fellow guests had incomes ranging from £500 to several thousand. Now he behaved even more clumsily than usual. He told a story no one could see the point of, and quoted something from the French, only to realize while he was doing so that he was forgetting certain words and could not pronounce others. A contemptuous silence, or rather several contemptuous silences, fell on the young men, none of whom Paul had ever met before. But Paul was rescued from disgrace by Ernst Stockmann who, although a German, took up Paul's clumsy English sentence and made what he was attempting to say fit explicitly, without jagged edges, into the surrounding talk. Dr Stockmann sat next to Paul at the table. Towards the end of the meal when they were all fairly drunk, he turned to him and said that Dean Close thought Paul had a great future, though perhaps not by standards strictly academic.

Paul said to him that during the long vac he intended to go to Germany, as he had to learn German for the Philosophy paper in his finals. Apparently overlooking all Paul's gaffes – indeed even appearing to find Paul delightfully innocent – Stockmann reacted by inviting him to stay with him and his parents at their house at Hamburg. Paul accepted at once: grateful perhaps not so much for the invitation, as for Stockmann's apparent belief in his talent.

There were several weeks to go before the end of the vacation. During these, Paul had time to reflect that this invitation, made by Dr Stockmann at lunch only an hour after they had first met and confirmed by him a few days later in a very friendly letter written from Hamburg, was rather strange. Paul began to wonder what Dean Close had told Dr Stockmann about him.

He was made apprehensive by a second letter from Stockmann, received on 10 July, saying that Ernst, as Dr Stockmann now signed his name, expected Paul on the 20th of the month. Paul booked a passage for the night of the 19th on the Hamburg–Amerika Line ship, the *Bremen*, leaving from Southampton for Cuxhaven, the port of Hamburg.

The night before he left for Hamburg, Paul visited William Bradshaw at his mother's small early Victorian stucco house in a quiet, garden-like square in Bayswater. As he was walking up the front steps the door was opened by a lady soberly dressed in the style – though it was ten years since the Peace – of a war widow. She looked at him through eyes as large and watchful as William's but, as it were, in a minor key of sadness and resignation, looking back on the past, where his were in the major key of the future. In spite of its far-away dreaminess, the veiled expression of Mrs Bradshaw's face did not entirely conceal a look of fixed determination. She said in a voice through which the friendliness seemed forced: 'You must be my son's guest. He has been a little out of sorts, so I know that he will be delighted to see you,' (dissociating herself quietly from this pleasure, Paul thought). 'I am afraid I have to go out to see an old old friend who is far from well. If you walk up that first flight of stairs you will find William in his study which is the first door on the right at the top. Our invalid is doubtless waiting for you.'

Shutting the door gently, she left Paul standing in the hall. He ran up the stairs and knocked at the study door. As soon as William had let him in, Paul asked: 'Was that your mother?' 'Who else?' asked William bitterly. 'Doubtless she was waiting in her lair, looking out through the curtains so that she might form an opinion about my guest before going out herself. Any friend of mine is suspected of the worst. She wants this house to be a prison and herself my warder. God, how glad I'll be to leave this Hell-hole. Simon tells me that you're fleeing the country.'

'I'm going to Hamburg tomorrow.'

'How I envy you. The moment I can get out of here, I intend to go to Berlin.'

'But can you get away from the hospital before you've completed your finals?'

'That's the question my mother asks me every morning at breakfast. "In this world we have to stick things out, however difficult we find them. Remember, William dear, your father stuck the war out." I've been told this so often that today I asked her, "After all, mother – which would you prefer? – my father sticking it out and getting shot? Or his not having stuck it out and sitting here at this moment at this table having breakfast ?"'

'What did she say?'

'What she always says on such occasions – "Dear William, I think you must be a little out of sorts this morning."'

'All the same, can you stop being a medical student before taking your degree?'

William shrugged. 'I've as good as told them that I've learned all I want to know about dissecting human corpses. Now I intend to dissect human lives. As soon as I've saved enough for my fare out of the tiny income my pervert rich uncle William – after whom I'm named – gives me – if and when he remembers to do so – I'll go to Berlin. I want to leave this country where censors ban James Joyce and the police raid the gallery where D. H. Lawrence's pictures are on show.'

'Did you read today in the *Mirror* about the policewoman arresting the nude bather?'

'No. What was it?'

'Somewhere on the coast near Dover a policewoman who was standing on the cliff watched through a telescope a man far out at sea, swimming naked. So she went down to the beach and arrested him as soon as he got out of the water.'

'Really, Paul, you must have invented that,' William laughed. 'I just don't believe it.'

'Not at all. And the funniest part is that when he got out of the sea he was wearing his bathing trunks. He'd only taken them off when he was in the water swimming, holding them in his jaws, like a dog.'

'Well, we should congratulate the policewoman on being spared the sight of the swimmer's penis.'

'Perhaps the swimmer can plead that he was in offshore non-territorial waters and therefore not in England.'

William laughed but then relapsed into self-dramatizing silence. With a sense of taking an enormous risk of being snubbed, Paul asked: 'How is your novel going?'

'I can't write a word in this house.'

Saying this, William had assumed a look of infinite weariness. To Paul's eyes everything in the little study seemed to weigh on William: the tidily arranged row of English Classics on the bookshelves, the two armchairs in which they were seated by the fireplace, the table with William's typewriter on it, and, over the chimney-piece, the watercolour of *Bluebells in a Forest* painted by his father, Colonel Bradshaw who, on 15 February 1916, had been 'reported missing' on the Western Front, never to be heard of again.

'What is your novel about?'

Paul asked this question for the simple reason that he passionately wanted to know.

William looked at Paul resentfully, as though determined not to be drawn out. Then, abruptly, changing his act, he said: 'I haven't discussed it with anyone, not even Wilmot, but after all, we are here to talk about each other's work. We're Colleagues. We are fellow writers like Henry James and Turgenev discussing our writing. Perhaps if I tell you my idea for the novel I will be able to write it.'

He was silent again for a few moments. Then, suddenly raising

17

his head, he looked at Paul with intenser glance. 'In order to explain my idea, I had better first tell you how it started.'

There was another pause, then William said: 'It began at school really, at Repton, when Simon and I were in the History sixth. At the beginning of our last year there was a new master, not much older than ourselves, twenty-two or, at most, twenty-three. He was called Hugh Salop and he was an absolutely galvanizing teacher. Instead of names and dates, he gave us living people and a sense of being switched back into whatever section of the past we happened to be studying, the moment he came into the library where he taught us. It was as though everything was news, some past battle or *crise* was happening now and no one knew the result . . . Just to give an instance – there was this little man, a mixture of a modern newspaper proprietor like North-cliffe and a very intelligent scientific popularizer like H. G. Wells, who came from Corsica where he'd played war games with his brothers and sisters in his childhood, and who, when as a young man he came to the French mainland, got very excited about science and all the revolutionary ideas of that revolutionary period. Well, he was a wonderful reformer and administrator, only he couldn't stop playing those war games – that's silly, I know. The point I'm trying to make is that Mr Salop made history seem as if it was going on like today's latest newsreel. He also excited Simon and me for quite another reason – because he had fought on the Western Front – he had joined up at the age of seventeen – had been shell-shocked. There were moments when we felt that with part of his mind he was still on the Western Front. In the middle of telling us about French history he might suddenly break off in mid-sentence, make a terrifying grimace and say something such as "Passchendaele – that was a bad show!" and then, a moment later, go on lecturing. And sometimes he'd say something quite crazy . . .'

'For example?'

'Well, I can remember one example because Simon made it a line in a poem. He was talking about the early English peasantry, tillage etc, and suddenly he broke off, walked to the school library window, stared across some recently ploughed fields – they were already beginning to sprout with corn – and said: "The ploughshare cuts a scream."'

'What did he mean by that?'

'Simon and I worked out that he was thinking of fields being ploughed in Normandy – landscape of the Western Front – where farmers, of course, still turn up relics of war – helmets, belts, Iron Crosses, shell cases. Anyway, at school Simon and I made quite a cult of Mr Salop. We tried to find out what he thought about the War but we could hardly ever get him to talk about it. And when he did, we could not be certain that he wasn't pulling our legs. Or perhaps he was just being crazy. For instance, he once said: "I loved every moment of the War. I had a white horse which I used to ride behind the lines." Once we asked him whether he hated the Germans.'

'What did he say?'

'He said: "I loved all the soldiers in the trenches, whichever side they were on, but specially the Germans, just because we were taught to hate them. Public hatred breeds private love. Love your enemies! My God, I'm *in love* with England's!"'

'How did you react to that?'

'Wilmot, already knowing a great deal about psychoanalysis, became suspicious. Mr Salop, I think, rather fancied me. Wilmot said: "Be careful if he takes you out and starts pinching your bottom."'

'Did he ever take you out then?'

'Of course, I was just dying for him to do so. But before he or, rather, *we* could, he was sacked.'

'Why?'

'The headmaster told us he was ill: but in that tone of voice where for "ill" read "sex".'

'And what happened to him after that?'

'Well, that's what my novel's about. We never knew.'

'Then what happens in the novel?'

'It begins at the school with this master who's back from the War and is school-teaching but who with part of his mind is still in the trenches. Well, school is a kind of war, isn't it, between boys and masters? He is a master who is on the side of the boys just as, in a manner of speaking, he was on the German side. He is shell-shocked and neurotic and one particularly sophisticated boy realizes this. That boy's character is of course based on Wilmot. In my novel "W" (let me call him) gains a kind of ascendancy over "Mr S" (let me call him). In the novel "Mr S" isn't sacked, he has a nervous breakdown, perhaps because the clever psychoanalytic boy, "W", in a too-objective way, tells him too much that is true about himself: as, I suppose, Rimbaud told Izambard, his schoolteacher. What happens is that without "W" knowing about it, "Mr S" goes to Berlin and has some psychoanalytic treatment, perhaps with an American woman who is an analyst. (I need a woman in the novel). Two years later, "W" goes to Berlin and there, quite by chance, he meets "Mr S" in a bar. They are delighted to see one another: for "Mr S" now thinks that he can pursue "W" outside the inhibiting circumstances of school life and "W" is quite happy to resume exercising power over "Mr S". But within a matter of weeks "W" has become very bored with "Mr S" who gives him the feeling that they are both back at school, just when "W" wants to be free of all sense of restraint. "Mr S" also disgusts him physically, especially since on one occasion for theoretic psychoanalytical reasons he goes to bed with "Mr S". I make that scene *hilarious*.' He giggled.

William stopped talking for at least a minute.

'What happens next?'

'Well, this is the terribly difficult part. It is the kind of problem Forster failed to solve in *The Longest Journey*. The fact is that I've pushed myself into a corner in which the solution simply has to be melodramatic. At any rate we have to go through the motions of melodrama.'

'What happens?' Paul asked impatiently. 'What happens next?'

'Well, as I now see it, I have to go back over the past and invent some reason for providing "Mr S" in Berlin with the service revolver he had in the trenches during the War. Obviously, in an attack of shell-shock he has to shoot either himself or "W" – perhaps both. And being unable to choose between the two, one night "Mr S" gets very drunk. He shoots himself through the roof of the mouth, but fails to put the bullet through his brain (it comes out at the top of his cheek). Then, bleeding terribly, he goes in a taxi to "W"'s rooms where, having rung the door-bell, he hands him the revolver and asks him to finish him off. Very sensibly – but rather too clinically cold – "W" says "You should have done your own dirty work", hands him back the weapon, gets him back into the taxi, and takes him to the nearest hospital.'

'And how does it end?'

'That's what I haven't decided. Can you suggest an ending, Paul?' he asked a bit maliciously.

'Well, if the novel were by Ernest Hemingway it would end with "Mr S" falling in love with his nurse in the hospital. They could get married.'

'WHEE! How right you are!' William howled with laughter. 'But I've got a still better idea.'

'What's that?'

'Can't you guess? Humbled and shamed, "Mr S" crawls back to the dear little house of his mother in a quiet little old-fashioned square in Kensington. His mother forgives and takes pity on him, sheltering him there for the rest of his life, which ends with his more successful attempt at suicide a few months later.'

'But seriously – '

'Seriously, I suspect that imprinted in "Mr S"'s mind from the trenches is an image of a German boy whom he has to seek out in the lowest bars and dives of Berlin. So he doesn't leave Berlin. He goes to the dogs there. There are some people who, to be redeemed, have to go into the lowest kennels of the gutter – like Ibsen's Wild Duck diving to the bottom of the pond among the mud and weeds...' Having been serious for a few moments now he started laughing again.

Paul said: 'And he takes the Berlin street-boy back to the little home in Kensington and introduces Karl – for that is the boy's name – to his mother.'

'Brilliant!' –

William walked over to the fireplace and lifting up his hands said: 'And mother LOVES Karl and takes him away from "Mr S". She WINS! Mother WINS!! Mother WINS!'

They both roared with laughter and then fell silent. 'I must go now,' said Paul. He knew that somewhere in all this teasing William had found the clue to writing his novel. '"Mr S" adopts Karl,' Paul said. 'He has found his son. But now I must go to Hamburg.' He stood up.

'If I ever manage to get myself out of this Hell-hole I'll join you there, unless you come and join me in Berlin.'

'You write your novel about Berlin, I'll write a story about Hamburg.'

'Oh, do! Paul, do send it to me!'

On the stairs Paul passed Mrs Bradshaw. 'Good evening' she said, with restraint, adding very sweetly and with the faintest touch of malice, 'Is our invalid recovered?'

'He's much better' said Paul, running out of the house and continuing to run when he got into the street, words running through his mind as if he was already reading William's novel. And in his head he was already planning the novel which he would write about Hamburg and send to William, and to Simon, a love letter.

PART ONE

THE CHILDREN OF THE SUN

THE STOCKMANN HOUSE

On 18 July, as the boat train from Cuxhaven drew into the city, Paul felt increasingly apprehensive. Arriving by train at Hamburg in the evening when the first lights showed through windows of rooms in which Germans were standing alone, or seated together eating meals and talking to one another, or putting children to bed, or perhaps even making their German love, was an eerie sensation. Before reaching Hamburg, the train proceeded over a complex of bridges and stone embankments, and Paul (now standing up in his compartment to take his luggage from the rack) looked over streets of slums, tenements, back-yards. He experienced a pang of intense loneliness, as though each German light that shone in a window mocked his Englishness, each drawn-down blind shut him out. The train clanked over terminal points, and as it entered the vaulted gloom of the great station he felt homesick for English friends. For an instant all memory of what Ernst Stockmann had looked like vanished. He wondered whether he would recognize him at the ticket barrier where in his last letter he had said he would be waiting.

He recognized first the Downing College, Cambridge, blazer, and after that, his host. At Oxford Dr Stockmann had looked like a foreign student who could be taken for English. Here he looked not at all English, nor for that matter distinctively German, but international, as though he belonged nowhere or everywhere, floating. Paul knew he would never again see him as the politely grimacing young German student at Cambridge quite fitting into English life. It was probably because Paul was now meeting Stockmann with the knowledge that he would be staying with him for some weeks in Hamburg that he seemed so different from the young man who had given him lunch at the

Mitre. Behind the ticket barrier on the railway platform his face seemed the caged head of a bird of prey with bone-coloured beak. He wore spectacles through which his eyes gleamed. The nervous tension of smiling seemed to give him pain.

As they drove in a taxi towards the Stockmann house, Paul began to feel better about Ernst. He seemed intelligent and sensitive. He spoke English with a precision which was sometimes a delight, sometimes slightly annoying, on account of his pedantry. In the half-light of the taxi, Paul studied his face. It had a masked, permanently injured, oversensitive expression.

Ernst enquired about Paul's journey. Paul noticed that when Ernst smiled at his account of twenty hours of social life on the *Bremen* there was no humour in his smile. He switched it on and off, in his pallid way. However, when Paul described any scene with remotely sexual innuendo – how an ash-blond waiter accidentally dropped a tray of drinks so that they formed a pool of gin on Paul's trousers – he smiled ambiguously as though he could discern all sorts of deeper implications in Paul's description. Paul felt self-conscious and looking down at his trousers, saw that they were stained. He regretted having told the anecdote.

The taxi arrived at the great, varnished, stone-framed oaken door of the Stockmann residence in the millionaire district to the south of Hamburg, separated from the commercial section of the town and the port by the lake, the Alster. There were sails of boats, white, or pink, or blue, which seemed to brush across the lake like airy brooms. Ernst opened the front door with two keys and they passed beyond a lobby into the panelled darkness and loftiness of a heavily furnished hall. They stood there for a few moments, waiting for the maid to take Paul's suitcase.

Ernst said: 'If you care for modern art there are several pictures here that should interest you.' Paul saw a Matisse nude, a Van Gogh *Still-life with Irises*. He started walking from picture to picture while they waited for the maid. Ernst seemed a bit annoyed that Paul was anticipating what would later be a properly conducted tour of the art. He said, 'Shall I show you your room first, Paul?' There was emphasis on the word 'first'. He added, 'My mother began making this collection when she was studying art history in Paris. I am sure she will want to show you the pictures herself.'

They followed a maid up the oaken staircase with its polished banisters.

Ernst left Paul alone in his room to unpack. It was large, handsomely furnished, thickly carpeted. As soon as Ernst was gone, Paul sat on the bed, then on each armchair in turn, then on the chair in front of the writing table. Before unpacking his clothes, he fished out from under them one of the two or three books he had brought with him and continued reading from the place where he had left off in the boat train. It was of essays by D. H. Lawrence. Then he took out his foolscap notebook and started looking over a poem which he had begun before he left London, and which he hoped – not having looked at it for three days – he would now be able to judge with the detachment brought to a poem read by some other poet – perhaps by his friend Wilmot – heard for the first time. He read it through several times but each reading seemed to weaken his capacity for judging it objectively. It became horribly over-familiar. Now he tried saying it to himself out loud. Just as he was in the middle of the second stanza, there was a tactful knock at the door. Looking round he saw that Ernst had entered the room at the same instant he knocked. Paul felt caught *in flagrante*. There Ernst stood, smiling blandly at him from the doorway. Paul sensed that Ernst was aware of having a slight advantage over him. Tact, evidently, prevented Ernst from advancing into the middle of the room. He put his hands on his hips while he surveyed Paul, appraisingly:

'I hope I'm not interrupting! Was that a new poem you were reading? How very exciting!' he exclaimed, indicating that he was proud that a Paul Schoner poem was being written in a bedroom of his house.

Paul felt embarrassed.

Ernst continued, 'I was only coming to tell you that dinner will be ready just as soon as you are. We don't change for dinner tonight.'

Paul took this literally and appeared in the dining-room a few minutes later in the clothes he had travelled in – a tweed jacket and much-rumpled grey flannels with the slight stain of the spilled gin on them. Fortunately he was wearing a tie.

The dining-room had a large mahogany table, and a massive marble and brass-handled sideboard, over which there was hung a painting of apples – emerald and vermilion on a grey table cloth against a background of a kind of coral brown – by Courbet. Ernst's parents, Herr Jakob and Frau Hanna Stockmann, were already seated when he came into the room. Frau Stockmann was a wiry, assertive-looking woman each of whose features seemed enclosed in a separate system of wrinkles; those circling the eyes, those framing the mouth, those going vertically down the cheeks. The eyes were dark and clever, the mouth expressive. The cheeks had a bit too much rouge on them, giving them an overdressed look in contrast with the gown she was wearing, which was of a pastel grey and fluted like a Greek column.

Ernst came down to dinner, still wearing the blazer of Downing College. Under this, he had changed into a white cricket shirt with collar spread either side in two triangles over lapels. With his white, carefully manicured hands laid like kid gloves before him on the table and his eyes staring from behind his hornrimmed spectacles at Paul, he seemed a bit austere for a cricketer.

Jakob Stockmann, whom Paul guessed to be about fifteen years older than his wife, was a businessman whose interest in life appeared to have narrowed down to his meals. He had a drooping moustache, prominent ears and dull, leadenly observant eyes. When he emerged from his absorption with knife and fork, putting food into his mouth, it was either to grouse about what his palate tasted, or to make some cynically humorous remark. His wife threw him alarmed looks from time to time.

Directly his father, looking up from his plate and laying down his knife and fork, noticed Ernst's spread-open collar, he protested. Ernst, twenty-five years old, was sent up to his room to get a tie. He went, smiling with brave forbearance, and glanced meaningfully at Paul as he left the room.

Frau Stockmann laughed noisily, and said: 'You know, my husband's so particular about little things. He doesn't like Ernst to be without a tie. We say he is a pedant, quite a pedant.'

Her husband raised his hands.

'All I say is why should Ernst be dressed to play cricket at this time of night? I want to eat, not play cricket. Seeing him dressed to play cricket puts me off my food.'

She laughed uproariously.

'You ought to play cricket too, you old pedant! I tell my husband he ought to play cricket. It would make him less fat.'

The rolling of her eyes, the gleaming of her teeth, the curling of her lips, subsided and then, when Ernst, wearing a tie, re-entered the room, started up again. She said: 'I say, your father ought to play cricket, Ernst! It would do him good!'

'Father play cricket? He wouldn't be able to!' said Ernst with a diplomatic smile.

'I only say that I don't want you to dress to play cricket at meals,' said his father, looking up from his soup, a trickle of it clinging to two hairs of his moustache. 'It puts me off my dinner.'

'Isn't he greedy!' screamed Frau Stockmann.

'Well then, I'll play cricket if you like, now,' said Ernst, taking up a table knife. He held it above the table like a bat in his two hands. 'Let's see, we must have a ball. What will do? Oh, I know – ' He took a fragment of bread, rolled it into a pellet, and gave it to his mother to throw at his table-knife bat. All this time he was looking across the table at Paul.

'Ernst, what are you doing?' cried his mother. 'Why, really, you might be in the nursery!'

'Not at all. I'm playing a very grown-up game of cricket. Would you like to play?' He offered to throw a pellet at her. She roared with laughter, shaking her head at him. Then she gasped, 'Yes, I'll play!' and then collapsed again unable to hold her table knife for laughing. Whilst mother and son were both helpless, Herr Stockmann looked across this happy family scene at Paul with an expression of pitying forbearance, his arms spread wide. Then, quite suddenly, his mother and Ernst stopped laughing and wiped the tears from their eyes.

'When you're at home do you torment your parents like this?' Frau Stockmann asked Paul. 'Are you as cruel as Ernst is to us, to your father and mother?'

'I don't have parents,' Paul explained. 'My mother died when I was eleven, my father when I was sixteen.'

She looked apologetic. 'Oh, how sad, what a pity, *wie Schade*! Where is your home, then?'

'I live in London in the house of my grandmother.'

She paused, and then asked crudely, 'And what is your grandmother's family?'

'My grandmother's family is Danish. But my grandfather came from Frankfurt and was Jewish. The Schoners emigrated to England.'

Ernst and his father fell silent. Frau Stockmann asked: 'When did they come to England?'

'Fifty years ago.'

'Do they go to the synagogue?'

'Oh no, my grandfather is dead. My grandmother is a Quaker.'

'Well, then you do not have to worry, they are not Jews,' she said decisively. 'Your family is English. In Germany here what count as Jews are from Eastern Europe – Lithuanian and Polish refugees – not Germans who have been here a great many years. My husband employs some real Jews like that in his business. Some are very clever. Some are good people. Clean, sober, well-spoken. I myself do many charitable deeds to them. Some are my friends. From far back, my own family came from Eastern Europe, from Kaunas, in Litauen, of a very cultivated family.'

Herr Stockmann and Ernst looked as if they were waiting for an unpleasant smell to stop.

The telephone saved what was evidently a 'situation' by ringing. Ernst got up, saying that he expected a call.

Herr Stockmann said: 'I thought this was to be a family meal with your guest, not to be interrupted by that machine.'

Frau Stockmann explained to Paul effusively: 'Ernst's friends often ring up at dinner, because that's the only time they are certain to find him in. He's so popular! But we do not want some of his friends in this house. We do not approve of them all. He works all day, you see, and is out often later in the evening. But any interruption while we are sitting at dinner always irritates my husband.'

At the ends of wires were people who cared about Ernst, loved him perhaps. Every evening his life with his parents was interrupted by voices from afar, voices perhaps of boys and girls who sailed on the lake.

After dinner, they took coffee in the hall. Paul could not keep his eyes off the pictures – the Van Gogh, a Derain, a 1905 Picasso drawing of a child. One that greatly puzzled him was of a scruffy, slightly mad-looking young man with corn-coloured hair tugged down over his forehead, partly obscuring his large, intensely blue eyes and the bridge of his strong, curved nose. The lips which were the shape of slices of melon were wide in a mournful grin.

'Who is that of?' Paul asked.

'Oh, I am glad you like that,' said Frau Stockmann with enthusiasm. 'That is very rare. Even experts when they visit here do not guess what it is.'

'What is it?'

Ernst interjected: 'My mother bought it when she was studying art history in Paris before the War.'

'And it cost me nothing,' laughed Frau Stockmann.

'Mother had an eye for what would go up. Now it would cost a fortune.'

'It cost nothing. The artist was almost starving.'

'What was his name?'

'So crazy, so young, always drunk, so ugly and so beautiful. Desnos.'

Paul had never heard of Desnos, but he liked the picture.

'Now he is for long dead,' said Frau Stockmann with a big sigh, but a sort of satisfaction. 'Does he not look happy in spite of the picture being painted on canvas like sackcloth – which I had to have re-lined – and in cheap paints that have faded in some places I have to have repainted with costly colours. So expensive!'

'Mother made all this collection. As a collector she is a true genius.'

'*Was*! I would not collect any of the filthy things they paint today. Disgusting! Everything now so hideous.' She turned away from the pictures and said: 'Now I am afraid I have to leave you, I must go out to a committee meeting of the Friends of Hamburg Music. I leave you in safe hands with Ernst. Ernst, don't introduce him to your friend Joachim Lenz,' she said laughing, but meaning this. She turned away from the hall and went to the front door.

Ernst followed her out of the house and then returned into the hall. He and Paul drank another cup of coffee, then Ernst said: 'Shall we go out into the garden? At the back of the house, it goes down to the lake.' They walked down a path along the side of the house to the large back garden with its lawn and shrubs. At the end of it there was a row of willow trees fronting the lake. Here branches bent over the water, the ends of some of them dipping leaves into it. Through the screen of willow boughs as through down-curved iron railings they looked out over the dense summer evening on the lake – swarming with boats.

Standing here with Ernst, Paul saw canoes only a few yards from them beyond the willow boughs. They seemed extremely near with their cargoes of girls and boys in clothes like leaves over flesh. He thought he felt their warm colours press through the darkness.

Paul could hear the rustling of the boats through the water, a throbbing bass under the splash of paddles and the laughing and shouting of the canoers. One canoe was very close to where they stood. It had penetrated right under the willow boughs which barred off the lake from the Stockmann property. Seeing Ernst and Paul, and with a decent sense perhaps that they were trespassing, two boys plunged the blades of their paddles into the water and moved away powerfully, the lifted shining varnished side of their canoe resembling the swishing side of a dolphin sheering away from a ship's prow. The stooping willow boughs, the scent of lime trees, the browns and pinks of flesh, the summer clothes, the murmuring laughter, the distant sails further out on the lake, and beyond them the lights of the city, rectangles and triangles of walls and towers reflected, gave Paul the strongest sense of young foreign life. The dusk seemed like the lake just below their feet, flesh into which he could penetrate, but from which he was shut out by the willows bending over into the water.

It was beginning to get dark and a bit chilly. They went back into the house. Ernst took Paul upstairs to his study and, sitting beside him on the sofa, showed him photographs of places he had travelled to, people with whom he went to parties. They were dully conventional pictures. Paul could imagine Ernst taking them. Only occasionally there was a self-consciously

32

facetious one of young people in fancy dress, making faces or gesturing at the camera.

One photograph, which was loose in an album, fell out on to the floor. Paul picked it up and looked at it intently. It did not appear to have been taken by Ernst. It was of a young man seen full-face leaning forward, his chin resting on his right hand. He had a high forehead, dark hair brushed back, and a hawk-like nose, a bit Mexican-looking. The eyes were like those of a bird-watcher, attentive, and as though he were instructing the photographer. He seemed slightly amused by whatever or whoever it was he seemed to be surveying so intently: the photographer, a friend. Or perhaps he himself was the photographer.

'Who is that of?'

Ernst gave a little, insinuating laugh, 'Oh, I suspected that you might be interested. That is my friend Joachim Lenz. I am afraid my mother does not like him. Perhaps you heard her say so.'

'He has extraordinary eyes.'

At this, Ernst, looking as directly as Joachim had seemed to look out of the photograph into Paul's eyes, said: 'Your eyes are more beautiful than Joachim's.'

Paul laughed. Then, seeing that Ernst was offended, he took up the photograph again.

Ernst said: 'Would you like to meet my friend Joachim?'

'Very much.'

'Well, as a matter of fact, he's giving a party in two days' time. You are invited. He asked me to bring you.'

'What will the party be like?'

'Well, it may seem strange, after Oxford. Can you dance?'

'I'm afraid not.'

'It doesn't matter.'

Soon after this Paul said he was tired after his journey. Ernst showed him to his room. Alone, Paul wrote in his Notebook:

> Now I shall begin to live.
> Resolutions for the Oxford Vac:
> To do absolutely none of the work set for me by my Oxford tutor.

Now that I am away from England, I shall do my own work, and, whether I stay at Oxford or leave, from now on, I shall continue to do that and no work except that.

My own work is to write poetry and fiction. I have no character or willpower outside my work. In the world of action I do everything my friends tell me to do. I have no opinions of my own. This is shameful I know, but it is so. Therefore I must develop that side of my life which is independent of others. I must live and mature in my writing. My aim is to achieve maturity of soul.

I shall now begin to keep this Notebook. It will contain descriptions of people, specimens of dialogue copied down from life.

After my work, all I live for is my friends.

The next morning, Ernst having gone to the office, Frau Stockmann, as arranged, took Paul to the Hamburg Art Gallery. As they left the house, she made it clear that she was not going to entrust him with its very complicated keys. If he went out alone, she said, he must, on his return, always ring the bell for the maid. But he must not come home by himself after 11.00 p.m. For him to do so would keep the servants up.

'You know, nothing was safe during the period after the War, when there was the Inflation. Then money became worth less than the paper it was printed on. There was no order. There was a great deal of robbing, and still in Germany it is safer to keep everything shut up. Always now I lock both locks.'

Paul agreed that it must have been awful. Before she closed the door, he looked back into the house, dark as the interior of a pyramid, with the pictures hung on chains like victims of a cult of art-worship. Outside, the sun seemed like some mad artist who had daubed road and leaves in blues and greens, twisted branches of trees into loops held up against the magnifying sun, and thrown inky blots on road and pavement.

'How hot it is!' complained Frau Stockmann. 'Ugh!' and she waved her hand before her face, partly to fan it, partly as though to brush the sun away.

She sat down in the taxi and seemed gratefully to breathe in the dark of its interior. She signed to Paul to sit beside her. As soon as the taxi had moved off, she began: 'I am very glad that you get on so well with Ernst. Ernst is a very nice boy . . . Yes, I think that you and he are – what does one say? – yes, you are very well attuned for one another, harmonious, *sympathiques*.'

She looked at him with a provocative appraising look. Then she went on, in a harsher tone of voice: 'But I hope you won't prevent Ernst from working. His work is very necessary to us all. His father is not well.'

'What work does Ernst do?'

'At present he is doing experimental work for an importing firm down at the docks. They import chemical products, you know, drugs and everything like that. But that's not for long. Soon he will do more important work. Eventually he directs the firm.'

'It sounds important.'

Frau Stockmann did not seem quite sure what impression she had made. She went on, insistently. 'You know, Ernst is very clever. He is brilliant. He passed all his examinations top here, first class in Heidelberg and top first class in Cambridge. First class. You know what that means?'

Paul did, indeed.

'What did he study?'

'Economics. He is very good, and at physics, too, he is very good. Of course, at languages he is very good. French and English and perhaps, too, Spanish. His Italian's not so good as those. I do not speak English well, but his English is very good, is it not? Brilliant.'

'Yes, brilliant. You speak very good English too. But I would have mistaken him for an Englishman.'

'So. You would have taken him for an Englishman. Really?' she repeated in her heavy way, staring at Paul with her great serious eyes.

Paul looked at the street through the taxi window, wishing he could jump out. People there seemed free, as though dancing because they were outdoors, not sitting next to Frau Stockmann in a taxi. Sunlit buildings shone satin behind striding purple silhouettes of walkers.

Before they reached the gallery, Frau Stockmann stopped the taxi and told the driver to wait for them while she did some shopping. She chose everything to please Ernst. At the fruiterers, she said, 'You know, Ernst's funny. He won't eat strawberries.' She bought cherries. She did not ask Paul whether he liked strawberries.

One modern picture in the gallery greatly impressed him: the portrait of a woman seated at a café table, her shoulders wrapped in a shawl drawn close round them, her hair hanging down in a distraught mass, her head bowed, a little glass like a poisoned chalice in front of her. The closed eyes and compressed lips, the shut-in face seemed those of someone totally imprisoned in her own world of misery. Lettering on a small brass plaque at the bottom of the frame said this was Picasso's *Absinthtrinkerin*. Paul wandered away from this picture into a gallery where there was modern German Art.

'Do not look at those monstrosities!' Frau Stockmann shrieked. Here were paintings in primary yellows, reds and blues – some of them crudely sketched on the bare canvas like graffiti on white walls – of jagged men and women grasping at each other's jagged bodies in jagged pine-tree landscapes. They were pictures of the new Germans living their primitive lives of primitive passions, like ancient Saxons in tents with skins painted blue in woad and tearing out each others' hearts. There was one of a man with penis erect like a spear approaching a bushy woman crouching against a background of transparent crimson flames.

'Do not look at those. They are disgusting, a disgrace to Germany that they should be there. *Ein Skandal!*' said Frau Stockmann. They left the gallery and went back to the still waiting taxi.

During lunch, Ernst rang up, and asked Paul to join him and Joachim and his friend Willy at a swimming bath, giving him instructions how to get there. 'I wish your son would learn some manners, and not telephone while we are eating,' growled Herr Stockmann to his wife. She replied grimly: 'I wish he did not see Joachim Lenz and his friend Willy,' she said.

The open air baths were immense, and crowded with people. When he got there, Paul was glad that Ernst had explained where he should find him and his friends. With only scanty bathing slips many of the bathers were ugly. Nakedness, Paul thought for his Notebook, is the democracy of the new Germany, the Weimar Republic.

He found Ernst standing with hands placed on his hips, showing off the muscles of his arms and the set of his shoulders. Ernst and he, Paul thought, were the only two people here who seemed self-conscious. Ernst was smiling expectantly. Paul felt he was being scrutinized by him as he approached as though he were some property Ernst was proud to show off, though a bit anxious that it might do him no credit. Ernst said, 'Good afternoon! So you found your way here all right?'

'Perfectly, thank you.'

'You slept well?'

'Beautifully.'

'Good. Well then, the others are in the water already. Will you undress first, and then shall I introduce you to them?'

Paul undressed and then rejoined Ernst. Joachim and Willy were with him. Ernst introduced Paul Schoner to Joachim Lenz who stared at him with a kind of humouring appraisal, not approving of his unathletic body, but ready to be on good terms with his talking head, it seemed. But, after glancing knowingly at Ernst, Joachim turned away from Paul.

Willy Lassel, Joachim's friend, had fair hair, blue eyes, gleaming teeth, a candid smile. Mind and body trained to charm. He said in a most friendly way that he would be glad to carry on English converse with Paul, as training – he was to be an English teacher. Joachim watched and kept silent.

Willy continued to speak to Paul a little, and then Ernst interrupted him. All three, Ernst, Willy and Joachim began talking in German. Ernst was joining in enthusiastically. He made the others laugh. Then Willy and Joachim moved away from Ernst and began playing with a large coloured rubber ball. They ran about, throwing it at each other over the heads of the crowd staring at them. Paul almost forgot Ernst, who remained standing beside him. Paul lay down separate from Ernst and watched Joachim and Willy laughing in the sun. Joachim and Willy disappeared into the crowd, also moving in the sun, playing on their faces and bodies and falling like a shower of arrows beyond them on the water.

Paul lay back and felt the light fall on him. He looked up directly into the sun. The lashes of his eyes fringed like black reeds the down-pouring stream of light. The words which ran through his note-taking mind were blotted out by this enormous light. Physically, the sun seemed to penetrate into his bones. He felt as though it sucked the thinking consciousness from him and drew him up to it. He was no longer an individual.

He felt a shadow fall between him and the sun, and, looking up, saw Ernst.

'Are you going in?'

'Yes, I suppose so.'

They walked down to the swimming pool, Ernst looking from side to side at all the people, especially at those who were beautiful. Paul began to feel embarrassed by the nudity all round him as Ernst walked on ahead, stepping so lightly, looking round him so intently, smiling so coyly.

They passed Willy and Joachim. Willy grinned at Paul, his body turning like a column pivoting in the light as he threw the ball to Joachim. Joachim lifted up his hands and caught it, glancing only a moment at the ball, and then, with shining eyes, back at Willy.

After Ernst and Paul had bathed, Joachim and Willy were already dressed and preparing to go home. As they shook hands to say goodbye, Joachim invited Paul to his party on the twenty-fourth of the month.

24 July

Joachim's studio was a section of the penthouse of a block of modern flats. It consisted of a large, plain room, lit by a skylight and sparsely furnished. One end of it was partitioned off with a double bed behind the partition. There was also a large divan at the other end of the studio. Furniture consisted of tubular chairs, and tables with glass tops, lamps which were glass cubes like ice-blocks lit from within.

Ernst and Paul arrived early. Joachim took Paul's arm and led him round the studio showing him various objects: the bowl of rough cast glass, the Mexican rug, the books on art. There were also a few books on the Far East, and African art. There was Oswald Spengler's *Decline of the West*.

'Have you read all these?' Paul asked.

'No, I don't read very much now. I bought most of these books just after I left school, when I was eighteen or nineteen. But now I don't read so much. After the day's business, I bathe always with Willy or some other friends. Then for the weekends, I go away to the Baltic. I like the sun mostly, and doing things – not reading.'

'Oh.'

'Well,' he said, pronouncing the word almost as though it were 'wall' – and pulling down an enormous tome from a top shelf, where it lay longways – 'There is this book which I sometimes read when I come home late at night – though I prefer looking at the woodcuts to reading the stories.' He opened the volume with its thick biscuit-coloured paper and the dense black woodcuts of forests, castles, maidens, knights, horses, heraldry and monsters done in the expressionist style, clear, crude, sinister, printed very black. It was Grimms' *Fairy Tales*. 'Often I lie down late at night and look at the woodcuts and think they are about the lives of people I know. The illustrations seem to fill my head as though it were a cavern with them on its walls.'

He spoke English slowly but correctly, with a slightly American drawl. He watched Paul with eyes that also seemed to watch the English words he was saying, as though they were fish swimming in a bowl.

'What do you do?' Paul asked.

'My father is an importer of coffee from Brazil, and I am supposed to be learning to manage the family business. But surely I don't think I will ever become a coffee merchant.'

Paul asked whether a drawing pinned up on a wall of two sailors leaning over a harbour wall was by Joachim. Done in sepia ink, it had strong clear, dried-blood-coloured lines.

'Oh, I did that a long time ago. Now I have given up drawing for photography.' He said he would show Paul his work some day.

By now a good many guests had arrived. Paul left Joachim and strolled round the room, trying to avoid talking to anyone: he did not want to force a conversation in English upon a fellow guest. Outside the front door of the studio, down some steps, there was a scullery. Here he found Willy, washing up dishes. Willy welcomed Paul, grinning broadly. Paul said, 'Oh, but do you do the washing up?'

'Joachim is so busy all day. He could not do his own housework. That is my business.' He went on: 'Do you like Joachim's studio? Have you ever seen those metal and glass tables before? And the glass cube lights?'

'No. Never.'

'Really? You know, it was all Joachim's idea. He ordered from the Bauhaus from Dessau the furnishing of this room, and he made the designs. He's so clever . . . Oh, I am so tired . . .' He swept a hand through his long hair and he laughed. 'I've been tidying up here ever since three o'clock. You see those books on the shelves in the studio? Well, they were in a heap on the floor when I first came here this afternoon, and I have moved them all. I've swept the whole studio too.'

They went into the main part of the studio. Paul was introduced to several people by Willy. Joachim walked up to him with a small rumpled man with bandy legs and a wrinkled wizened face like a monkey. 'Paul, you must meet Fedi. He is a heroic Zeppelin commander, shot down by the wicked English when he was innocently bombing their contemptible little island – weren't you, Fedi? He also speaks English perfectly – don't you, Fedi?'

Fedi smiled tiredly. He and Paul walked across the room and stood side by side looking out of one of the studio's vertical slot-like windows across the Alster towards the harbour gleaming with lights, and distantly red with flame.

'What was it like, being shot down?' Paul asked.

'We were hit as we crossed the English coast, after a raid. We managed to make our way to the Baltic, where we came down.'

'Didn't the Zeppelin catch fire?'

'Well, we were in the sea. Part of the envelope remained floating above it. We six survivors climbed on top and sat there and waited till dawn, when we were rescued.'

'Were you very frightened?'

'The worst was that we couldn't light a cigarette because we were sitting on top of all that escaping gas.'

'When was this?'

'It was the summer of 1916. After that, no more Zeppelins!'
He gave a wry, monkey grin, and lit a cigarette.

'Why no more Zeppelins?'

'You', said Fedi, as though Paul had personally made the
invention, 'invented the phosphorous bullet which set alight the
gas in the Zeppelin when it had penetrated the envelope. Boom!
After that *Schluss*! Goodbye our nice Zeppelin.'

'Perhaps you were one of the crew of the Zeppelin I saw fly
over our house when I was seven years old. That must have
been the summer of 1916.'

'How then?'

'Our family lived in Sheringham right at the edge of the
Norfolk coast. One evening we all ran out into the garden and
there was a Zeppelin flying very slow, and very low down, as
though it might scrape the chimneys off the roof. You could
hear the whirring of the engines. My father and mother, my
father's secretary and the cook and housemaid, and my brother
and sister – we all watched it there in the sunset glow, the most
beautiful thing I ever saw, like a furled autumn leaf with all its
ribbed veins showing, moving so peacefully through the sky. I
can't think why we were allowed by our parents to run into the
garden like that. Next day, the family were all evacuated to
Cumberland.'

Fedi laughed. 'Then at least we had some success! Yes, it
might have been our Zeppelin. Over the *Ostküste*, the *Nordsee*. *Ja
ja*, that might have been us.'

'Did you happen to drop a bomb?'

'We jettisoned bombs, not to damage, to gain height.'

'I remember there was a bomb in a neighbour's garden that
didn't explode. An oval, whitish, pock-marked thing, like an
ostrich egg, but larger, I suppose.'

'Like an ostrich egg!' he roared with laughter. '*Ja ja*, that must
have been us.' He put his arm round Paul's shoulder and his
head against his chest, embracing Paul.

Paul imagined them: the little crew of England's enemies,
sitting on top of the still floating bulge of the Zeppelin's
envelope, just a few feet above the icy Baltic. Waiting for a
chugging motor boat to rescue them. Paul felt touched by this
little German hero with the domed bald head like the top of that

Zeppelin above the waters. Paul was English and Fedi was German, but now ten years after the War all the hatred between nations had leaked away like the gas from the airship's envelope. A pity Fedi was so wizened and ugly.

Fedi went away, and Paul remained standing by the window, as before a spectator. He watched the young Germans. They had a style which he thought of as excitingly 'modern'. The fashions that they wore were sun and air and their bronze skin. The boys gentle and soft, the girls sculptural, finely moulded. There was something brave about the show of happiness they put on. He liked them.

Ernst introduced Paul to a girl.

'I want you to meet Irmi, a very special friend of mine.'

'I spik no English. You are staying with Ernst, no? Ernst is very nice boy.' Smiling, she took Paul's hand.

She insisted on Paul dancing with her, though he protested he could not dance. She had hair cut short in an Eton crop, pale blue eyes, a boyish figure. She danced pressing her body close to Paul's. The top of her head came up to his lips, and he wanted to kiss her hair. He did so, very lightly. Suddenly he could dance.

After the dance, she ran towards Joachim who was resting on one of the mattresses. She put her arm round his neck, smiling up at Paul. She beckoned to Paul.

'This is English, is it not?' she asked, pointing down to her skirt. 'A kilt, you call it?'

He said yes. The skirt was of a woollen material, very short. She wore plaid socks with little tabs stuck into them. Her knees were bare. He imagined her in a boat on the lake. 'In Hamburg we so much like all that is English,' she said.

Ernst smiled at Paul, a bit reproachfully. 'You told me you couldn't dance. Now I see you can, you have to dance with me.' But as soon as Paul and he started dancing Ernst realized that Paul was not lying when he said he could not dance. They abandoned the attempt, and stood in a corner of the room, talking.

'You find this very different from England?'

'Very different.'

'You prefer England?'

'No.'

'I thought perhaps from the tone of voice in which you said "very" you were angry with me.'

'Did I say "very" in a special tone of voice?' Paul was half in love with everyone else in the room for not being Ernst.

'Perhaps you would prefer me to go away and leave you here alone?'

There was agony in his face.

Paul remembered how pleasantly Irmi had spoken to Ernst – how warmly Joachim and Willy had received him.

'I only wish you wouldn't fuss over me like an old hen.'

'In some ways I prefer parties I have been to in England, but this sort of thing, well, it does have certain advantages.' Ernst looked enigmatic.

'Did you like Cambridge?'

'It was the most wonderful experience of my life. Oh, Downing College.'

The dancing had stopped. Silence fell on the room. Ernst said *sotto voce*: 'I expect you find this an odd set of people.'

'I like your friends.'

'I'm glad you like them. I hoped you would. I felt sure you would. Of course, I knew you would. I already knew you well enough for that, even that first luncheon at Oxford. And I had read your poem about your friend Marston. He seems to have an innocence which reminds me of you. "His mood was thunder in anger, but mostly a calm English one." So English! You know I'm quite glad that you were angry with me just now, because it made me think of that line. For a moment, I almost imagined you being Marston.' He went on in his insinuating tone of voice: 'I'm particularly interested in the party tonight because there's a lot going on under the surface.' Then he asked:

'Do you like Irmi?'

'I think she's charming.'

'Charming,' Ernst laughed. 'I'm glad you said that! Charming's the *mot juste*. Irmi's always happy, so gay, like a butterfly flitting from flower to flower. And she hasn't had too easy a time, either. As a matter of fact, she got into very bad trouble, about a year ago. She almost had a child. Of course that's a great, great secret.'

43

'How do you mean, "almost"?'

'Well, she had to go to the hospital and have an operation . . . Then it was all put right.'

Paul had felt as though he was the first young man she had pressed her body against. He thought they would never forget each other.

'It was just a little cloud in her life, you know. It sailed over. And now she's as happy as ever.'

Joachim called out. '*Bitte setzt euch!*' Everyone sat on the floor in order to see the film shown on a screen fixed to the wall above the bookshelves. Willy turned out the lights, and sat down beside Paul who, by this time, was a bit drunk with absinthe. The idea of Irmi having an abortion was mingled with his memory of dancing with her, which had now regained its sweetness. Colours, sounds, scents, the taste of absinthe, wisps of remembered conversation, wove patterns in his brain, as he sat there in the dark, waiting for the film to begin.

The picture leaped out of the darkness, a new sequence of images in his head. Boys and girls skiing jerkily down a snowy slope. The sky black against the snow. When they reached a bump at the bottom of the slope they lifted their sticks in order to propel themselves forward. A girl looked up into the camera. She seemed to be greeting someone in this room. Joachim. They all laughed and clapped and called out 'Joachim!' Now the scene was on board ship, under a hot sky. Iron shadows drew straight and curved lines across a deck. Joachim leaned on railings, staring out to sea. His face was motionless. He turned – and laughed at his friends in this room – skin wrinkling in the sun. Now he was playing deck tennis, laughing and gesticulating from that deck towards his friends in this room. Paul was his friend. Now on the screen there was a party held in this very studio, with boys and girls dancing. Some of them there then, some of them here now – dancing. The camera sauntered among twisting and turning figures, taking in the interior of the studio, the tubular furniture, the cube-shaped lamps, occasionally singling out a pretty face, a stripped torso, a thigh, a bare foot. Suddenly they all fell on top of each other on the floor, some of them now present in this room. Looking up with flashing eyes into the light, Willy lay stroking the head of Irmi, on the ground beside him, beside Paul. Willy turned, his face thrust up into the light, and kissed the top of her head, then his head seen from above with its thick curls, covered the light on her lips. Everyone laughed. Paul heard Willy, lying beside him on the floor, laugh. Paul laughed.

The studio lights were turned on again. They all stood up, for a moment speechless, vibrant. Two or three couples started dancing softly, to no music. One couple stopped dancing, frozen in a tableau embrace.

Paul heard Irmi say 'Willy!' and walk away with him. Paul felt drunkenly jealous. Willy and his companion had left the room. Paul waited by the blue slit of a window, leaning against the sill, for what seemed a very long time. He wondered what Irmi was doing with Willy.

Then suddenly Paul had fallen to the ground, was lying on his back on the floor. For a moment he was unconscious. Then he was staring up at faces staring down at him. His fellow guests formed an irregular frame of heads and shoulders beyond which he saw the ceiling like a mirror reflecting electric light. A girl broke away, tearing a gap out of the frame, and returned a moment later with a sponge of cold water which she pressed gently to his forehead, his cheeks, his lips. She stroked his hair. It was Irmi. He clambered to his feet. 'Are you all right?' asked Joachim, looking at him, eyes big with amazement. 'Yes, perfectly all right.' Joachim went away at once. Ernst came over with the concerned parental look of one who has brought a fellow guest who has committed a social gaffe. 'If you feel all right now, I think we should go home,' he said severely.

'I want first to say good-night to Willy.'

'Where is he?'

'He left the room with someone.'

Ernst looked at Paul inquiringly, then went away, returning a moment later with Willy.

'What do you want, Paul?' Willy asked, smiling.

'I only want to say good-night to you, Willy.'

'Oh, is that all? How funny!' he burst out laughing.

'Shall we go now?' Paul said goodbye to Willy who shook his hand warmly and said that he would go downstairs to say goodbye to them outside. Whilst they were standing at the door talking, Joachim came out with several other departing guests. They all, stumbling rather, went down the eight flights of stairs.

Outside, in the street, Joachim said to Paul: 'I always say that my friends must love me very dearly if they come all this way upstairs to visit me.'

'They do love you very much, Joachim,' Willy said laughing excitedly.

All shook hands, saying goodbye in the road outside.

Now Paul and Ernst were alone. 'Are you all right?' asked Ernst.

'Yes. I'm quite recovered. I can't think what happened to me. I've never fainted before.'

'Well, it was nothing. No one noticed really. Willy's happy now. I'm glad. He hasn't been happy most of this evening.'

'What do you mean?'

'He's gone back upstairs with Joachim. I think he was afraid at one time he wouldn't be asked. But there it is, everything has turned out for the best. I'm glad.'

The presence of Ernst gave Paul the sensation of being forced back on himself. He tried to look at trees and buildings around them, here in the street below, in order to shut Ernst out of his consciousness. They came to a bridge over a deep stream which flowed into the Alster. Leaning over the parapet, Paul looked downwards and across the lake. Something was happening to the sky. There was no sunrise yet, but no longer completely dark, the sky was growing transparent. It was filling up with light drop by drop like a tank with water. Against the paling sky Paul saw tresses of leaves hanging down like hair, all detail blotted out.

'How extraordinary, the way they hang!'

'Yes, *hanging*. That's the *mot juste* to describe the foliage. I can see now how it is you write poetry.'

'Do you ever write poetry, Ernst?'

He took this portentously. 'Well, I haven't done so for a long time. The funny thing is that when I do think of anything to write, it's always a line of French or English that comes into my mind, not a phrase in my own language.'

He bothers, he fusses, he persists, he imitates, never leaves me alone, he's my shadow tied to my ankles.

'It's dawn!' cried Ernst suddenly, shooting his right arm up like a railway signal.

'I know. I know. I know.'

They were at the Stockmann residence. Through the grey light Paul saw silhouettes of the mansions of that millionaire neighbourhood. Two lines of poetry kept running through his head:

> *J'ai fait la magique étude*
> *Du bonheur, que nul n'élude*

Ernst unlocked the immense doors and they tiptoed into the house, creeping upstairs as quietly as possible. As they went past a room on the first floor, Paul noticed a light showing under a door. Ernst started slightly, and turned back. Then he followed Paul again, asked him to go up to the next floor to his room, and said that he would join him there immediately. He whispered that his mother had almost certainly stayed up all night waiting for his return from Joachim's party, and that he must speak with her.

Feeling strangely guilty, Paul waited in his room. In a few minutes Ernst returned. He was looking quiet and determined.

'Well?'

'It's nothing. My mother is often like this, but it makes no difference. It is distressing, of course, because she is one's mother. She seems to have taken exception to you. But I always do what I want. You are my guest, not hers.' He turned and came towards Paul. He repeated: 'I take no notice. I get my way. I do what I want.'

'Can I help?'

Suddenly, Paul felt sorry for him.

He shrugged as though to imply that he needed no help.

'Why are you so unhappy, Ernst?' Paul asked, thinking of questions Wilmot might ask.

'That shows how little you understand me. I am not unhappy. You are here.'

Paul got up to go, thinking this was the end of their conversation. Just as he reached the door, Ernst said:

'You might help me. You are the only person I have ever met who might.'

'How?' Paul knew there was something he could do at that

moment which might save Ernst. Something that Wilmot might recommend doing. He was trembling. Ernst, a different person, happy. A miracle performed. Ernst stood now quite close to Paul. He put a hand on his shoulder. It was not so much that Paul was repelled by the action when suddenly Ernst kissed him as by the expression in his eyes.

After the maid had brought him his breakfast of coffee and rolls, he spent the morning in his room writing. Ernst had gone to the Stockmann office. Thinking that he must give the maid time to tidy the room, Paul started downstairs with the intention of letting himself out of the house and taking a walk along the road by the lake. When he got to a door on the first floor landing – that under which the previous night (or rather, morning) Ernst had seen his mother's light still burning – the door opened abruptly. Frau Stockmann emerged and walked out on to the landing. She was in a dressing gown, her hair falling loose over her shoulders, her face not made up, crinkled and ugly, her breasts sagging. Obviously she had not slept. She commanded: 'Come into my room, Herr Paul Schoner. I want to speak with you.'

The room, which was large, gave the impression of being all Neapolitan red damask. The walls were lined with cloth that colour, as were the curtains and sofa, and two walnut-wood armchairs. There was a dressing table with an oval mirror, and a very handsome writing desk. It seemed a luxuriant frame for an immense water-colour of rust-coloured frayed-petalled chrysanthemums. He disconcerted Frau Stockmann by at once asking the name of the painter. It was Nolde.

Having snapped out this information, Frau Stockmann seated herself in one of the armchairs, telling Paul to draw up the other, opposite her. She barely produced a smile as she said, 'I hope you have been happy in Hamburg during your short visit.' He noted the past tense.

'I have been very happy. Thank you very much for your kindness in having me.'

'When Ernst told me he had an English visitor, I was so very content,' she said, 'I thought, at last my son has a nice friend, a promising young poet – Ernst told me – who is serious. He will be able to share all intellectual interests with Ernst. In my mind's

48

eyes, I see them go to concerts together and the art galleries and visit the architecture of this city, which is world famous. There is so much culture in Hamburg. And nearby there are the Hanseatic cities, Bremen and Lübeck, in the neighbourhood also to see. They will hire a car and Ernst will drive to show him where Thomas Mann wrote his *Buddenbrooks*, I thought.'

'I do want very much to see those places. But – '

She took up the word 'but' and said, harshly, 'But you are too busy going with Ernst to parties with Joachim Lenz and his friend Willy.'

'I think I must tell you, Frau Stockmann, that I very much like Joachim Lenz.'

'Joachim Lenz? You like Joachim Lenz? Joachim Lenz used to come here often with Ernst. He is not stupid so I invited him. I thought, maybe Ernst will influence him to being better. But I soon saw that it was Joachim Lenz who influenced my son, Ernst Stockmann, for the worst – the very much worst, more bad than I can tell. I cannot tell you what things. A young *Engländer* would never understand them. Decadence! That's what there gives now in Germany where there is so much decay among the young! Always going about naked! That's what began it all! In canoes at the end of this garden, boys and girls like those expressionist pictures we see in that Art Gallery! I say to Ernst: "Do not ever bring that dirty young coffee merchant to our clean house where my son remains unsoiled." Ernst, thank God, is still pure.'

'Joachim does not like being a coffee merchant. He told me so himself.'

'So much the worse. He is not even serious about coffee – the only decent thing he sells – you tell me.' She broke off, contemplating the enormity of Joachim Lenz. 'Those photographs!' she exclaimed and went on: 'I always thought an English poet – such nice poetry they write, the *Engländer*, so admired in Hamburg – would not want to meet *gemeine Leute* – low people. In Hamburg we think of the English as so clean, upright, so respectable – only for good influences always – so you can see how disappointed I am! However, all that is of the past. What I have to tell you is I am very sorry to say that you no longer after next week can be my guest. That has nothing to do

49

with what we have been mentioning. The truth is now I must have other *Gäste* filling each spare room. Art collectors from Düsseldorf. And, after the terrible war, we do not have the servant for many *Gäste*, only now four maids to clean up all.'

'But Ernst said only last night I am *his* guest, not yours.' Paul instantly regretted having said this.

'Ernst does not decide who stays in this house. He does not understand our conditions – his guests are not like my guests who do not make all this work and bring bad influences here, like Joachim Lenz!' Suddenly she changed her tone again and said, rather pathetically: 'I am sorry, I have not slept. Not one minute all last night. I do not know what I say in a foreign language. Excuse all of what I said. When I was in Paris I spoke French like German, and my English was good, though not good like that of Ernst.'

'You have been very kind. Whatever Ernst wishes, I agree that I must go. I did not mean to tell you what he had said about my being his guest, meaning that I was not yours. Please forgive me.'

'One favour I ask you,' she said, smiling and even friendly now. 'Do not tell Ernst we had this conversation. Else it all falls back on top of me. I cannot stand that he and I should quarrel over you. I think he likes you, truly he likes you; truly.'

'What I shall tell him is that I myself have decided to leave. And of course, after all you have said, that is true, but I won't say it has anything to do with you.'

'It is true I really do have three guests next week,' she said getting up from her chair with a certain pathos and a look of fatigue near to collapse, tired even of being angry.

Then she surprised him by holding out her hand. 'Well, we do not have to say goodbye quite yet,' she said, as though it had been her intention to do so. She asked: 'Do you know what Jakob, my husband calls you?'

'No.'

'"*Der Engel!*" He calls you "*Der unschuldige Engel-länder*" because, as he says, you look so innocent. "A fallen angel," I laugh at him. But now perhaps I think you are only a falling one. But do not bring down my son with you in your fall. He is clean.'

Paul reflected that their conversation had lasted long enough for the maid to take away his breakfast things and make his bed. But he no longer wanted to walk by the lake. He went back to his room and wrote a long letter to Simon Wilmot.

At the *Schwimmbad* that afternoon Paul for the first time was alone with Joachim and Willy. Ernst was still at his office. The two friends seemed relieved to be with him without Ernst. They asked Paul whether he enjoyed staying at the Stockmann residence. Paul said that the house and pictures and furniture and garden were beautiful. Willy said: 'Yes, it is all very wonderful, but do you get enough to eat?'

'Of course I do.'

They laughed.

Joachim said: 'We always say that if you go to dine at the Stockmanns' everything is served on silver plate, but there is very little to eat.'

Willy asked: 'Do you like Hanny?'

'Hanny? Who is Hanny?'

'Haven't you heard that everyone calls Ernst's mother Hanny?'

Joachim said: 'Two years ago, when I was twenty-four, I was very friendly with Ernst. I was always going to his home, he was always coming to mine. But soon Hanny suspected that I was coming between her and Ernst. She said nothing, but after that Ernst stopped inviting me to his house. For a time Ernst went on coming to my parents' house, but then suddenly he refused whenever I asked him. Ernst and I stopped meeting at each other's homes. Then, finally, we only met at places like this, or at Sankt Pauli, where none of our parents would want us to go at all! The last place they would want us to meet, I guess.'

'And what do you think of Ernst?' Paul asked.

'I think that most of what I do not like about Ernst comes from his mother,' said Joachim. 'I used to go on seeing him because I thought he would become free of her. But now I think that as long as he lives with his mother and father, it is hopeless to try and help him. So I do not see him so much.'

Paul felt liberated knowing how Joachim and Willy felt about Ernst. His friendship with them was now separate from his friendship with Ernst. He felt disloyal to Ernst. But, he told himself, that was because it is difficult not to be disloyal to someone who implicitly demands an exclusive relationship with you.

Ernst arrived. They all shook hands. Joachim asked him, with an exaggerated amiability acted out before Willy and Paul, 'Well, Ernst, how are things going just now with you?'

Bridling, Ernst replied: 'Oh, pretty nicely, Joachim, but of course I haven't got your luck.'

'How do you mean? How do you say you haven't got my luck? I think you are very lucky, Ernst.'

'Well, I haven't such a charming way with me perhaps, as you have, Joachim.'

'Oh, I don't know. I think that you are lucky too, Ernst. Surely you are lucky also, Ernst, very lucky.' And suddenly he looked at Paul and laughed outright. Then he said to Willy: 'I think it is time that we should go into the water now.'

'Oh yes, do let us go now,' said Willy.

Paul lingered, thinking that perhaps he should stay with Ernst.

Joachim called back: 'Paul, are you coming too?' Paul hesitated.

Ernst said in an offended voice, 'I'm going to stay here. I don't think I'll go in yet. Perhaps later.' Paul followed Joachim and Willy.

Directly they were out of earshot of Ernst, Joachim began: 'You know what you have always to remember about Ernst is that he is a Jew. Therefore, I think he is an actor. He acts always, you know, in everything he says and does, hoping he will make you admire him.'

'I am partly Jewish – half-Jewish in fact.'

'Oh, we do not believe you, Paul!' exclaimed Willy, laughing extravagantly. 'You are the most English Englishman I have ever met!'

'Well, I guess everyone is a little bit Jewish,' laughed Joachim. 'I have a Jewish great-aunt in Brazil.'

'Oh, Joachim, you never told me that!' exclaimed Willy, laughing harder than ever. Now they were all laughing, very hard – all three of them, harder than ever.

'I feel sorry for Ernst,' Paul said.

'You feel sorry for Ernst!' said Joachim looking at Paul. 'Why? Surely he's clever enough to look after himself?'

Paul knew he had been hypocritical saying he was sorry for Ernst.

'I am sorry for him too, Joachim,' said Willy. 'It is true that he is clever, but he seems able to do nothing to make himself happy, with all his cleverness.'

'He is clever, he has money, he has friends, he has Hanny, he has everything! What more could he want?' Joachim exclaimed, half indignantly, half amused, and he dived into the water.

The Stockmanns always had five o'clock tea (part of the English style and tradition of Hamburg) so now Paul said *'Auf Wiedersehen'* to Joachim and Willy and went in search of Ernst. There he was. By this time Paul knew well his white skin, which the sun never seemed to turn brown, polished like wax out of which grew black hairs like minute wires. As if to match these black hairs, Ernst wore black bathing drawers. Along his thighs other wiry black hairs coursed almost down to the ankles. In his most characteristic pose, he had a hand on a hip, and his right foot was only just touching the ground, the toe pointed downward in order to display the firm single stance of the left leg. He was looking at a boy who had fresh pink cheeks and limpid light-blue eyes and whose body was soft, not hard with that mechanical rigid muscular hardness of Ernst. Ernst encouraged the boy to speak, asking him soft, dove-like questions that seemed to peck all over his pink body. Just as Paul approached, he was taking some remark of the boy's seriously and advising him considerately on a point.

As soon as he saw Paul, he called out buoyantly: 'Hello-ah! Good, then you have come back!' Then, turning to the boy, he said, *'Das ist mein englischer Freund,'* giving him a quick smile. *'Comprenez?'* He threw in the French word, for good measure. Then, looking at his watch, 'Oh dear me, I didn't realize that it was so late. We must go at once or we won't be home in time for tea.'

He turned to the boy. *'Also, auf Wiedersehen. Bis übermorgen.* The day after tomorrow, remember.'

Ernst and Paul walked to the tram stop.

'A very nice boy, that,' he said. 'So *frisch* and simple. I like young people to be simple. He's just the type I most like to meet. You feel at once when you first look at him, that he's honest, direct ... But tell me about your day. It's the first time you've been alone with Willy and Joachim, isn't it? How did you get on with them?'

'Very well.'

'Good. Tell me. You still like Willy, don't you? Do you like him as much as when you first met him, I wonder?'

'I haven't had any reason to revise my opinion of him.'

'I meant something different from that. I thought at first you were specially fond of him and now you might feel differently. That's all.'

Paul found the conversation stifling and did not answer. But Ernst did not mind. This afternoon nothing could damp his high spirits. After Paul got into the tram, Ernst lingered until the car started, then sprang neatly into it, jumping springily from the pavement.

Entry in Paul's Notebook:

I realize now that I am more consciously happy here in Hamburg than I have ever been before, because some need I have always felt is fulfilled in this relationship between Joachim and Willy. I feel as if a new life had begun here in Germany. I do not know precisely in what the newness consists, but perhaps the key to it is in these young Germans having a new attitude toward the body. Although I have never been puritanical in outlook, I confess that till now, whatever I may have pretended to myself, I have always regarded my body as sinful, and my own physical being as something to be ashamed of and to be overcome by compensating and atoning spiritual qualities. Now I am beginning to feel that I may soon come to regard my body as a source of joy. Instead of an obstacle which prevents me achieving satisfactory relationships with others, it may become the instrument by which such a relationship is attained. Perhaps, after all, I may become a complete human being, not just someone who overemphasizes and overdevelops the idealistic side of his nature, because he is incapable of accepting his own physicality. Yet I still hardly think such fulfilment possible for me, because I recognize myself as condemned to the ideal. Yet it is life-giving to have realized the quality of this friendship between Joachim and Willy.

Note: Willy is really nothing. Joachim is the creator of Willy and of their whole relationship.

Note: of the people I have met here, the one with whom I have most in common is Ernst. He and I are both Jewish. Hanny, his mother, is *brilliant*.

Paul was sitting in his room writing the above in his Notebook. He was feeling happy. Joachim had rung him up that morning, inviting him to dine with his family. As he was writing, the door opened – as always with Ernst, its opening coinciding with a warning knock. When Paul looked up, Ernst was already in the room. His appearance was so strange, Paul almost fell off his chair. Ernst ran forward springily saying, with a light affectionate laugh, 'Why, you're all nerves!'

He was wearing white rubber gym shoes, grey flannel trousers and a white zephyr running vest. Paul was now fairly accustomed to his extraordinary changes of attire, but this he found gruesome. In the white, tight-fitting vest, the light-coloured trousers, the pink socks in off-white sneakers, with his horn-coloured face behind black-rimmed spectacles emerging above these clothes and his dead expression, he made Paul think of – what? Perhaps an ancient Egyptian mummified and wrapped in bandages prepared for the tomb.

'Why are you dressed like that, Ernst?'

'Why, Paul, you look quite alarmed. There's nothing the matter. I like to keep myself in training. I've been doing a little gym with Karl.'

'Who's Karl?'

'Surely you know who Karl is? But no, perhaps you don't. He's the boy I was talking to two days ago, on the beach at the *Schwimmbad*. Didn't you hear me say to him, "*Auf Wiedersehen, bis übermorgen*"? By now you should know enough German to understand that. I've been teaching Karl a little boxing. I think the training of the body is very important. Yes, very important, especially for us Germans now.' He looked at Paul closely. 'If you don't mind my saying so, you yourself could benefit from some gymnastics. You are a bit round-shouldered, and your pectoral muscles need developing. Too much poetry doesn't improve the flesh, even if it does the spirit. In the new Germany, people like our friend Joachim prefer poems written on the body to those on paper.' He broke off suddenly and then, raising his arms, said: 'Look, I'll show you.'

He stood in the middle of the room, his hands slightly clenched and loose, swaying his arms to and fro, to and fro, with clocklike regularity, in front of his body. Paul had never seen an exercise like this before. Ernst's body was absolutely relaxed, he leaned forward like a marionette. His hands now moved round and round, in front, behind.

He moved beautifully, precisely, repulsively. He was completely absorbed in movement. Then he looked up at Paul, with his little smile.

'Won't you try now?'

'I'd rather not. I couldn't possibly do that.'

'Oh yes, you could. It isn't at all hard, once you've got the rhythm. Come into the room where I keep my instruments. What do you call them?'

Paul could no more think of the appropriate word than Ernst could. Was he forgetting his English?

Ernst took Paul up to a room at the top of the house. It was a large garret with heavy black beams and a floor of bare boards of pine, varnished, reflecting the light from a skylight in the roof.

'Now try,' said Ernst.

Paul moved his hands in a feeble effort to imitate the exercise.

'No, no. Excuse me, but that's not at all right. Look, you must lean your body forward, so, quite loosely, and then, still keeping well forward, you must let the weight just lean from one side to the other, and, at the same time, let your hands swing by themselves, from side to side, so . . .'

He stood in the middle of the room, to show Paul. Again, Ernst yielded himself to the exercise. Paul noticed the back of his head swaying slightly, like a pendulum, with the black beams above, and below, on the floor, the polished reflections from the window. Before he had finished Paul started imitating Ernst.

'Oh no. It still won't do, I'm afraid. Let me help you.'

He stood behind Paul and put his arms on his shoulder.

'Now,' he moved his body to one side. 'And now.' He swung it round to the other.

'Yes,' Ernst meditated, as though he were a doctor addressing Paul, 'I thought so. Your muscles are very stiff. You ought to do this often. You should practise with me sometimes before breakfast. Now, right – left – '

Paul felt Ernst breathing on his hair. 'I can't do it!' Paul cried, jumping away from him. 'It's no use! I can't do it!'

Paul hated Ernst.

'Why, of course, you needn't go on if you don't want to. Not now. Perhaps some other time. You are a little tired now, I think. I'm sorry to have made you come up here at all.'

'I'm not at all tired. But I simply can't do things like this. I associate them in my mind with institutions and discipline. For some reason I've always resisted improving my physique. I used to hate drill at school.'

Paul was afraid Ernst might notice how physically repelled he was by him. He tried to cover this up with talk.

Ernst said: 'Then let us go downstairs to my room again.'

When they were back in his large, comfortable room, with its venetian shutters closed to protect the books, papers, furniture, from the summer, Ernst said: 'Sit down on the sofa. You're a bit tired, aren't you?'

'I'm not in the least tired.'

'I think you are tireder – "more tired", should I say? – than you realize. You look tired. It was thoughtless of me not to have noticed that before. I blame myself for it.'

He sat himself down beside Paul on the sofa. He seemed to be watching Paul from a height.

'What are you reading?' Paul asked, pointing to a book that lay on Ernst's desk.

'One of Valéry's essays. I haven't ever shown you my books, have I? I have some rather rare books on art, which you might care to look at.'

They spent a quarter of an hour pulling books down from shelves. Paul found Ernst's books interesting, but his enjoyment was spoiled because he was always conscious of Ernst leaning over him, commenting, criticizing, wondering whether he would like this book more than that, hoping he would not soil the pages with his fingers.

Ernst had taste, and Paul found it pleasant to discuss books with him. When Ernst started talking about the poetry of Rilke, he even forgot himself in the endeavour to express his meaning lucidly in English. He spoke English with the pleasure of an artist of language.

He said, taking down a volume of essays by Walter Möring: 'As it happens, the man who wrote this is a particular friend of mine. He is a very interesting man indeed, an able critic both of books and life; and, I think, perhaps even a great satirist, although, of course, I am not unaware of his faults.'

An abrupt little insidious laugh, then he went on, showing Paul the inscription beginning *'Lieber Ernst'* in the flyleaf of a volume: 'I wonder if you are interested in handwriting. If so, you might like to see what Möring has written in this. You see, there is a certain spirituality in the finely penned words. I think that one can discover a great deal about the writer's character from his handwriting. I always look very carefully at the handwriting of the letters I receive.'

Taking down another volume with an autographed dedication, he said: 'You can tell at once that the person who wrote this (it happens to be André Gide) is both energetic and deeply sensitive. The lines of the rather long dedication slope upwards on the page, the words themselves lean forward, like runners, and when the writer has reached the end of a line he is impatient at having to go on to another line, and the last words of it twist defiantly downwards. There is a certain aesthetic unity of effect over the whole page, which reveals, I think, a touch, if only a touch, of genius. And yet,' – he smiled – 'there is a weakness as well as strength here. There is something almost effeminate, almost petty – or would it be correct English to say "petticoaty"? – about the hurriedness of it all. Well, perhaps I shouldn't go so far as to use the word "effeminate". In German the word would be *weiblich*, which isn't quite as strong as that.'

Whilst he was saying all this, Paul had the impression of Ernst flying about the room.

Ernst went to another bookcase and started to take out an immense volume. Then he said, 'No,' and began to put it back again. He stood up, tapping his knee with one hand, consciously weighing a question in his mind. He looked at Paul quizzically, smiling coyly, his head cocked on one side.

'Well,' he said, 'you might like it. We'll see. Yes, I think that you would. After all, you are a poet. Surely . . .'

He took the book across to the table in front of the sofa on which Paul was sitting.

'This is a very curious book indeed. I wonder if it will interest you. A great work in many ways, of anthropological and scientific interest. Yes, in its way a masterpiece.'

The book was an illustrated history of pornographic art: primeval pottery in the shape of sexual organs; Greek vases with images of satyrs, centaurs, men and women copulating; a woman being fucked by a donkey; obscene sculptures on medieval cathedrals and in cloisters; gargoyles; Boucher's girls with legs upraised to exquisite courtiers of Versailles pulling down their satin breeches.

Paul would gladly have spent a week alone studying the encyclopaedia, but not with Ernst leaning over him. 'Why should this stuff interest you?' he asked in a voice that seemed smothered.

'You don't like it? I am sorry. I thought you were broadminded, interested in every aspect of human life throughout history. *Nil humanum mihi alienum est.*' Ernst said this in an assertive schoolmaster's voice. Then he added, more mildly: 'Of course, I quite understand your objections, but surely it is very immature of you to dismiss a great masterpiece of scientific scholarship simply as "disgusting"? But then, Paul,' he went on severely, 'you are very young, even for your twenty years, in many respects. It's delightful that you should be in some ways so naïve. It's part of your charm. All the same, this is a very famous book, which perhaps you are too young to appreciate. Indeed, it is a classic.'

'I dare say. But the interest is too specialized for me,' Paul said. He felt as if he were being cross-examined by a smooth inquisitor.

59

'As a modern writer, with the scientific outlook, you ought to be interested in everything. Have you read *L'Immoraliste?*'

'No.'

'Well, you ought to read it. Perhaps if you read some modern French writers, you would see what it is to have a completely open mind about everything. I feel sure this should be the attitude of our generation. The next generation in Germany feels like this. Joachim does.'

'Anyone who is not completely dead warms particularly to a few things, and is repelled by other things.' Paul thought of the essays by D. H. Lawrence he had been reading.

'I condemn nothing,' said Ernst stiffly. 'So perhaps you think I am dead?'

He smiled tensely. Paul, seeing here an opportunity to seize, said:

'I intended nothing personal. But now I do have something personal to tell you – about myself. I have to leave your house.'

Ernst stared at him blankly. Paul went on:

'It has been very kind of you to have me. And very kind of your mother. But I can't make demands on your mother's hospitality any longer.'

'Aren't you happy here?'

'I have enjoyed myself very much, but I can't go on staying here any longer.'

'Why not?'

'Well, though she hasn't said anything, I do have a slight feeling that your mother doesn't altogether like me. You yourself said as much.'

'You are my guest. I can have my own guests.'

'Then shall we say that I leave in two days' time?' Paul got up decisively, as though to leave at once.

'You prefer to be alone, perhaps?'

'It's not quite that – '

'Perhaps I have done something to upset you? You must say what is the matter. I shan't be offended.'

'Ernst, it isn't as though we'd known each other a long while. After all, we scarcely know each other. I just want to be independent.'

'I don't feel like a stranger with you, Paul.'

'Thank you very much for all your generosity.' Paul stood up and moved towards the door.

'Are you leaving then?'

'The day after tomorrow.'

'Well, where are you going now? You don't intend to leave this moment?'

'Surely I told you I have to go out. I am dining with Joachim.'

'You seem very fond of Joachim.'

Paul left him then. He felt exhausted. He did not even want to see Joachim. He thought: 'Perhaps Joachim will find me as much a burden as I find Ernst. I am like Ernst. Perhaps I repelled Marston as much as Ernst repels me.'

Situated in a garden which faced the road in front and the lake at the back, the house of the Lenz family was only about ten minutes' walk from the Stockmann residence. But it was not in the millionaire quarter. It had two perky-looking gables, a stucco front through which rust-coloured beams protruded, and a porch above concrete steps leading from the garden: a suburban house, that seemed to express bourgeois standards the very opposite of Joachim's life.

When Paul rang the bell, Joachim, accompanied by the family's noisy fox terrier Fix, opened the front door. Fix yapped and Joachim's fifteen-year-old brother Klaus, smiling shyly at Paul, appeared at the far end of the passage-like hall. Joachim conducted Paul to the heavily furnished sitting-room where, waiting for dinner, were Hans Lenz, his father, Greta Lenz, his mother, and an uncle, whose name Paul didn't catch. They went into the dining-room almost immediately. They sat down at a long table, where Joachim's mother and uncle were opposite Paul. Frau Lenz had hair looped either side of her head, over her ears. She wore around her neck a velvet band with a little diamond in front, and over her shoulders above her dress a white lace collar. She looked like a late Victorian daguerreotype of a lady at some spa.

His father was a diminutive version of Joachim with deeply lined forehead and shrewd half-shut black eyes, contrasting with Joachim's, which always seemed startlingly open. The uncle was a slightly larger version of Hans Lenz, but still, compared with Joachim, shrunk and somehow petty. On the wall was a large framed sepia photograph of the most famous member of the family, another uncle, the bemedalled General Siegfried Lenz, a distinguished field commander during the Great War, and today a close collaborator of Field Marshal Hindenburg. Paul asked about this very striking picture: Joachim told him that General Lenz lived in ferocious retirement on his estate somewhere east of Potsdam. 'We are all terrified of Uncle Siegfried,' said Joachim, growling like a lion. 'Gr-r-r!' he said. Klaus giggled.

After a few polite enquiries in stumbling English about his reasons for being in Hamburg ('*Ach*, to study German with Herr Doktor Ernst Stockmann? *Ach so! Ja! Ja!*') not much was said to Paul by members of the older generation. 'You are my son Joachim's English friend? It is good for his English that you talk with him,' was about all Frau Lenz said to Paul in the course of the evening. There was something about her Paul liked greatly – perhaps most of all her unconcealed manner of resenting him as Joachim's friend. Evidently the understanding of the family was that Joachim and Paul were there to talk English, while the others talked German in the background. Paul noticed that when, from time to time, Joachim talked in a bantering tone of voice to his brother Klaus, Frau Lenz frowned slightly. The frown matched the white lace collar.

Supper consisted of *belegtes Brötchen*, cuts of various meats, slices of sausage and of cheese, black bread, and potato salad. This paper-thin diet seemed appropriate to the stiff and straight two-dimensional photographic cut-out which Paul saw as the Lenz family. Here perhaps the English were still the enemy, the War was not over.

After coffee, just as soon as they could decently make their escape, Joachim said to Paul, 'Let us go for a stroll in the garden.' Klaus made an effort to dart out after them, instantly frustrated by his mother. Joachim and Paul strolled past the back of the house to the end of the garden, set against the lake, where there was a little boat house. Joachim seemed not in the least perturbed by the atmosphere of disapproval left behind them. 'Poor Klaus! My mother won't let me speak to him, if she can prevent it. She's certain I'll ruin him. It's a wonder you're allowed to come with us, Fix!' was his ironic expression of regret, which he addressed to the fox terrier. He seemed highly amused at their reception of Paul. 'I think they suspect you of being a very, very bad influence on their virtuous son. You see, in Hamburg, the English have a reputation for all sorts of immorality. That's why English sailors are so loved in Sankt Pauli.'

He became serious, as they leaned against a fence and looked across the lake. 'My family', he said, 'are all merchants, all of them so bourgeois except for my uncle the general who never got married and so is very suspect. Anyway, we never see him. But I intend one day to go to Potsdam and introduce myself. I think he might be glad to see my photographs. My mother spends her life trying to prevent Klaus from becoming like me. They want me to become like them. But I cannot. There is a great division in Germany today between the older and the younger generations.'

'Well, so there is in England, among my friends.'

Joachim did not respond to this. He stared out across the lake with its canoes and sailing boats, his attention gone. Then he deliberately focused it on the present state of Germany, as he turned back to Paul.

'The older generation belongs to the period before the War when all values for the middle class seemed fixed, materialistic. The aim of Germans in Hamburg of my parents' generation was that of merchants who only want to make money.'

'Did Germany's defeat in the War change that?'

'It wasn't so much the defeat as what happened afterwards. What really made the new generation so different from the old was the Inflation. For a year or so in Germany money became completely worthless. To mail a letter you had to stick on the envelope a postage stamp for a million marks. To buy a loaf of bread, you had to fill your suitcase with bank notes, and you hoped that the price of a loaf hadn't gone up so much by the time you reached the bakery that you wouldn't be able to buy the loaf. Of course, this didn't affect people like the Stockmanns who had property, which went up in value all the time – it was during the Inflation that Hanny Stockmann bought most of her art collection, apart from one or two things which she boasts about having got in Paris earlier on – or even my people very much, though times were difficult for them. But it impressed us who were children then, if we had friends at school whose parents didn't have any objects they could sell.' His eyes seemed to be watching past German history as though it were a movie. Then he turned back to the present.

'The new generation doesn't want money in the same way as their parents did. Of course, just to do what we want, we have to have *some* money. But what's the use of accumulating a lot of money, if it can all disappear overnight? And we don't want many possessions either. All we want is to *live*, not to acquire things. And sun and air and water and making love don't require a great deal of money.' He looked out at the boats on the lake again.

'But what will happen when you get old?'

'Well . . . We shall change, I guess. But for the time being, all we want is just to live. Maybe other things will arise later. Already in Germany there is wonderful new architecture and interesting art, but the best architecture is cheap and bare and plain, designed for young people who don't want houses which are mausoleums they fill with things they have acquired, like the Stockmanns do with their pictures.'

'But you can't remain young always.'

'That's what my parents are always telling me. But I don't want to become like them or like Ernst's parents. Most of all, they want me to be a merchant. I don't want to be a heap of coffee. But my parents are reasonable, nice people. They say that if I am interested in the arts, then I should go to art school and become an artist. Artists also make money, and if you are famous as an artist you can become rich like Picasso. There are very good schools for artists in Germany, for example, the Bauhaus where I bought the furniture of my studio.'

'Then why don't you go to art school?'

'As soon as you become an artist, if you are successful, you have to develop a style by which you are well known, which means turning yourself into the maker of a certain type of product for which you are famous. I don't want to do that. For the time being I want to live my physical life, not make stereotypes of my soul for art dealers.'

64

'Is young people living their lives the new Germany? Is that the Weimar Republic?'

'For very many members of this generation, yes. Perhaps, after all Germany has been through, we Germans are tired. After the War and years of starvation, perhaps we need to swim and to lie in the sun and make love in order to recharge our lives like batteries. We want our lives to replace those who became corpses.'

'But how will it end?'

'I don't know, perhaps something marvellous – an under-standing of the values of living, nothing but living, life for its own sake, life, a new world, like the new architecture, not material-istic.' He laughed. 'Or perhaps not that at all, perhaps something terrible, monstrous, the end!' He held up his hand and his eyes shone, as though he were looking at an immense screen on which he saw moving pictures of final war – the end of everything.

Joachim suggested that they go to his studio, which was only ten minutes' distance to walk. As they walked, Paul observed him closely. Joachim was wearing a dark brown suit, a garish tie, a grey felt hat. There was something a bit flamboyant about his appearance, a bit vulgar, but entertained – by himself among other things – and warm, as though he invited spectators to share his pleasure in his sheer vitality. He walked conscious that many young people in Hamburg knew about him and admired him. He was entirely Joachim. He combined display with privacy.

They climbed up the eight flights of stairs to his penthouse studio. When they reached the top, he held Paul's arm affectionately and, pointing to the ceiling under the roof of the penthouse, said: 'Tell me, Paul, would you like to walk up and up stairs, higher than these, round and round and round, until you reached heaven?'

'I suppose I would,' Paul admitted, a bit ashamed, yet proud of this.

He looked into Paul's eyes, seriously mocking, with a shade of contempt.

'Yes, I think you would.'

He fumbled in his pocket for his keys and, having found them, unlocked the studio door, and threw it wide open. Standing on the threshold for a few seconds, he seemed to be watching with delight its bareness and emptiness, its blank wide oblong, the vertical slots of windows and the slant parallelogram of skylight, the transparent blue shadows along the walls. Satisfied, at last he switched on the light by the door and, whistling, with hands in pockets and hat pushed back on his head – guying almost the Chicago movie gangster – he strode into the room. The studio, Paul thought, looked like a film set.

'I always love to come back here,' Joachim said, throwing his hat down on a table and taking off his jacket. 'This is my real home, not with my parents.'

He put his arm on Paul's shoulders with the gesture of someone who is accustomed to physical displays of affection – as a way of exercising power over his friends. Then he walked to the far end of the studio and put a Cole Porter record, 'Let's Fall in Love', on the machine. He came back to where Paul was standing and started questioning him about England, English public schools, Oxford University, the censoring of books. 'We hear such strange things about England – that so many things are forbidden there that are permitted here. And then that books are banned. Is that true? I read in the newspapers about *Ulysses* being banned and then recently there was another we were told about – *The Well of Loneliness*. Can all that be true? Doesn't anyone protest?'

'My friends and I all do protest. But – '

'But why are they banned?'

Paul tried to explain the attitude of the British authorities. But all the explanations sounded ridiculous even as he said them. Joachim just stared at him in astonishment. He changed the subject: 'Do you have friends in England? You are a poet, Ernst tells me. Do you know other young writers and artists?'

Paul attempted to describe Wilmot – 'the most extraordinary person I know.' How Wilmot, when he was working, hated daylight and, with the curtains of his room closed sat at his desk writing poetry. How he had read the works of Freud and could diagnose the neuroses of his friends. How he was very funny, looking a bit like Buster Keaton in his comedies. Wilmot, Paul said, was also very serious. He went for long walks near Oxford and also in the English Lake District. He was blond, almost albino, and had a mole on his left cheek. He had lived in Berlin and stayed for a time at the Institute for Sexual Science of Magnus Hirschfeld. He liked young men. He said he had many affairs. At this, Joachim who had been listening carefully, with a puzzled expression on his face, brightened up a little. 'You say he is amusing, and always acting a role. Perhaps he is like a friend of mine who was in Hamburg, the actor Gustav Gründgens. He also is always dressing up and is very magnetic, very funny. Do you have any friend who is not so amusing, not so clever, but perhaps for love? For love I myself do not like intellectual people.'

Paul told him about Marston. By now he had by heart the myth he had made himself about Marston, the walk along the Wye, the day they were followed by the dog – a record that he played over to himself again and again.

At the end of this recital Joachim asked, 'Did you make love?'

'No.'

'Then why did you go on liking him?'

'Because I found him better and more beautiful than anyone else.'

'Why?'

'His character was like he himself looked. He was very English. In fact he was just like that countryside we walked through.'

'That wouldn't interest me so much if he didn't respond to my great passion for him.'

The false and deceptive word 'pure' was on Paul's lips but he resisted saying it. Instead, he spoke deliberately using English words that he thought beyond the range of Joachim's under-standing of English, words which he would not dream of using to Wilmot or Bradshaw who would see right through them to the hypocrisy they concealed. He murmured, 'My idea of his perfection embodied in us both my conception of friendship as a shared state of perfection.'

Joachim certainly did not take this in. He said:

'I think I would like to go on talking with you a great deal. I find I like my friends either for their minds or for their bodies. It is strange how often those who have beautiful minds do not have bodies that seem physically beautiful, whereas those who have such bodies I can make love to, do not have minds. Your appearance is like your mind, I think. Perhaps you should do exercises to make you know what you are.'

Paul flushed furiously.

'Why did you come to Hamburg?' Joachim asked.

'In order to learn German.'

'Why, though, to Hamburg?' he asked mockingly. Paul explained the circumstances of his meeting Ernst – which made Joachim laugh – and of Ernst's inviting him to stay.

'But you can't have come to Hamburg simply in order to stay with Ernst Stockmann – and with Hanny!'

'I didn't know anything about them. So I thought I might as well come here as anywhere else.'

'Is that all? Don't the English come to Germany for better reasons than that they are charmed by the beautiful eyes of Ernst Stockmann? Or of Hanny? Have they never heard of the Rhine or Heidelberg or the Black Forest or Berlin? Didn't you ask Ernst what Hamburg was like?'

At this Paul remembered something that had slipped his memory.

'Now I do remember that at lunch, that day at Oxford, I did ask Ernst what Hamburg was like.'

'And what did he say?'

'He looked down at the tablecloth and said with his insinuating smile, "Oh, you know it is a port and has all the strange pleasures and strange customs of a port." How odd of me to have forgotten that!'

'Well, shall we go and see the port?'

'When?'

'Tonight.'

'I'd love to, but I have no key to the Stockmann house. And after 11.00 Frau Stockmann says is too late to ring the bell.'

'*Typisch.*'

Joachim thought for a moment, then decided: 'Well, we'll have to take Ernst with us, that is all. Surely he is allowed a key. I'll ring him up and ask him to come too. Willy will be with us anyway, as he is coming round here later.'

He rang Ernst, and it was arranged that in an hour's time they should meet him at Sankt Pauli, the port area of Hamburg. While they were waiting for Willy, Joachim showed Paul some of his photographs. To see them was, for Paul, to see the expression in

Joachim's eyes when he looked at someone or something. The object photographed seemed contained within them. Each photograph was the record of how, at some particular instant, face or scene or thing had concentrated itself into an arrangement of lines and masses, lights and shadows which summed up the comedy of its own existing, interpenetrated with Joachim's perception. He trapped the coincidence of disparate objects within a frame of time and space: steel-rimmed spectacles lying on the balustrade of a balcony above a sea enveloping a Greek island; the underpants of a pauper, pegged on a line high up above a narrow Neapolitan street, blown by the wind into a shape like a face sneering at the dress and ropes of necklaces of a fashionable Roman lady walking in the street below; the contrast of black children playing in the park against skyscrapers on Chicago's lake shore, of rich white bodies opposite poor brown ones on the beaches of Rio de Janeiro. Objects in his photographs seemed to draw attention to themselves, pointing and speaking – 'Here I am! Look! How extraordinary we are!' and – an exclamation Joachim used frequently in conversation – 'How FUNNY!' A portrait said, 'I have caught the expression of Gustav Gründgens just at that split second in his life when he looks more like himself than anyone will ever see him look!'

There were many photographs of young men. One, in particular, struck Paul. It was of a bather standing naked at the reed-fringed edge of a lake. The picture was taken slightly from below so that the torso, rising above the thighs, receded, and the whole body was seen, layer on layer of hips and rib-cage and shoulders, up to the towering head, with dark hair helmeted against a dark sky. V-shaped shadows of willow leaves fell like showers of arrows on San Sebastian, on the youth's sunlit breast and thighs. 'Oh, wonderful!' said Paul, 'The temple of the body!'

Joachim laughed, 'I like that – the temple. It's always seemed to me like a pagoda, layer on layer, tier on tier, but I suppose that's what a pagoda is, a temple!'

'You say you do not want to do anything. But you do this: you are a photographer, an artist. You should make that your work!'

'I don't want to be a professional photographer. Doing that means pretending to everyone that you are an artist, but I do not think photography is an art. It is a skill, and having a good eye, like shooting, which is what it is quite rightly called. It is a technique only. A good photographer is not like an artist who transforms what he sees, he is like a hunter who is in search of some particular animal which he happens to see more clearly than other hunters, at some particular moment, his particular vision. But the animal, however special to him, does not come out of his own particular soul. It is given to him by the world outside, on which he is totally dependent for it. Photography is impressions the world provides, beautiful scenery or beautiful girls or boys, trapped when perhaps he alone sees them looking as they are at that moment. But that does not make him an artist,' he persisted. 'I would sooner be a coffee merchant than pretend I am an artist because I take photographs. To do that would be cheating.'

'But in that case you are only taking them for yourself.'

'Well, some of my friends seem to like them. Isn't that enough?' he grinned.

'Why do you take photographs?' Paul persisted.

'Haven't I told you? For myself and my friends. Just to provide myself with memories of boys and other things I have seen and shot, like a hunter hanging skulls and stuffed heads in his lodge. What I like is the truth of how something that struck me very much was at that instant. That is just the opposite of art. Even a drawing like that bad one,' he pointed to his drawing of two sailors looking over the quayside, which was pinned up on the wall, 'somehow separates itself from the moment it was done and belongs to the moment at which you see the drawing. What I like about a photograph is that it always looks exactly like it was when it was taken. It fixes a time which rapidly recedes into the past. A photograph of you when you were a baby looks older than you will ever look, even at ninety. It is embalmed in the moment when the photographer took it. I like that. That is very FUNNY. Photography is comedy of life and death. Terrible comedy sometimes. Under the flesh the white skulls of slaughtered soldiers.'

Paul turned next to a photograph of Willy, clasping a large rubber ball and laughing. Joachim asked Paul what he thought of Willy.

'I like him enormously.'

'Yes. I also like him very much. But, you know, he is too nice. There are some people who are so good, there is nothing one can criticize them for, and then they become rather boring. Willy is perhaps one of those. He does everything for me. He is always good-natured. There is nothing in him I can ever complain about. But the result of his being so nice is that I do not want to see too much of him. Often I like people who are nasty, wicked even. They interest me if I understand the human thing in them that makes them bad. I think I would like to fall in love with someone really WICKED. Quite soon, I would like that.'

Joachim said: 'Before Willy comes, now I would like to take your photograph, Paul.'

He fixed up his camera, a Voigtländer Reflex, on to a tripod, and told Paul to stand at the end of the room, as he wished the picture to be full-length. He arranged the lights so that they shone on Paul from above, gleaming on the hair, the forehead and, especially, the eyes, with the lower part of his face, apart from the lips, in shadow, and then falling on the shirt whose whiteness was bisected by a tie like a quill feather, and leaving the trousers, which were a herringbone tweed and tied round the waist with a neck-tie, in shadow. Paul looked like an El Greco acolyte attendant at some shrine, his body slightly bent in a bow, his hands naïvely dangling against his sides, his eyes, brilliantly lit and with an appearance of being cast heavenwards, a smile of trusting innocence on his full lips. He was awkward and absurd and this was why Joachim liked him. 'I have tried to make you look like a very tall wax candle on an altar.'

A few minutes after this Willy arrived. They left the studio and went to the Metro station.

They got out of the train at a station called 'Freiheit' after the wide avenue in which it was situated. They found Ernst waiting for them outside the station. Nearly every building in the Freiheit seemed to be a restaurant, café or bar, brilliantly lit. They went down a street which led to the harbour. They came to the quayside beyond a waterfront of very old houses. Men and women and boys were standing, looking out over the water, vacantly waiting, leaning over railings. They stared at these, who stared back at them. It was as though each group regarded the other as figures on a stage set. Paul looked across the people to the harbour. There was a jetty connected to the quay by a miniature toy-like suspension bridge. Beyond the yellow lights of the jetty there were distant starry white lights from ships, and, beyond those, cranes and other installations. There were harbour smells of oil and tar. From the distance came sounds of hammering, an occasional shout, an explosion, a flare.

They stood there, waiting, while Joachim tried to remember the way to a particular *Lokal* which he thought might amuse Paul.

Facing the quayside he saw the lights of The Fochsel, the place he was looking for. Ernst, walking beside Paul, started up a running commentary on the evening:

'Joachim's wonderful at this. He knows every amusing *Lokal* in the city. Of course, he manages to get here more often than I do. I admire his enterprise.'

The Fochsel was so small and crammed with people (it was obviously a tourist attraction) that they had difficulty squeezing into it. Ernst whispered to Paul that it reminded him of Dickens – *The Old Curiosity Shop* – and it was certainly Dickensian, though, Paul thought, still more Rabelaisian. Its owner–bartender was a misshapen Old Tar with square bristling chin and bulging Mussolini eyes. He seemed to have collected in his tavern souvenirs of many voyages. From the ceiling hung stuffed alligators, so low that Paul, even when seated at the bar, had to bend his head to avoid banging into them. Huge, leathery bats with wings spread out were hammered as armorial escutcheons on to wooden walls. At the end of the bar there was a fence made of dried pampas grass. A porcupine, with eyes of bright glass beads, crouched under the stool where Joachim sat. Willy translated for Paul inscriptions, written in Gothic script on parchment labels. Two inflated bronze-coloured pumpkins, 'the genitals of Hercules', were, an inscription said, taken from the pillars of his name. Every label was an obscenity, but the Old Tar, standing behind the counter and serving drinks, never moved his features when his customers laughed out loud.

They walked back to the Freiheit, down a side street. Signs for shops and the *Lokale* were written in Chinese. Joachim told Paul of fights between sailors free with their knives. In some streets it was dangerous to walk alone. Someone might throw a handkerchief over your face, search your clothing for valuables and leave you stripped and beaten, dying perhaps in the gutter. Bars were haunted by drug pushers. All this excited Paul greatly.

Joachim left Paul and joined Willy who was walking a bit ahead of them. Ernst – at Paul's side – went on and on as though continuing the afternoon's conversation begun in his study. 'By the way, Paul.'

'Yes?'

'You remember what we were talking about this afternoon?'

'I don't want to remember it now.'

'You upset me very seriously at the end of our conversation by suggesting that you may have to leave our house. I am still deeply hurt by your having said that.'

'We agreed that I am to leave the day after tomorrow. It is all settled, surely.'

Two whores scuttled past them in the alley.

'We arranged nothing, Paul. We had just left everything undecided. But now I am afraid that I must ask you if you can go away on the first of August.'

Joachim looked round to see if they were following.

'That is what I told you I intend to do. That is what we arranged.'

'I'm glad that you take so well what must be quite a blow to you. The fact is my mother has just announced to me that she has three other guests coming on the first, so she will be wanting the room that you are in . . .'

'She has told me that herself already.'

They entered an immense beer hall, where an orchestra, dressed in Bavarian Lederhosen accompanied a chorus of yodelling Alpine maidens. The walls were daubed with murals of Bavarian lakes and Alps. At the far end of the hall, a painted cow three times life-size pendulously wagged its head from side to side, lifted its tail, dropped something damp on the floor and mooed. They drank beer and ate slices of raw turnip – Bavarian diet, Paul supposed. They left and went into the street again.

Ernst caught up with Paul and went on, '. . . Had hoped we weren't going to have any guests for some time, while I got over this little disappointment, but it seems that I am not to be spared . . .'

'Yes, yes, I understand.'

'. . . my mother . . .'

They came to a *Lokal* called The Three Stars. But for some rough wooden chairs and tables, it was unfurnished. It had the air of a *louche* Parish Hall with a platform at one end on which a band of untalented musicians were playing jazz. Couples danced cheerfully. There were some freakish youths in women's dress. Rolling their eyes, they went from table to table, chucking men under the chin, shouting lasciviously inviting obscenities at them. At some tables there sat perfectly respectable, better-dressed citizens, bourgeois husbands and wives, who seemed to have strayed in here by chance (but perhaps everyone was here for a reason). Seemingly unaware of the depravity surrounding them, when approached by the macaw-like transvestites they nodded their heads and smilingly rejected their screeching calls.

Leaning against the wall, or standing talking to one another near the orchestra, there were working boys wearing cloth caps, and a few sailors. There was a curious solemnity about them, as though they moved in another time and place.

Joachim and his friends pushed their way through. At the table next to theirs sat an old man with a long white beard who gazed with eyes of unwavering desire at a young boy and girl dancing together. With strong, nervous hands – those perhaps of a sculptor – a genius – he fingered the rim of his glass.

A young man was dancing by himself – seemingly only for himself. He was black-suited like a bank clerk. He had pale features, and he wore pince-nez. From the way in which he held himself, he seemed to suffer from some partial paralysis. As he wove his way in and out of the dancing couples he whirled his hands above his head: they looked like maimed wings or cardboard propellers. People looked at him and laughed as he went swaying and staggering around the room. Perhaps the reason why Paul could accept the bank clerk's grotesqueness, feeling only sympathy for him, was that despite his illness – whatever that might be – he was fulfilling himself. The bank clerk had reached his private heaven in this den. Simon Wilmot would approve.

The room was incandescent. Always reminded of pictures, Paul thought of Van Gogh's canvas of men playing billiards in a brilliantly lit hall in Arles. 'This makes me want to paint,' he said to Joachim.

'To paint what?' Joachim asked coldly.

'The room. The people here.' Now he remembered a Picasso Blue Period scene, the *Absinthe Drinker*.

Ernst, who had stuck a monocle into his left eye-socket, said: 'I understand just what Paul means. This room does stimulate one's creative urge, doesn't it? All the different characters here seem to form a picture, a pattern, a unity, a composition like the petals of a sunflower. That man dancing alone reminds me of a scene in Rilke's *Malte Laurids Brigge*. I feel like you, Paul, that somehow one enters into a hallucinating vision of these couples dancing. One has distinct aesthetic pleasure. You and I, Paul, are one with all humanity.'

Joachim stood up, looking round the room and bowing in every direction. Extending his hand like a showman, he said: 'You see, they all come here: statesmen, clergymen, bankers, merchants, school teachers, soldiers, poets, they all end up in The Three Stars.'

Ernst held up his hat to hide his face. 'Why are you doing that, Ernst?' asked Willy, laughing uncontrollably. 'You look absurd, Ernst!'

Ernst said in a prim, offended voice: 'I have to be rather careful here. You see, I am known. There is a banker, a colleague of my father, sitting over there, by whom I particularly wish to avoid being seen. By the way, Paul, I had not finished what I was trying to say to you just now in the Freiheit. Our friends here interrupted us. Of course, it is very upsetting to me that you should be leaving my family's house so soon, and that is why it is particularly difficult for me at this moment to enter into Joachim's unshadowed – or should I say unbridled? – enjoyment of this evening. Joachim has a wonderful capacity of living just for the moment and dismissing all serious concerns. I envy him it. I wish I had that capacity, but I don't. I feel I have responsibilities thrust on me by my family. In order to make me a bit happier about the future, I wish that you would promise me something . . . Will you come on a trip to the Baltic with me soon?'

During this speech Joachim and Willy had left the table. They were dancing together.

Paul said drunkenly: 'Of course, Ernst. I will go on a trip with you to the Baltic. I've wanted to see the Baltic ever since the Zeppelin commander Fedi told me about coming down in it.'

'You promise?'

'No no, I never make promises.'

'If you promise, you will make me extremely happy.'

'Then of course I promise, of course I want to make you happy, Ernst.'

Ernst said, 'That means a great deal to me. Now I am happy already. Can't you see that in my eyes?'

Willy and Joachim came back to the table. By Joachim's side was a bald, red-faced man in a dark suit of respectable appearance.

'Let me introduce you', Joachim said, 'to a friend of Willy.'

Willy, who had gone very red, roared with laughter. 'Oh, Joachim, you are telling lies! How can you say that? It is a shame. He is no friend of mine!'

'He is not a friend of yours, Willy? How comes it then you dance with someone who is not your friend? How can that happen, Willy? I do not approve of that.'

Ernst whispered to Paul in an aside, leaning over so that his lips almost touched Paul's ear, 'How exquisitely funny! Joachim is so amusing doing this sort of thing.' All three started talking to the stranger in German, encouraging him. The man put out his hand and stroked Willy's hair.

'Oh! Oh! Oh!' protested Willy.

Joachim was talking rapidly and earnestly to the man in a low voice. Suddenly a terrified expression came over the man's face.

'Wonderful!' exclaimed Ernst, seizing Paul's hand and squeezing it. 'Joachim is now pretending he is a plain-clothes policeman, and that he has come here in order to obtain certain confidential information about the customers. He has named a price for keeping silent. The poor man is terrified.'

Ernst now joined in the conversation with the other three. The man had the joke explained to him. Paul could not ignore the fact that Ernst was making a witty and sympathetic impression. The others roared with laughter at his quips. Joachim and Willy and the man were laughing uproariously. Ernst shone. Paul wondered whether, in German, there was a funny side of Ernst not present when he talked in English.

The excitement at their table had attracted attention. Three boys came over from the far end of the room and stood over them at their table, puzzledly listening to their conversation. They had intent expressions on their faces as though they were in class. An English lesson. One of the boys asked:

'Zigaretten?'

Ernst offered him a cigarette. Joachim gave cigarettes to the other two. He said: 'Setzt euch!' The boys sat down.

Joachim offered the boy who had asked for the cigarette the chair between Ernst and himself. Willy drew up chairs for the other two boys. One sat by Paul. Paul said to the first boy:

'Was ist deine Name?'

The boy looked puzzled. Joachim corrected: 'Wie heisst du?'

'Lothar.'

Joachim ordered more drinks all round.

Lothar was silent for a moment, looking at each of them in turn. Then he looked at Paul, and asked Joachim: 'Ist er Engländer?'

'Jawohl.'

Lothar smiled, raising his glass to Paul. Then looking at Paul he said: 'You – Englisch.'

Paul laughed. Finding that he could grasp these primitive exchanges in German, the boys started to talk to him, sometimes using Joachim, Willy or Ernst as interpreter. Paul asked Fritz, the third boy, what he did. Unemployed now, once in Liverpool, a sailor.

The boys listened to Paul's replies to their questions with a kind of awe, as though Paul were a strange visitant, the enemy returned from the trenches to say kind words. Out of the trenches. Blood and mud and rats. Joachim asked Lothar whether he had a job. Lothar said:

'I work at the amusement arcade across the road. I help to look after the place with my father. But I must work such very long hours, and earn so very little. Oh God', he laughed, 'I do not like it! Have you another cigarette? Give me two, please.'

Joachim gave him two. 'What sort of a place?'

'Oh, there are filthy pictures they show there, where I work. And then there are games: billiards, shooting, try-your-strength machines, wheels-of-fortune, oh and everything else of that kind. I tell you, man, it is ripping. *Knorke.* You might like to come and see it one day. The pictures would interest you,' he said, looking at Paul.

'Yes, I would, I would. I will come one day,' Paul said, seriously looking at Lothar, who had a head like a poster of a Great War fighter in the trenches. A promise to remember had been made.

'What kind of a sailor?' Joachim asked Fritz, who told him that he was a stoker. He clenched his fists and bared his arms on one of which there was an anchor, on the other a snake-like temptress. He said gravely to Paul: '*Ja, ja,* one has to be awfully strong for my kind of work and also if one lives in Sankt Pauli. Always exertion, shovelling coal, ready to fight every moment, awful things, never stopping, many accidents.'

The third boy, whose name was Erich, dully said he was unemployed, adding that he had eaten nothing that day. Joachim ordered sausage and potato salad for him. The food, and some beer, stimulated Erich and a few minutes later he was saying, his eyes gleaming, that he had eaten nothing the whole of that week.

'I do not believe you,' said Joachim, delighted. 'Tell me, do you come often to this *Lokal?*'

'About three days a week. Only three days are good.'

'Is it any use here? Much trade?'

'No, not much use, but I must make money as I can.'

'That is right, we must have money. What he says is true,' said Lothar. The one whose name Paul had not caught said: 'The German people can only win through if each one fights regardless of others, for himself. We must have money. Have you got another cigarette?'

'Money, money,' said Fritz the sailor to Paul in English, opening and shutting his fist. 'Have you got money? If so, I want it!' He roared with laughter.

Ernst handed his silver cigarette case to Lothar. Lothar examined the case meticulously. 'Please take two,' Ernst said generously. Each boy took four. Lothar examined carefully his

78

four cigarettes, fingered them. He undid his jacket, putting them, with an effort of his fingers, into an inner pocket. Cautiously, he did his jacket up again, tugging at the lapels, and smoothing them down, as though they were sealskin. Then he took a fifth cigarette. He lit it from Ernst's lighter. Ernst gazed deep into Lothar's eyes.

Ernst said to Paul: 'Lothar has such very nice eyes. So sincere. A little sad. In fact, altogether I think Lothar is particularly nice. I don't like the sailor Fritz and his friend *quite* so much. Of course, Joachim is very uncritical, but I don't feel altogether at ease with Fritz, somehow . . .' He put out his hand and stroked the lapel of Lothar's jacket.

'Where did you get this? It's smooth as sealskin,' he said, incidentally feeling Lothar's shoulders and chest with both hands.

All the time that Ernst was fondling his jacket Lothar looked away from the table into a far corner of the hall. There was a peculiar, withdrawn, gleaming expression in his eyes.

Ernst got up from the table, and explained that for various complicated reasons, to do with his mother, Paul and he must leave. Joachim and Willy also decided that it was time to leave, at which Lothar said that he would accompany them part of the way on the train because he had to go back to his parents' house. Shouting and laughing, they ran through the streets to catch the last train. Chased each other. Leaped. Danced. Lothar turned a cartwheel in the street, 'Like Puck in Shakespeare's *Midsummer Night's Dream*,' Ernst said in an aside to Paul.

The carriage was almost empty. Joachim and Willy started running up and down it, Joachim chasing a moth that had flown from the upholstery of a seat. When they were wearied of that, clinging with both hands to the strap-hangers, Lothar lifted his body until his head touched the ceiling. He turned a somersault.

Ernst got up from his seat with an expression which implied that gymnastics must be taken seriously. 'Let me show you,' he said, pushing Lothar to one side. Standing at attention between the strap-hangers, with a disciplinary movement he placed each hand on a strap-hanger, holding firmly on to them. Although his face wore his social smile, there was something so rigid about it, they all stopped laughing. Then Joachim said, '*Sei doch nicht so ernst, Ernst'* – 'Don't be so earnest, Earnest' – which set them off again.

Very slowly, Ernst raised his body up on the strap-hangers and, with clockwork precision, turned a somersault. Hands and arms and legs seem to creak as he did so. His eyes looked dead. A yellow skeleton revolving between brown strap-hangers.

Back in his room at the Stockmann residence at 5.00 a.m., Paul did not go to bed, for he had made a discovery both upsetting and rather flattering to him. This was that his Notebook, containing drafts of his poems and a sketch of the dinner-table conversation on the occasion of his first evening at the Stockmanns, together with a rather vivid portrait of 'Hanny', had been taken from the suitcase where he always hid it and replaced in a drawer under some shirts. He concluded from this evidence that Ernst had been reading it – doubtless because he was curious about the poems Paul had been writing under the Stockmann roof. Paul wrote in his Notebook – for Ernst's perusal – the letter which follows:

Dear Ernst,

I am still rather drunk after our night at Sankt Pauli, a fact which may largely explain why I am sitting up writing this letter to you which I am leaving open on my writing table, where doubtless you will read it.

This evening you extracted a promise from me to go on a trip to the Baltic with you. Unless you are so offended by this letter that you make it clear that you never want to speak to me again, I will keep that promise. If you are so offended, let me know, otherwise perhaps it would be best to say nothing about this letter, as it is not an understanding between us that you rifle my suitcase to read my Notebook.

I have to admit that I dread our weekend alone together. I want to explain to you why I so dread it. This is because you have a way of making me conscious every moment I am with you of a self which is your idea of me, and of which I would rather not be made conscious. You attach yourself to me like my own shadow attached to the soles of my shoes, or, like a mirror nailed in front of me in which I am forced to see your idea of my image. You never let me forget myself (or, rather, your idea of my self). You are always making me conscious of being something which I do not think I really am – that is innocent, naïve, and forever giving a performance of my innocence, naïveté, before you, my audience.

Supposing that I were as innocent as you think I am, then by making me conscious of it you would corrupt that innocence. You remember those poems I wrote about my friend Marston, which Dean Close showed you? Well, I had a relationship with Marston which was in some ways like yours with me. I thought of him as innocent. I identified him with the English countryside, green lanes, rivers winding through wide meadows, wooded, rolling landscape, calm and temperate, a kind of mildness which yet had something threatening about it, angry with anyone who turned it into self-conscious self-advertisement, who did not let it dream its way unconsciously into life. Well, I attached myself to Marston out of admiration (love!) for qualities that I admire in him – his English innocence, his unselfconsciousness – until he became bored with me watching him all the time and resentful and angry. He might even have come to hate me, but seeing how he felt I arranged for us never to meet again. Ignore all this. I am so drunk.

I admire the relationship between Joachim and Willy because it is not like mine was with Marston, not like yours is with me. It is directed towards things outside themselves which they share, as though these things – their outdoor life – the sun – their own bodies – were passionate intermediaries between them. They are friends without tormenting each other with consciousness of what each thinks the deepest nature of the other.

The moment one person keeps on looking into the 'soul' of another (or rather, what he thinks that 'soul' is or ought to be) he becomes vampirish, blood-sucking, feeding his own conscious lack of certain qualities, or what he feels to be those qualities, in his friend. He is trying to make his friend his own spirit's prisoner, without giving his friend freedom to be himself. I am so drunk.

81

Well, unless you are so offended by this letter that you don't ever want to set eyes on me ever again (which, frankly, I hope will be the case), I must and will fulfil my promise to go with you to the Baltic coast. You insisted on my PROMISING to do this, and the one thing I learned in my philosophy course in Oxford is that one must keep promises, however trivial, and not break contracts. I am sure you thought about Oxford Moral Philosophy, when you extracted from me this PROMISE.

Thank you for having me to stay, and please thank your mother for her hospitality.

    Love,
    Paul

Paul had a window seat of their second-class compartment, opposite Ernst. To avoid meeting Ernst's gaze, he stared through the window at the landscape rushing past. There was an immense khaki plain of reeds and spear grass, broken at intervals by sheets of shallow water in which herons stood. The train passed villages where storks built straggling nests of twigs on top of squat church towers. As it approached the estuary of the Alta it skirted the coast which was fringed with pine trees. Paul saw glimpses of the sea beyond sand dunes.

The sky was sullen, sandy-looking, with a ceiling of foggy cloud like stacks of coke banked up. It had a core of smouldering fire, off-centre, that was the sun.

The train had left Hamburg at 14.17 hours, taking three hours and thirteen minutes to the ferry which crossed the mouth of the river Alta to reach, on its eastern side, the little holiday resort of Altamunde.

Made claustrophobic by his proximity to Ernst, whose eyes he felt to be never off him, Paul thought he was perhaps going mad. He certainly heard voices, at any rate a voice, his own, inside his head, accusing him: 'This journey is grotesque, absurd. The only reason you are here is that, three weeks ago, when Joachim, Willy, Ernst and you were all at The Three Stars *Lokal* in Sankt Pauli and all four drunk, Ernst extracted a promise from you to go with him on this trip to the Baltic. You agreed to go as the result of your total inability to anticipate what an engagement entered into will be like when it becomes fact. The future is to you a blank space of empty inconceivable time. Asked whether you will go somewhere or do something on a day distant from Now, you ask yourself only whether you have made any alternate arrangement on that day, and if you have made none, then you fill in the blank space with some commitment, without having any picture in your mind of that appalling moment when the handwriting will crystallize into fact: the fact now is Ernst sitting opposite to you in this train. This promise you made to Ernst three weeks ago has become the present you see as solid Now, petrified minutes. You have seventy-two hours alone with Ernst. Sixty times seventy-two is 4,320 minutes, each of which you must will yourself through, one by one, until you are released into Sunday night, back in Hamburg in your room.'

The sun broke through the clouds. Ernst leaned forward and exclaimed in a whisper: 'The sun is wonderful on your face. It flames. You look like an angel.'

At 5.30, they got off the ferry, carrying rucksacks. They walked along a path which brought them to a café, the shining new annexe of the part-frame, part-brick, white-balconied hotel where, as Paul assumed, Ernst had made reservations for them to spend the night. They set down their rucksacks in a corner of the café and seated themselves at a table looking out over the sea front. Paul saw the beach with holiday-makers splashing and swimming and running and shouting and laughing: each of them, he thought, happy in the fact of not sitting at a hotel café table at the other side of which there is Ernst with his face the skull of a predatory bird, and the skeletal upper half of his frame covered with the blazer of Downing College, Cambridge.

'But I shall insist on having dinner at 7.30,' Paul told himself. 'That is two hours from now – 120 minutes. After dinner, I shall get to bed early – by 9.30. Then I shall read and write in my room – alone. I shall write in my Notebook an account of my feelings about Ernst in the train and then I shall read Rilke's *Malte Laurids Brigge*.' Anticipating being alone in his room gave him a sensation like that of the most thrilling sexual fantasy.

'Surely I did make it perfectly clear, that evening at The Three Stars, that we would not share a room?' As soon as Paul thought this, intense distrust of the Paul of three weeks ago seized him. Did that feckless creature have the foresight to ensure that Paul now, sitting with Ernst at this table, would be liberated into his own separate room at 9.30? That Paul had been terribly drunk, today's Paul remembered, which was why he could recall so little about him. He put these thoughts aside, and continued anticipating the rest of the weekend. 'There will be all of tomorrow with Ernst, but not all of it alone with him, if we go – as I surely do remember him saying we would – to visit the young architect Castor Alerich and his wife Lisa, in their modernist house, built by Castor himself. "A small masterpiece of the New German Architecture – a functionalist jewel," Ernst had said.'

Paul, now making a stupendous effort, stopped looking at the beach scene and forced himself to look at Ernst. 'Let us walk by the beach before supper,' he said, thinking that physical exercise would speed up time.

'Perhaps before we set out I should ask at the hotel desk about our rooms.'

'I though you had already booked them in Hamburg, from your office.'

Ernst made a little *moue:* 'I didn't think that would be necessary.'

'Well, then, you had certainly better see about them now.'

'Will you come to the desk with me?'

'I think I'll stay here.'

Taking the rucksacks, Ernst went into the lobby of the hotel. Alone, Paul indulged himself in dreaming of their return to Hamburg on Monday night, Ernst back to Hanny and the tomb-like Stockmann residence, he to the room he had taken when he left without saying goodbye to Ernst's parents: a room bare of everything but chair, table, clothes cupboard (on top of which he put his suitcase), a scrubbed wooden table (for books and manuscripts), and a narrow bed.

Ernst returned from the interior of the hotel. 'I've fixed everything up. I hope it will be all right . . .'

'Good, then we can go for our walk.'

'As a matter of fact there has been a minor complication, though of no importance, as I'm sure you'll agree. It appears that today there is some sort of festival going on in the neighbourhood, so the hotel is overbooked. I had trouble persuading them even to let us have a room. It makes no difference, of course. The important thing is that we do have one. I'm sure you won't mind that it seems we have to share it.'

'Can't we get rooms at another hotel?'

'Naturally, I enquired into every possibility. But they said that this is the only hotel in Altamunde, and, on the western side of the estuary, everything is even more crowded.'

'Can't we go back to Hamburg tonight?'

'Even if that were possible, it would seem awfully strange if I did so, having told my mother that I would be away for two days. I don't really know how I would explain matters to her. And surely you have cancelled your hotel room in Hamburg for tonight?'

'I had to keep my room. There are my things in it.'

'Financially, surely, you're hardly in a position to pay for a hotel room which you aren't occupying. I should have thought that you would have made some economic arrangement with the hotel porter to leave your things with him overnight.'

Paul stared at him.

'I do wish you had told me how you feel about this trip a little earlier. After all, I could have gone on my little jaunt alone.'

Paul thought, 'Just as if in taking me he was sacrificing days of blissful solitude.'

'Ernst, you know perfectly well that you made me promise to come. I am simply keeping my promise.'

Ernst said, stiffly: 'It is hardly my fault that the hotel has so little accommodation. But it can't possibly be the fact that we are obliged to share a room that is so upsetting to you.' He looked straight at Paul. 'Why are you so hostile to me, Paul?'

'You know the answer to that question.'

'I don't.'

'Well, didn't you read the letter to you which I left in my Notebook at your house? Haven't you been reading my Notebook all this time?'

Ernst reacted with surprising calm to these questions.

'Yes, I have read both these – er – documents.'

'Well?'

'To tell you the truth, I didn't take what you wrote altogether seriously. I'm five years older than you, Paul. I suppose I thought, After all, Paul is only twenty, a young writer, and he is trying out his powers. I confess that when I read your description of your first meal at our house on the night of your arrival, I was more annoyed on my mother's account than my own.' He squeezed out a smile, quite parched of humour: 'Here and there I noted touches of journalistic observation – the description of my coming down to dinner wearing an open shirt – and of the miniature game of cricket with my mother after that – well, quite amusing I suppose, if published in an undergraduate magazine – the *Granta*, for example. You may be surprised to learn that my mother when I told her about your Notebook – not that I showed it to her, for to do so would have seemed not playing the game – took the same view as I did myself though perhaps she did feel a trifle more strongly than I – that perhaps while you were practising fiction on my family, it was a tiny bit caddish (if that is the correct English word) to go on staying as a guest in our house . . .' He broke off, and then said in a graver tone of voice: 'However, when I asked just now why you feel so hostile to me, I wasn't thinking of your literary achievements. I wanted to know why you show such revulsion at the idea of our sharing a room. I cannot believe that you would object to sharing a room with, say, Joachim – or Willy perhaps. This does seem to reveal a distinct antipathy to me. I would be grateful now to hear your reasons for having taken against me, Paul. I would like to hear them from your voice, that is, instead of reading them as written by your undergraduate pen.'

Here was an irony which took Paul aback. It was as though some character who existed for him as written about – a character in the novel describing the Stockmanns of which he was all the time thinking – suddenly stepped out of the projected printed page and announced in his own voice that he was real, the proof that he existed being speech that issued out of the present moment and not words written or typed or printed after the event. Paul had to admit that until now he thought of everything Ernst said as lines of print in Paul Schoner's novel, mentally written for the eyes of William Bradshaw. Now the words describing The Trip To Altamunde, which, as soon as spoken, Paul saw flowing into ink which dried, black and white, on paper in his Notebook for this fiction, suddenly dissolved into the ever-changing, never-fixed unpredictable stream of spoken language like the salt in that sea beyond the beach. Ernst, sitting in front of him across the table, suddenly became someone who might become someone else at

87

any moment and then someone else again and again for ever and ever. Paul looked at the sea. There currents ran, there tides ebbed and flowed, there the temperature never remained the same. There was all of life.

He said, guiltily almost: 'I don't know whether I was justified in writing like that about dinner at your house on my first evening there. Perhaps it was premature. We hadn't known each other long enough. We still don't know each other ... Probably my first impressions were false ...' He threw out irrelevantly, 'Your friends in Hamburg are fond of you, and I trust their judgement better than my own.'

Ernst assumed an air of judicious detachment, not unpleasurable, considering this question, cocking his head to one side: 'They are not really fond of me. They tolerate me because they have grown used to me. My mother and I provide material for them to joke about. Of course I know I am ludicrous. Often I laugh at myself as I did that evening when I came to dinner wearing a cricket blazer, you remember. I was very amused. I am fond of Joachim and Willy. I enjoy their little jokes about me.'

'They like you. They told me so, when I was at the *Schwimmbad* alone with them.'

'I wouldn't have gathered that from certain passages in your Notebook.'

Wishing to clear matters up between them, once and for all, by admitting the full enormity of his previous attitude to Ernst, Paul explained:

'I wrote those things about you in my Notebook because you struck me as being, in some way, dead.'

Ernst retained his head-on-one-side attitude of coolly judging things, assuming the tone of a professional philosopher considering with detachment the somewhat extravagant thesis of a young, a very young and naïve colleague: 'What precisely do you mean by using the word "dead" to describe one of two friends, in the context of a friendly argument between them, when, in fact, both of them happen to be alive? This is not a very precise use of language for someone who aspires to be a serious writer, I suggest.'

'When I am with you, together with Willy and Joachim, I

sometimes have the sense that you are battening on their vitality in order to prove to yourself that you are alive.'

Ernst gave Paul a soft glance: 'Perhaps I get a more genuine sense of being alive when I am alone with you than when I am with both of them. The difference is between something which is a purely physical sense of well-being with them, and something – well, dare I call it spiritual, or at least poetic? –with you.'

Paul spoke wildly: 'You don't really like any of us as much as you think you do. You want to become us – take on our physicality, and what you call my spirituality – which is something quite different from love. Loving is sharing of tastes between people who are different from one another – not one trying to absorb the other's life. Loving is when each delights in the other's difference from him or her. Under your wish to take as your own the qualities in another person which you think you lack in yourself there is a deep resentment, a wish to destroy the person with those qualities.' (Had he tried to destroy Marston?) 'You say you admire Joachim for his careless vitality, and that you would like to have his recklessness, but nevertheless you despise him for not being discreet and careful and for not caring exclusively for business. Deep down, you think that he ought to be a success in the business world according to your commercial standards, even though you know those standards to be death, the mausoleum, like your mother's house. You admire Joachim and Willy for their friendship but, although you so value friendship (and it is true that you do want it perhaps beyond anything else), ultimately you regard them as frivolous. When you analyse the handwriting of those French and German literary geniuses you so admire, you do so not so much in order to praise their strong qualities as draw attention to their weak ones. You assert your own power by discovering defects in people you consider to be more real than yourself. You are compelled to do this because their vitality destroys your belief in your own.'

Ernst looked very still and corpse-like. Then he said: 'Everything you say is true. I have known it all for a long time but never quite admitted it to myself. It is true. I am dead.'

There was silence as if they had reached an end. Triumphant,

89

Paul broke it by making himself laugh out loud. 'Of course, you're not dead, Ernst! Of course what I said isn't true! I got it all out of a book I've been reading.'

Ernst faintly showed an intelligent interest – 'Oh! Out of a book! How interesting! May I ask for the name of the author?'

He took a pencil and a little notebook out of a pocket of his blazer.

'D. H. Lawrence's *Fantasia of the Unconscious*.'

Ernst wrote this down. Then he said, with funereal sincerity, 'All the same, it is true that I am dead. But you can help me become alive.'

'Let us now go for our walk.'

The hotel was at the very edge of Altamunde. In front of it, the concrete promenade stopped just beyond the café. Below three stone steps there was a footpath along the edge of the beach, beside a pine forest, one of many on this coast. They followed along this path with the beach on their right, and beyond it, the sea. There were deck chairs and some tents. Bathers lay on towels or mattresses. Some stood up, drying themselves. The sky had now cleared. The sun shone. The beach was a shining, speckled-eggshell yellow, the waves moved in parallel sparkling chains towards the shore. Boys and girls were playing on the beach. Inshore, legs walked between the shafts of pinkish pine trunks, legs now in light, now in shadow, flickering.

Paul began to consider Ernst's problems clinically as a 'case', just as Wilmot might have considered Paul's own. He decided that what would 'save' Ernst was for him to do work that was 'creative' (Paul tended to think 'creativity' as everyone's available remedy. This, Wilmot would certainly not have done). 'I tell you what, Ernst, you ought to translate. You love the English language, and speak it better than most Englishmen. If you could release your love of English into beautiful German, then you would be happy.'

'I have tried that already. What it is impossible for you to understand, Paul, is that I simply haven't got the will to be creative – even though I myself do realize that, if I could be, it would be the answer to most of, though not quite all, my problems. I know myself better than you know me. There is no shred of creativeness in my nature.'

'But you want people to love and admire you, you are ambitious.'

'That is true, up to a point', he said, luxuriating in his self-despair, 'but can't you imagine someone having ambitions which he himself realizes to be only shadows, like a charcoal sketch on a canvas for a picture which the artist knows he will never paint and that will always remain a sketch? The ambition itself is only charcoal, it will never take on living colours. Yet the artist is good enough for the charcoal sketch always to remain there, for him to look at and torment himself with as the unrealized, unrealizable possibility. Well, I'm like that. But I know my own weaknesses so I don't take either my successes or my failures seriously. On the whole I am reasonably happy, I have books, and I have my study, and I have friends. And, of course, I have my dear, dear mother, who is half my world to me, and I love Hamburg and there is always Sankt Pauli to go to. My philosophy, if you can call it that, is that I am happy because there is no sufficient reason why I should be unhappy.'

'Let us go into the water now.'

They undressed beneath the pine trees. The water was very shallow. They had to wade far out to find a deep channel. They swam for nearly an hour, getting on much better when they were swimming side by side, shouting only an occasional word across the sea to one another.

Returned to the hotel, they went up to their room which was quite small. It had two narrow beds, put side by side, a wash-basin, with looking-glass above, a chest of drawers, a cupboard. Ernst went to the wash-basin and stared into the looking-glass. The better to examine his face, he puffed out his cheeks, like an orator about to make a speech. He was disconcerted by the sight of a small white spot on his cheek about half an inch from his mouth which threatened, he knew, to develop into a disfiguring, boil-like spot.

They went down to dinner in the dining-room with its pine-wood walls painted a chocolate colour and its few framed photographs of Norwegian fjords. Several tables were noisy with holidaying families. At others there sat young married couples. At one a sad, wistful, solitary 'queer'. (Thus did Paul diagnose his fellow guests.)

Written in purple jell-printed ink there were cards on each table announcing alternative menus at 2 marks 50 or 1 mark 75. Paul, never wishing to cause a host expense, said that he would have the cheaper of the two. Ernst said: 'That's cold. Are you sure you wouldn't like to have hot chicken, which is on the other menu? But . . .', looking hard at the card before him, 'perhaps you are right. At this hotel, cold cuts would certainly be excellent. I think I'll have that as well.' He went on, dubiously: 'Perhaps with your meal you'd like something to drink?'

'Oh no, really not. I never drink anything at meals except water.'

'All right. You're sure you wouldn't like some mineral water or lemonade?'

'I think I'll have some lemonade.'

'Oh yes, certainly.' His face fell as Ernst called out to the waiter: 'One lemonade!'

Paul realized that he ought to be making serious intellectual conversation with Ernst. But just at that moment he was overwhelmed by an irrepressible fantasy which blotted everything else out, preventing him seeing Ernst, far less hearing what he was saying. The door from the restaurant to the pavement suddenly burst open, and with grinning triumphant faces, Simon Wilmot and William Bradshaw rushed in. They looked eccentrically English. Simon was in a grey flannel, double-breasted suit, with shirt collar open at the neck. He had a straw hat, which he was now carrying in his hand, to protect his pale features from the sun when he was outside. A monocle dangled from his neck and he carried an ivory-topped cane which he had lifted up at right angles to his body. Obviously he felt he was dressed for the seaside. William Bradshaw wore grey flannel trousers, no jacket and a white knitted jersey with narrow blue stripes on it. He looked the brightest of jovial young sailors.

Their eyes were always on each other, as though they shared some tremendous joke. The joke was Paul. When they saw him they burst into a simultaneous roar of laughter. 'Paul!' they exclaimed in chorus.

'How on earth did you get here?' Paul asked them.

'Well', said Simon, 'I received your letters from Hamburg with your change of address when you left the Stockmann house, so we called for you and your landlady said you were in Altamunde.'

William Bradshaw said, 'I always wanted to go to the Baltic coast, so we took the chance that you would be somewhere around on the beach. We felt pretty certain that we'd run into you.'

'Before we went to Hamburg I was in Berlin,' said Wilmot. 'You got my letters?'

'About your life at Magnus Hirschfeld's Institute for Sexual Science? Of course I did,' Paul replied.

'Simon's made some sensational discoveries,' said William.

'What discoveries?'

'Well, it goes without saying . . . about love,' said William. He pronounced it LAHV.

'What about love?'

'So long as you don't feel Guilt, you don't catch anything,' said William.

'I never said that.'

'Oh yes, I forgot. The proviso is that you have to love the person concerned.'

'The person concerned has also to love you, my dear.'

'Good. They have to love one another. Then they are immune. Immunity is mutuality. Mutuality spells immunity.'

Bradshaw went on: 'Wilmot's proudest achievement is that he cured a bishop's son – who had run away from his paternal cathedral – of kleptomania.'

'Oh! How did he do that?'

'He stopped him feeling guilty about stealing. He turned burglary into a purely business pursuit (which is, after all, what it is – I mean what business is) thus making him feel no more guilty than any other businessman. I mean, as innocent as the Governor of the Bank of England.'

'How did he do that?'

'He bought a large ledger and made him write down everything he'd stolen in it, together with the money he obtained on the market for receiving stolen goods.'

'No, no,' corrected Simon. 'Today you get everything wrong.

He didn't receive money for what he stole. He just put the stolen goods in a cupboard in my room where I kept them for him.'

'What happened?'

'The extraordinary thing is that nothing whatever happened until one day he stole a set of silver spoons of the Twelve Apostles. When it came to entering them, with a description of what they were, into the ledger, the bishop's son fainted. When he came round, he insisted on giving back all the stolen goods to the owners.'

William added: 'You see, Paul, by making the transaction of burglary purely commercial, Simon had undermined the image of himself as a romantic hero, and made stealing merely sordid, like running a bank. And when it came to stealing Apostolic spoons, well that brought Dogmatic Symbolism into conflict with Romantic Dream, and his world collapsed.'

'What happened to him then?'

'Well, he ran away, but without the loot,' said William. He giggled. Simon looked slightly embarrassed.

Paul, in fantasy, had left the table where he had been seated with Ernst and gone over to the door where Simon and Wilmot were standing. Now they all three left the restaurant and walked on to the beach. Mysteriously, Paul had with him a camera and tripod which he had recently bought. The camera had a delayed-shutter release for self-portraiture. Paul now screwed the camera on to the tripod and set it up on the beach. Simon and Wilmot posed grinning on the pavement in front of the hotel. Paul set the delaying device in motion, quickly joined his friends, and stood between them, one arm round Simon, one round William. They all three stood, roaring with laughter, against the background of the hotel.

This fantasy was so bristling and bursting, so compelling, that Paul simply could not hear a word that Ernst was saying. Ernst was like someone on the far side of a river bank across which Paul could hear nothing, only see Ernst's lips moving assiduously. With a tremendous effort Paul forced himself to listen to him, feeling that he was pinning himself down to every separate letter of every word Ernst uttered. Paul heard Ernst ask:

'Tell me, when did you first begin to feel like this about me?'

94

'Like what?'

'When did you begin to feel antipathetic to me?'

'Perhaps it was the day you came to meet me at the station at Hamburg when I saw you waiting at the ticket barrier. You seemed so different from when we met at Oxford in Univ Lodge.'

'Why, at that particular moment?'

'You struck me as being very unhappy.'

'That day I was particularly happy. I was meeting you.'

Coffee was served. It tasted strongly of shrimps. Paul was prey to another fantasy which began with his wondering why a hotel situated on the Baltic, instead of serving cold cuts the texture of shoe leather, did not serve delicacies direct from the sea. Six broadly smiling elegant waiters, emerging from the kitchen door, bore on silver dishes lobsters, turbot, scallops, shrimps, whitebait. With another prodigious effort he banished this fantasy and clamped his attention back on to Ernst.

The prospect of going to bed directly after dinner and writing his Notebook and reading Rilke in his room having been replaced by that of sharing a room with Ernst, he was as anxious now to postpone going to bed as previously he had been to go there. He suggested they take one more walk along the beach. As they stood in front of the hotel, looking at the darkening sea and sky, he forced himself to start a conversation with Ernst about Thomas Mann, whose early novels and stories were often concerned with the life of burghers in the Hanseatic cities of Bremen and Lübeck, cities not far from here. Ernst confessed that when he was adolescent he had often masturbated thinking of Hans Castorp, the hero of *The Magic Mountain*. Paul said that in his first term at Oxford he had started to read that novel but had given up because the descriptions of the symptoms of consumption among the patients in the Swiss sanatorium were so vivid that he started shivering feverishly. Next, Ernst asked about the work of young poets of Oxford. Paul tried to describe the poetry of his friend – two years his senior – Wilmot, but found himself totally incapable of doing so. No, it was not like the poetry of Rilke, in so far as he understood that. Ernst put on his quizzical expression and said: 'Well, if you can't describe his poems to me, perhaps you can explain to me his attitude to life. Hugh Close told me it was rather strange.'

95

Very unwisely, Paul embarked on a discussion of Wilmot's philosophy, beginning with his attitude towards sex, for that was obviously on the agenda. 'He believes that Sexual Acts, in themselves, are not Important. What matters is that one should not feel Guilt about sex. If you do not feel Guilt, and if you are Pure in Heart, you will not catch a disease from an infected partner, for it is the Sense of Guilt which causes you to contract venereal disease. That is why, in the Middle Ages, saints could sleep with lepers without their catching leprosy. They were sleeping with them in order to communicate love and they felt no Guilt.' He quoted the saying of a favourite unorthodox psychoanalyst admired by Wilmot: '"Agape does not catch syphilis from Eros." The important rules in life are to Love and not feel guilty about what form the Love takes. Guilt is Failure to Love, which turns against you and causes Neurosis which, in turn, realizes itself as Cancer.'

At this point Paul began to get rather confused. Nevertheless he persisted, partly because he felt himself criticized by an argument which made him feel unloving and inadequate. Someone who found himself in the position of being loved by a person physically unattractive – repulsive even – to him would be acting in a saintly manner (that is, responding to love with love) if he accepted the physical advances of the person by whom he was repelled. Paul could not imagine himself achieving this degree of saintliness: sleeping, for example, with some wrinkled, mauve-haired society hostess, or a disease-ridden *poète maudit* – Paul Verlaine. But then perhaps Rimbaud was a sapphire-eyed seraphim because he slept with Verlaine.

Whether or not Paul really said all this to Ernst, the feeling of his having communicated his version of Wilmot's philosophy influenced that evening, as they walked along the coast where the sun was now so close to the horizon that, seen through veils of oyster-grey cloud, it was no longer dazzling. Looking straight into it Paul saw a disk of burning vermilion stone. He tried to look at the sun without seeing anything else, excluding from his vision the turfy sea and the land that now looked like a huge squamous octopus, its tentacles the headlands. When the burning disk touched the horizon, it seemed to become distorted, to bulge, with sides which, a few seconds later, palpitated like, he thought, Ulysses' plucked-out fiery heart. And then it changed once more. Now, he thought, it was like King Henry's tent on the field of the Cloth of Gold. Last, it was like a red sail driven by a hurricane over the horizon. The waves leaped up, pulled it down, flapping, and sank it; after which, he felt, rather than saw, transparent light flooding that part of the sky with blood.

They had reached a place where there was some kind of a holiday camp, with tents under trees. Solitary campers were preparing to retire for the night. Suddenly Ernst's face lit up and he hailed a girl who was standing apart from the others. 'Hillo –ah! Hillo! Who have we here? . . . However did *you* get here?' he said, in a quieter voice to Irmi, who was now approaching them. She was dressed in white shorts and a white shirt and white socks that showed above white gym shoes. Smiling, she looked across Ernst directly at Paul and said, 'Good evening.' He smiled back at her and said quietly, 'Hullo.' 'We've caught you red-handed. Who are you with?' Ernst asked her, archly. 'I am by myself, although I have friends here,' she said. 'And who is My Self? It sounds a rather oriental name to me. A Siamese gentleman? Perchance, the better half of a Siamese twin?'

'My Self is Baltic Travel Camps, that runs this camp. I am employed by My Self for the month of August, as lady camp leader. At the end of August, I go back to Hamburg.'

'Perhaps we shall see you tomorrow, if you come swimming here,' Paul said. 'I am sorry to have to remind you that that is most improbable,' said Ernst, with asperity. 'You seem to have forgotten that our trip to the Alerichs will take up the whole of tomorrow; and then, in the evening, you, I take it, have to be back in Hamburg. Isn't that what you insisted you want?' 'You'll have to have your swim at sunrise,' Irmi said in a voice soft as a feather just brushing Paul's cheek. 'Goodbye then, till Hamburg,' Ernst said, turning away. She met Paul's farewell smile across the retreating figure of Ernst as though he had lobbed a shuttlecock across an invisible net. Then Ernst and Paul walked back towards their hotel through what was now almost darkness.

They had not walked very far before they heard the sound of firing – spasmodic bursts of it – coming from the depths of the pine forest. 'What is that?' Paul asked. 'Young imbeciles,' said Ernst, deliberately casual.

'What do you mean by young imbeciles?' 'They call themselves the Sharpshooters,' said Ernst. 'Who are they sharpshooting?' Paul asked facetiously. Ernst became serious. 'I am afraid that in Germany there are still some members of the pre-War generation who do not recognize the War was really lost through Germany being defeated by the Allies. They think that patriotic Germans were stabbed in the back by unpatriotic international Jewish financiers. Tl e reactionaries who think like this attract to themselves young adventurers, thugs, like those you hear firing through the darkness now.' 'But isn't it illegal for them to have firearms?' 'Well, no one quite knows. They form themselves into so-called clubs for target practice. As our new constitution of the Weimar Republic is very liberal, these clubs are allowed to become what amount to private armies. They seem to be allowed to go in for what is really military training. They are planning the great awakening of Germany, when she will rise up to avenge herself and overthrow her enemies.' 'When is that going to happen?' 'It will never happen, I think. The Republic is too well established, and the German people are opposed to war, they lost too much in the last one. They have turned against militarists and reactionaries like Joachim's uncle, General Lenz. Besides, the French and the English together would never permit there to be a militarist Germany.' There was another burst of rifle fire from the depths of the darkness. 'Then they don't matter really?' Paul asked. 'Well, I wouldn't quite say that. They are a menace to stability.' 'Why?' 'Because they commit political murders, and because they appeal to the worst prejudices of some Germans' (Ernst said 'some Germans' almost as though he regarded Germans as foreigners), 'such as anti-Semitism.' 'Whom have they murdered?' 'Walther Rathenau, a Jewish financier and liberal politician – a great man, someone whom Germany very much needed. But don't let's talk about them tonight,' he said, with a shudder and a little nervous laugh. 'I don't want to let them ruin our weekend.'

They reached the hotel and went up to their room. They washed, undressed and got into their separate beds, side by side. Ernst put out the light, said 'good-night' and reached in the darkness for Paul's hand, all in the same moment. Paul's first impulse was to withdraw his hand, as soon as it seemed possible to do so without rejecting Ernst's friendship: but the words of Wilmot which he had quoted on the beach were still echoing in his mind, challenging him with alternatives of rejecting love, or returning it, making affirmation out of the negative fact that he found Ernst physically repulsive. The two beds were drawn so close together that there was no space between them. Instead of withdrawing his hand, Paul moved across into Ernst's bed. He was quick to discover that the decision of mind to respond to Ernst's advances was far more easily taken than it was easy to make his body respond to him. Out of a kind of nervous reaction of disgust – or perhaps out of the desire to get done with the physical as soon as possible – he came very quickly. This was the first time he had ever had sex with anyone. Then he realized that to return immediately to his own bed before Ernst had achieved his satisfaction would be a worse rejection than to have denied him in the first place. So he stayed in Ernst's bed with Ernst desperately writhing against him, struggling to attain orgasm. Paul realized that by Wilmot's standards he had already failed to show love. His involuntary reaction proved his incapacity to return love with love. But he could at least, he thought, show sympathy by simply staying with Ernst. There would be some kind of mutuality of shown affection in being with him until he had come. This took, it is true, an infinity of rock-like minutes while Ernst struggled towards his arid climax. Paul, lying by his side and being crawled over by Ernst, could not have felt more separate from him had he been in Hamburg and Ernst in Altamunde. Indeed he felt an aloneness which was beyond them both, beyond himself even, as though he had no existence except this being alone. Lying there in the dark he felt himself like a prisoner cast down upon a floor where he was compelled to look at a brilliantly illuminated mosaic on the wall of some Romanesque cathedral, of devils and demons with prongs and pitchforks tormenting the naked bodies of sinners. Nevertheless he was

not so mean-spirited – or he was too alone – to blame Ernst by
identifying him with any demon. He even felt sympathy for
Ernst. Hell was himself. And when at last Ernst fell into a deep
and silent sleep which Paul took to signify orgasm achieved, he
felt only a sense of relief on Ernst's behalf. Yet he knew that,
while Ernst slept, he himself was condemned to lie awake until
dawn, for only daylight would assuage his self-disgust.

There was absolutely no question of sleeping. He was
tortured wakefulness incarnate.

At last there were glimmerings of light in that north, in that
summer, overlapping the darkness with its assuaging calm. As
soon as all the objects in the room had clarified and identified
themselves as bed, cupboard, table, chair, linen, Paul dressed
(Ernst still snoring), snatched up a towel, opened the door of the
bedroom, ran downstairs and through the hotel hall out into the
cool air. He ran along the same sandy path between beach and
pines as Ernst and he had gone last night, until he saw the little
holiday camp with tents where he bid Irmi good-night. He
undressed on the beach and walked into the sea, wading
through shallow water until he came to the channel deep
enough to swim.

The morning was perfectly still, the pine trees at the edge of
the beach distinct in every detail of line and shadow, like figures
engraved round the rim of a glass bowl, the sea an expanse of
flat mirror under a sky of abstract colourless pure light. Paul's
awkward body – arms and legs plunging – seemed to churn the
water and turn it up in tillage, like a plough a smooth field at
dawn. Swimming, he seemed to make a noise which shattered
all that quietude.

Then he realized that someone was swimming beside him. It
was Irmi and she was laughing as she swam. They said only
'good morning' to each other then turned, and swam back to the
shallow water. They waded up the beach where, beside his
trousers and shirt and shoes, he had left the towel. As soon as
they had reached this place, without speaking (his lack of
German and hers of English providing excuse for communica-
tive silence) he started kissing her: the top of her head, her face,
her shoulders, her breasts. He put his hands around her
buttocks, and felt his penis harden against her stomach.

They were still dripping wet from the sea and, between kisses, paused to dry each other with the towel, before starting to kiss each other all over again. Then they spread the towel out on the beach and lay down. They made love.

Paul heard, from behind them, the sounds of a man coughing and then coming out of a tent just visible between pine trees above the beach. Irmi was the first to get up. She whispered '*Auf Wiedersehen*'; then, pressing a bathing wrap against her breasts, ran, with angular flopping movements of her arms and legs that suddenly struck him as those of a member of an alien species, towards the pine trees and the tents. Paul stood up, still exultant. Then, looking down at his body, he noticed a thin thread of fluid that ran from below the navel to his sex, still gummy from intercourse. He ran down to the sea and washed, then he returned to the beach and, taking up the towel, vigorously dried himself. As he ran back along the shore towards the hotel, the sense of triumph came flooding back in waves: and lines of Rimbaud, always haunting, seemed to run along the shore beside him:

> *O vive lui! chaque fois*
> *Que chante le coq gaullois!*

When Paul got back to the hotel, he went to the dining-room and waited for a long time. At last Ernst appeared. Paul explained that he had got up early to have a swim. Ernst looked solemn. He said he was upset because the pimple on his cheek had got worse. They ordered breakfast. Paul ordered two fried eggs, an 'extra' not provided for by the hotel (price included in bill) breakfast of coffee, rolls and butter. He felt two fried eggs were payment due to him. They discussed their visit to Castor and Lisa Alerich to see their house. Ernst surprised Paul by saying, 'Since we have to go by train that long journey to Hamburg this evening, I thought that after our restless night it would be too exhausting to go the two hours' journey to the Alerichs' village in the little local train, so I have ordered a car. I am afraid neither of us slept much last night: it was like that night you once described to me, when you were with your friend Marston.' Two hours later, when they were seated in the car and Ernst, driving, had changed into top gear along the smooth, sandy road through the pine forest, he said, 'Last night, you seemed so innocent and natural and spontaneous, Paul.'

3

THE ALERICHS' HOUSE

Castor Alerich was waiting for them at the front gate of his house, a white cube of concrete, like a greatly enlarged version of one of the lamps in Joachim's studio. A balcony surrounded the whole upper floor (there were only two floors). The roof was flat. Castor wore leather shorts, a shirt of coarse white linen with collar open at the neck, a jacket of what looked like faded brown corduroy. He had a pale thick skin and ragged yellow hair the texture of tow, over greenish eyes staring through gaps in it. His head was enormous and skull-like. His wide shoulders gave an impression of primordial strength. Looking at him, Paul found himself thinking of a period of history he associated with Picts and Scots living in caves that might well have resembled modernist architecture.

'How are you, Ernst?' Castor said, giving Ernst a hearty slap on the back.

Trying to put on a correspondingly hearty manner, Ernst introduced Paul. 'My friend Paul Schoner, an English writer.' Castor grasped Paul's hand and, bowing over it ironically, said, 'Welcome to you, my good sir.'

'We haven't met for a long time, Castor. I hope all goes well with you and Lisa,' Ernst said.

'Quite well. We haven't got any money, but that's nothing new,' Castor said in English, continuing without any break, 'I have something to tell you now. It is that Lisa isn't feeling too well. So she may not be able to see you. She caught a little cold last night and, you know, at this time one has to be careful.' He turned to Paul and asked abruptly: 'Do you like gardens?' – opening the gate – 'because I have rather a nice one, or shall have. All one can see now is shit, but I am working on it every day now so that it will be blossoming, I hope, by next summer.'

They went through this garden. Castor opened the front door of the house. It gave directly on to the living-room which took up three-quarters of the ground floor area and reached above to a skylight. The furniture was of white-enamelled wood: tables and chairs, and two settees with cushions in covers of primary colours, and the texture of sacking. Lamps had shades of white or yellow, thick transparent paper. There were two or three abstract paintings done in very thick pigment. On the floor there was a red and black Tunisian rug, a pattern sewn in thick thread on coarse-meshed string. There was a large, rectangular stone fire-place. The room and everything in it, except the contrasting fabrics, gave an impression of Wagnerian comfort, as though, after wassailing, you chose your place on chair or settee and flung your bare hairy limbs down upon the brightly coloured cushions for athletic love-making or centennial Valkyrie slumbers.

Castor said: 'There are no books in this house, absolutely not one book except the telephone directory and some architectural journals.'

He made tea. Ernst and Castor struck up a conversation – part German, part English – about girls and friends they had in common. All these people, familiar to Ernst were, Paul suspec-ted, scarcely better known to Willy and Joachim than to him. Ernst had different sets of friends, whom he kept apart and before whom, it seemed, he played entirely different roles. Paul thought once again that when he spoke English or French Ernst had a personality less relaxed than when he spoke German.

As soon as tea was over, rubbing his hands together, Castor roared: 'There is a lot of rubbish in the garden to burn. You've had tea, now we go outside and make a bonfire.' Under Castor's terse commands, Ernst and Paul spent the rest of the afternoon duti-fully collecting twigs and branches. Then they had a light supper of salad and ham and cheese. After this meal, Castor went upstairs to see whether his wife felt better. He returned to say no, Lisa still suffered from a cold and headache. But he added that, as the night was so warm, when they had lit the bonfire, perhaps she would come out on to the balcony to see it.

When Castor had finished putting together the twigs and branches which they had collected, he crushed the heap down with his foot and said: 'This business of my wife having a child is too much – really too much. As soon as the time comes near, I will ride away. I cannot be present at this Woman's Business.'

'You will go – really?' Paul asked, incredulous.

'Yes, really. I shall take my bicycle and ride through Holland and France and Spain and Italy.'

'That's the modern husband for you,' said Ernst.

It was now almost dark. Castor put a match to the shavings below the heaped up bonfire. They burned brightly, some of them catching light on the ground outside the heap, flames licking empty air. The fire began to burn, crackling and thrusting back darkness over a widening circumference. Then it died down, seemed almost to have subsided, but for a roaring which came from the centre. Through crevices in the branches Paul peered into the glowing heart of the fire hidden almost by clouds of pulsing smoke and hissing jets of steam. At last the bonfire was well and truly alight. It blazed and roared.

Excitedly, Castor shouted, 'Lisa, come and look!'

Paul turned towards the house on whose white walls the blaze, reflected, danced. The garden smelt of smoke and earth. Castor rushed indoors and upstairs to the bedroom. A moment later, Lisa came out on to the balcony. Castor came down into the garden again.

Lisa wore a red nightgown of exotic silk – perhaps Castor had got it in Burma. She smiled down at Paul, saying 'Good evening!' in English.

She looked so ethereal in the glow of that intense light, and it seemed so difficult to raise his voice against the triumphal roaring of the bonfire, that he did not answer, only stared up at her, too dazed to smile even. Meanwhile Ernst, determined to strike an attitude, put his arm round Castor's shoulders and, laughing, hid his face against Castor's chest, raising his other hand in a gesture of pushing the wall of heat coming from the fire away from him.

The fire burned higher and higher. Great sparks shot far above it, drifting out of sight, dissolved in air, or joining the company of stars. Lisa stood there leaning over the railing of the balcony. Sparks seemed to fall in a shower all round her.

Just when she stood back from the balcony railing to go into her room, the fire, fanned by the wind, threw up a yet intenser shaft of light. Her dress was lifted slightly by this breeze, and, under it, Paul could see the swelling of her body.

They went back to the living-room to rest after the bonfire which had produced on them a peculiar kind of drowsiness, as though their senses were drugged with aromatic smoke. They lay on the floor with the large cushions spread out round them, their heads resting on their arms. Castor provided them with refreshments consisting of lager and some kind of bread the texture of dog biscuits. It was growing dark but no one wanted to turn on the lights. Paul enjoyed a sensation of wakeful dreaming.

Getting up, and going to a corner of the room where there was a gramophone, Castor, winding its handle, said: 'I don't have any books, but I do have records. Didn't some English writer or philosopher or something like that say that architecture was frozen music? Perhaps that's why I adore music so much. Because I'm an architect. My wife can't abide it.'

'Ruskin perhaps,' said Paul.

Castor put on the adagio of Mozart's Clarinet Quintet. Paul lay back completely, taking his arms from behind his head and resting them on the cushions at his sides. The music seemed to make the room expand as though it could enclose first the garden, then the forest, then the sky, then the stars, then the universe, then God. The sound of the clarinet was a waterfall flowing white over rocks, there were notes glimpsed between the pine trees which sometimes concealed, sometimes revealed them. Breezes shaped the sound to their own hidden impulses. The tune went on outside him and yet entirely filled his head, his skull, his brain, sounds in which he could live or, equally happy, die. It was music, transforming all things seen into things heard.

At the end of the movement Ernst got up to say that if they were to catch their train to Hamburg, they must leave now. Paul was feeling that he could lie like this among the cushions on Castor's floor for ever. He got up to go.

As they went back on the train to Hamburg, Ernst said: 'I no longer have the spot on the left side of my cheek which was bothering me. The heat of the bonfire, when I was standing near, made it burst.'

Paul thought of Castor, head bent over handle-bars, hair falling over his green eyes, staring straight ahead, riding through

European lands, Holland, France, Italy, Spain, looking at their architecture. He wondered: What is his goal?

In Hamburg, they joined Joachim and Willy for dinner, very late, at a restaurant situated on the Alster. Before they went to their table, while they were standing at the bar having drinks, Joachim drew Paul aside. He was going, he explained, on a business trip to Cologne in early September. He suggested Paul meet him there. 'We could spend a couple of days seeing Cologne and then go together for a walk along the Rhine. You will see a part of Germany that is not Hamburg, nor will it contain Ernst and Hanny Stockmann,' he said. Paul said he would be delighted.

4

THE WALK ALONG THE RHINE

September 1929

Joachim met Paul at Cologne station. Paul was rather horrified
to find that Joachim had taken a room for them in one of the
most expensive hotels in the city. Joachim explained that he had
to stay there on account of his representing his father's
business. Anyhow, they were only due to stay three days in
Cologne, and then to start on their trip down the Rhine.

Paul had arrived just before lunch. After lunch at the hotel
they went to swim. Paul wanted to unpack before going out, but
Joachim said in his slowest drawl: 'Well, I think that you may
unpack later.' He seemed impatient even of the slight delay
while Paul collected his bathing things. However, directly they
were outside the hotel he was in a good humour and Paul
ceased feeling irritated at his high-handedness. As they walked,
Paul asked him how he had liked his business dealings. Joachim
said he enjoyed having interviews with people when travelling
for his father's firm, because he always succeeded in making
them buy what he wanted to sell them – even things they did
not want.

They crossed a wide bridge over the Rhine. Whilst they were
on the bridge they had to walk single file along the pavement,
there were so many people there, and so much traffic on the
road. They could not talk. Paul observed Joachim closely. He
was dressed in the pseudo-English Hamburg style, which
looked rather foreign in Cologne. He wore grey flannel trousers
and a jacket of a light blue colour. Striding along, Joachim stood
tall and straight, his head erect. He held the little case
containing their bathing things and his camera lightly in his left
hand in a manner nonchalantly self-aware. The sun beat down
on his tanned skin. He stared round him almost defiantly and

always with that air of entertaining and being entertained. People turned to look back at him.

On the far side of the bridge they followed a broad path which left the road and went through a garden past the long modern building for international exhibitions. Everything seemed clean and new and polished like gun-metal on this side of the Rhine. The Exhibition Building, with its long lines of low walls and symmetrical windows, stretching far away from each side of its central tower, looked diminished, microscopic almost, under the immense glare of the afternoon.

'Isn't it wonderful?' said Joachim, grinning at Paul. He put up his face toward the sun, and lifted up an arm to shield his eyes. 'It is so bright,' he said. 'I can hardly look at it.' Then he let his hand drop against the concrete parapet in front of the river. He drew it quickly away again. 'Oh, it is so hot! You can scarcely bear to touch it! Let us go and swim at once.'

They soon reached the *Schwimmbad*. After they had undressed, they walked slowly down to the water. Paul lagged behind. Joachim said: 'Why can't you keep up? Is it so awfully difficult?'

The current of the Rhine at Cologne being very strong, when Paul got into the water he was immediately swept off his feet. Joachim said, grinning: 'What is the matter with you, Paul? You don't seem able to stand on your feet at all.' But he said it teasingly and he laughed.

Paul struggled to his feet, and then walked further out, whilst the stream tugged at his legs as if they were being pulled by cables.

'Try and swim against the current now!'

Paul swam as hard as he could but he was carried backwards by the stream.

'Swim! Swim!' Joachim shouted, laughing. 'I'll race you!' He threw himself down into the water beside Paul and appeared to be advancing rapidly. But when Paul looked at the shore he saw it was gliding forwards, not backwards. Even Joachim could not quite hold his own against the current.

Paul abandoned any attempt to conquer the Rhine. He swam downstream, enjoying the incredibly swift motion of the water carrying him. Joachim, after diving under the floating wooden platforms which surrounded the bathing place, moved far out into the centre of the river. When a string of barges came downstream he climbed up the side of one of them and then dived off its deck the other side. Being liable to cramp, and not able to swim well, Paul was grateful that Joachim had gone away. He no longer had to behave athletically. He began to enjoy himself, floating on his back and thinking about poetry.

After swimming, they lay on the beach, drying themselves in the sun. For a long time, closing their eyes and feeling the light touching their bodies, they did not say anything. Later, they sat up and, as though convalescent, began to take notice. Joachim talked about his childhood: how, when he was five, his mother had prevented a working-class man from giving him a groschen. Since then, he had always wanted to talk with working-class men. Suddenly he touched Paul's hand. 'Look!' he said.

He was pointing at a boy who lay on the sand a few yards distant from them. The boy's face was pressed against the sand and his arms spread out, almost embracing it. The sun was so strong on his hands and thighs that the flesh seemed a transparent vermilion.

'Well?' Paul asked.

'It is so funny. He knows all the time that I am watching, and he is pretending not to notice. He is so glad.'

'What are you going to do about it?'

'Wait here. I will go and get a newspaper. Then I will pretend only to be interested in it, and he won't be able to hide any longer how much he wants me to be looking at him.'

Joachim got up and walked leisurely away. Directly he was gone, the boy looked up, leaning on one elbow, turning round with an air of disappointment. The boy scanned the shore, and then, a few moments later, seeing Joachim returning, he looked back again towards the Rhine. When Joachim was near, he blushed.

'What are you laughing about, Paul?'

Paul told him what had happened.

'Oh, is that so? I thought he was expecting something from me. Well, he doesn't have to wait very long now.'

He unfolded the illustrated paper and began to look at the photographs in it very carefully. He held it out in order to show Paul a picture. He whispered: 'Look at the boy now.'

The boy was leaning forward on his elbow, unable to conceal his eagerness to look over Joachim's shoulder at the picture.

Joachim finished looking at the picture and then, after folding it very carefully, he threw it down beside him. Then, as if by an afterthought, he turned round quickly, and, taking up the paper again, handed it to the boy, saying in German:

'Would you care to look at this?'

The boy smiled gratefully, taking the paper.

'Thank you very much. It is nice to have something to look at in the sun.'

'Yes, it is a wonderful day, isn't it?' Joachim gave the sky and river and city an encircling glance.

'Wonderful. One can bathe all day in this weather.'

'Yes. Unless one has to do something else. Have you work to do?'

'I? Work? Not yet. I am only seventeen. I am still at school. I am free all day now, because it is the holidays.'

'I wish I still had such long holidays. Will you have a cigarette?'

'Oh yes. Thank you very much.' He took a cigarette and examined it closely. 'Yes, I like Egyptians.'

Paul got up.

Joachim said in English: 'Where are you going? Are you leaving us?'

'I'm just going to walk round a bit. I want to watch the people who are doing exercises over there.' He pointed to a place a little removed from them where men and women stood twisting and turning their bodies, as though they were grilling them on a spit.

'All right. Don't be gone long.'

He turned to the boy. 'Do you speak English?'

The boy shook his head, flattered, smiling.

'May I introduce you to my friend Paul? What is your name?'

'Groote. Kurt Groote.'

'Oh, Kurt. That is nice. My name is Joachim.'

They all shook hands. Paul walked away towards the place where people were doing gymnastic exercises.

He watched the writhing figures of the mostly middle-aged members of the German youth movement. As he looked at them

– men, women, boys, shrimp-pink, yellow or mahogany – they struck him as ludicrous, even the beautiful ones, and some were beautiful. After being in Germany for just over two months, he found himself beginning to tire of the self-conscious insistence of the Germans on their bodies. They worshipped the body, as though it were a temple. But why can't they accept themselves for what they are, he thought. I am sick of all these people who strive endlessly to attain a perfect physique and who wear themselves out with exercising, simply because they are unable to accept themselves physically as they are. They are unable to forgive themselves for having the bodies they were born with. Joachim, of course, is wonderful with boys. He moves from boy to boy, and will continue to do so, even when he grows older, always pursuing beauty and the love affair, always having to act the boy himself, having to judge himself by the standard of the most beautiful boy in the world.

Out there on the sand dunes, these brand-new Germans twisted their bodies round and round, like agonized contortionists, each one denying his own separateness, trying to become the perfect Child of the Sun.

Paul wondered whether he should attempt to live up to Joachim. For a few moments he realized so completely that he would not be able to do so that he ceased to want to. He turned away from the ever-gyrating athletes of the sand dunes, a scene from the *Purgatorio*.

He walked back slowly towards Joachim and Kurt. Joachim was laughing with his new friend, whom he watched closely all the time. Joachim sat on the sand, with knees drawn up close to his chest, whilst his hands touched his ankles. He held a cigarette in his hand. He flicked the ash off his big toe, as he began to tell another anecdote.

Kurt's face glowed with pleasure as he lay back, bewitched, his body relaxed and his elbows dug into the sand. His eyes followed every gesture of Joachim's hands. And Joachim never ceased to watch the expression on Kurt's face.

When the story appeared to be finished, Paul joined them.

'Hullo, Paul,' said Joachim in a rather drowsy voice. 'What have you been doing? Have you been in the water again?'

'I have been watching those people doing their exercises.'

'Is that all? It must have been rather dull, I think.'

He stood up and held out his hand to Kurt: 'I think that we ought to be going. Remember tomorrow. *Auf Wiedersehen!*'

Whilst they were having supper at the hotel, Joachim talked without stopping about Kurt: 'I have arranged that we shall go for an expedition with him tomorrow. I hope you don't mind.'

'No, I'd love to.'

'That's fine. He will meet us outside the hotel at 9.00.'

After supper, he yawned and said:

'What would you like to do now?'

'I don't know. I haven't thought. What would you like?'

'I was asking you,' Joachim said a bit impatiently. 'Isn't there anything that you want to do for yourself? Do you always want to do what I want?'

'I would like to walk round the streets and by the river, and look at people and the shops. But that must seem very dull.' Paul could think of nothing that seemed exciting enough for Joachim.

'Well, I would like to do just that. But I would like also to have a drink at the end.'

They walked through the square past the cathedral. They came to a street through which traffic was not allowed to go in the evenings in summer, for at that season it was then used as a promenade. People strolled up and down, all walking on the right side. Joachim walked slowly, almost down the centre of this fairway, with his arm under Paul's. Joachim stared outrageously at the passers-by. He seemed to see everyone as actor or actress of a role in a parade.

'I always like to watch people. I can feel so much from seeing the way they walk or look at you. When I am at a party, I will watch each person who comes into the room. One person comes in and he is nothing, no one notices him. But then, maybe, there comes another, at once everyone feels his presence. He looks at you and you feel that he is alive, keen.'

They did not speak very much, only occasionally, to make the briefest comments, like signals to each other, on the people coming towards them. All the time Paul and Joachim watched the same things, each of them enjoying the light and movement of the street far more because they were together than either would have done alone.

They had reached the end of the brightly lit promenade, and turned down a road that led to the river. When they arrived at the river, Joachim leaned over the balustrade looking down on it, and said: 'You know, I like it when I am together with a boy like Kurt. I would like to swim or to walk or do something active with him all day, and not talk very much.'

They came to a café where they had drinks. At a table nearby there was a young man wearing a black felt hat who watched them closely as they drank beer. Joachim, in his usual manner, was soon talking to this young man – and offering him a drink. His name was Nicolas. He said he was a Russian émigré living in Paris. He described his life there, his debts, his friendship with Cocteau, the Russian ballet.

They walked back to the hotel slowly, arm in arm. Most of the way they talked about Nicolas, by whose stories they were half amused, half touched.

They went up to their room. Paul undressed quickly and got into bed. Joachim, however, took a long time over his toilet, which culminated with his putting on a hair net to keep his hair set back. Paul thought this un-English.

However, at last Joachim was finished. Taking Paul's hand, he sat on the edge of his bed, looking at Paul with his wide attentive eyes, that always seemed amused behind their darkness like that of a theatre. Now, holding both Paul's hands, he kissed him good-night.

'I think it is a good thing that we have come here together, Paul. Don't you think so? I hope that we shall like our trip.'

He went back to his own bed, and they both slept.

Joachim had arranged for them to meet Kurt the next morning at 9.00, in the street, outside the hotel door. Exactly at 9.00, they stood in the street beside the hotel porter, who was not a little annoyed at their presence, which seemed to rob him of dignity. But he could not do anything except shoot indignant glances at them from time to time. The morning sun again was very bright. Most of the street lay in the shadow of the cathedral, except for a strip of light a few yards wide and deep in front of the hotel, where traffic glittered.

When the bells of the cathedral struck 9.30, Joachim asked

Paul if he would mind waiting a little longer whilst he went inside the hotel to telephone Kurt.

Paul waited, for half an hour, in the street. At 10.00, Joachim emerged from the hotel and said that he had searched the telephone book but found no number under the name Groote that could be where Kurt lived. Paul did not express his feelings to Joachim at having been kept waiting.

'Well,' Joachim said, 'we will have to go out alone. I cannot think what has happened.'

'Perhaps the boy forgot where we were to meet.'

'No, I don't think so. I suppose he went home and told his parents how he had met us, and they have not allowed him to come. That is most likely.'

All that day he kept on talking about Kurt. They went to the same bathing place on the chance of meeting Kurt there. But they did not see him. As they lay on the beach, Joachim said:

'It is such a pity. You know, I cannot stop thinking about him. Every minute I hope that he will come, and that we shall talk together again, like we did yesterday.'

Paul was too dazed to reply to Joachim's remarks. Joachim explained to Paul that he would like very much now to meet someone with whom he would fall in love.

Before they left Cologne, Paul wrote in his Notebook:

Last night I had a touch of sunstroke. I had a bad headache so, before supper, I lay down to rest. An extraordinary sensation. Directly I shut my eyes, I saw vividly the white, burning sky of that afternoon. And I no longer loved it. I hated that intense sun. It made me ill. I dreaded being out of doors another day, as I might dread seasickness. Now I no longer imagined the sun as a healer, but evil, poisonous, serpent-like: as it appears at the most dreadful season, when the sky is a stage set, empty, waiting for the cyclonic storms: silent, waiting for the voice of thunder. I pictured a sky where I could see no clouds, but a greyness like a piled-up continent of sand, round whose brindled edges showed the livid pallor of the sun. Perhaps there really was some dry electric evil in the air which had corrupted everything. But, if so, it was a frown on the face of summer which quickly passed, for there was no storm. I think it is myself who is being corrupted.

Joachim was very busy during their last day in Cologne. In addition to work for his father's firm, he spent a lot of time shopping. He bought three shirts, a pair of corduroy shorts, a beret, socks and stout leather shoes for their walk. Paul went to the art gallery and the museum. He bought no new clothes. He was conscious of being unable to compete with Joachim. Also he had no money to buy anything except books.

Next morning, they took the train from Cologne to Bingen on the Rhine. After they had put down their things at their hotel, they walked down to the road running alongside the river. It was evening. Behind them, from restaurants and *Weinstübe* in the little town, they could hear the voices of Germans singing. The days were now shortening. Lights were starting up everywhere. Behind them, on the hillside, Bingen looked as if its houses were cut out of cardboard. They could hear the clinking of wine glasses from a restaurant where there was some celebration going on. Figures moved mysteriously beside them, suddenly stopping, then moving, then stopping, a man and a woman, two men, a man, a woman, alone, then not alone, looking across the Rhine to the mountains on the further side. Paul felt the end of the summer of 1929 chill in the air.

'Look, Paul.'

Touched by Joachim's singleness of purpose, Paul looked at the boy by whose side Joachim was standing. Unlike that one of yesterday, this one of today wore Bavarian *Wandervogel* outfit: Lederhosen, embroidered shirt with collar open at the neck, a jacket green like hunters wear, through the front of which there showed a band on which stags were embroidered, attached at each end to straps of leathern braces.

Paul said: 'I don't trust him.'

'You don't like him?'

'No.'

Joachim seemed pleased. The boy turned round and Paul admitted, 'He is beautiful.'

'Will you have a cigarette, Paul?'

'Yes, please.'

Joachim gave Paul a cigarette. Then he offered one to the boy, who accepted it, more gracefully than gratefully.

Joachim began talking to the boy. His name was Heinrich. Joachim said: 'We are going to have something to eat and drink, Heinrich. Will you join us?'

'*Gern* – gladly.'

They all three walked up the hill through the village to a restaurant with tables outside looking out over that sensual dim evening view of the river and the mountains.

To Paul, Joachim's moves now seemed as familiar as the opening moves of a game of chess. They held a fascination which excited him, as though Joachim was putting on this show for Paul's entertainment. Paul was the ideal spectator whom Joachim had brought along with him to watch the performance.

The evening was still warm enough for it to be pleasant to eat outdoors. Paul ate in silence, watching Heinrich, and watching Joachim watch Heinrich. The boy had long fair hair swept back from his temples and falling in waves over his brow and ears, as if it were blown back by a gentle breeze. He had a very fair complexion. His skin was not in the least coarsened through exposure to the sun but the colour of alabaster, which it also resembled in smoothness. His face was one of sensual eagerness, fixed anticipation that might have been poetic had there not been something petty about it. The mouth was full. A kind of over-fastidiousness of the nostrils was emphasized by the eyes which seemed narrowly focused, close together like a small wild cat's. It was the eyes with their rather cruel look that had made Paul, at first glance, find him repellent.

'Where do you come from?' Joachim asked the boy.

'Bavaria.'

He named a village and said just how many times he had been to Munich. He answered all Joachim's questions promptly, quietly and sweetly as if those lips were a tiny bugle blowing a hidden tune. Yet there was a slight, naïvely subtle hesitation as if he was considering what would be the most effective answer to the question asked. When Heinrich was talking, Paul watched his face, and he imagined a photograph in which, behind the surface likeness, there was a scarcely discernible second truer-likeness. The ghost image behind Heinrich was someone old and arid: a cunning commonplace peasant villager. Paul noticed that when Heinrich spoke, until he had finished what he was saying, he always looked away from Joachim into the distance as though into his own dream: then, immediately, he would glance back at Joachim, excluding Paul.

Joachim asked: 'What are you doing here on the Rhine?'

'Wandering.'

'Oh, wandering! Why did you leave Bavaria? Did you have work there?'

'Yes, I was employed in a shop for selling all the trivial knick-knacks required by the villagers,' he said, hinting faint distaste for these humble peasants. 'My dear dear mother was delicate, so I worked in order to earn money to support her ... My mother, you see, is dearer to me than anyone else in the world.' He said this as though, whether it were true or untrue, he wanted to believe it. He paused, glanced at Joachim and then, with a little laugh, continued: 'But I found I could only make very little money. You know how small wages are in a village. There was just enough money to support me but not enough to support Mother as well. Mutti was ill, and although I worked so hard, I could not support her. Well, then at last she did get a little better, so that she could manage alone at home without me. I hated my work and was making enough money only for myself. So I thought, It's no use my staying here. I do no good to Mutti, I am only a burden to her, and I myself am unhappy. Now that my mother can manage for herself, I shall leave. So I put on my little Lederhosen, and I started to walk. This is where I have got to, as you see.'

'For how long have you been walking?'

He laughed, shrugging his shoulders with a movement that made his hair fall over his face. Then he jerked his head up with a fine open-air gesture. The hair fell back into place.

'I can hardly tell how long. Perhaps ten or twelve weeks.'

'And this is all you have with you?' Joachim asked, touching the satchel which he carried at his side.

'Yes, yes, that is all I have,' he smiled. He opened the satchel and laughed gaily. 'Look, that is all I've got in it.'

He drew out of the satchel a shirt, a comb, some shaving things, and a small leather-covered notebook. He opened the notebook and said: 'Here is a poem which I wrote about my mother. Shall I read it?' He held the notebook in front of Joachim, and Joachim put his hand on Heinrich's shoulder. Heinrich read out the poem very slowly, in a sentimental voice.

Joachim said: 'My friend Paul also writes poetry.'

Paul resisted an impulse to get up and never come back.

Heinrich smiled at Paul with interest. Then he looked enquiringly from Paul to Joachim. Joachim touched his shoulder again.

After supper, Paul left them together. He saw that in Joachim that machinery of self-persuasion was beginning to work which might end with his loving Heinrich. He foresaw that if he were with them both, Joachim and Heinrich would soon come to resent his observing, listening, envious presence. Paul went to a café by the Rhine and ate an ice. Then he read from a selection of Hölderlin's poems which he carried in his jacket pocket. Ernst had given the slim, beautifully printed volume to him as a farewell present.

Later, he walked back to the inn where they were staying. He was about to enter the room they were to share when he observed a note pinned above the door handle. It was from Joachim. He wrote that he had taken a room on the opposite side of the corridor for Paul as he was now sharing this room with Heinrich.

Paul left the inn again and climbed the road away from the village, up through vineyards. Soon he came to open fields. While he was walking through the darkness, feelings of anger, shame, self-pity and forgiveness were playing thoughts through his mind like variations on a theme in music. Sometimes he thought resentfully that Joachim had deliberately meant to insult and hurt him by arranging that he should sleep in a room alone. Sometimes it seemed a reasonable, if a bit inconsiderate, decision to have made. In his desire to share a room with Heinrich there was no wish to offend Paul. After all, he thought, nothing in our relationship – his and mine – is betrayed by his doing so. For what is our relationship? I am the friend with whom he can talk about things which he cannot talk about with boys like Kurt or Heinrich. If Joachim had done him an injury, Paul wanted to forget about it. They were on holiday.

From the field which he had reached at the top of a hill, he saw the lights of a village the other side of the Rhine strung out along the railway. The wind was cool. Suddenly he remembered how much he had resented having to share a room with Ernst, at Altamunde. I am being absurd, he thought. Now I have got the room I wanted so much. Looked at like that, he was glad to be alone, and to read, and write notes by himself in his room. To be a poet, he thought, I must be alone. Perhaps the reason why Joachim, who was so gifted, did not want to be an artist was because he could not bear to be alone. His idea of being alive was to be with living statues of flesh and blood, not to make dead ones out of marble.

Paul soon got himself into a state of mind in which he began to feel sorry for Joachim, doomed always to be running after some Heinrich or Kurt.

The next morning, after breakfast, Paul took Joachim aside and said: 'Joachim, of course I must leave.'

Joachim stared at Paul: 'But why, Paul? What are you meaning to say?'

'Well, now you have another walking companion.'

'Surely you aren't jealous of Heinrich?'

'No, but the two of you will want to be alone, Joachim.'

'What are you talking about?'

It was so obvious that it had never occurred to Joachim that Paul would want to leave, Paul was taken aback. 'All right. I shall stay and see what happens.'

'Good.' Joachim seemed delighted. Then he burst out irrepressibly: 'Oh, I must tell you how wonderful he was last night. Heinrich told me everything about his adventures on his journey here. I think he is the most interesting boy I ever met. Don't you think that he is wonderful? Didn't I tell you I wanted to meet someone I would want to stay with all my life on this trip?'

'How has he been supporting himself during the past few weeks, since he left Bavaria?'

'I don't know. I don't quite like to ask him that yet. Perhaps he had saved himself a little money from his earnings at the shop. But I shall find out, surely. I think that all he tells me is true.'

That morning they went through a little wood up the hills, so as to cut off a bend in the Rhine. The sun was brilliant. The morning light between shadows of leaves dappled their path, or lay in great pools on the grass below high-up gaps in the tree tops. That morning gave a feeling of early autumn as the burning counterpart of early spring.

Joachim talked to Heinrich in German, breaking off only sometimes to translate for Paul one of Heinrich's remarks. Paul could not help being caught up by the elation of their meeting. He began to like Heinrich.

They had reached the edge of the wood. Here they looked out through a fringe of leaves over a little valley, beyond which, on the side of the hill, there were vineyards with terraces silhouetted against the light. Joachim took a photograph of the sunlit valley with, high up, the lines of stony terraces and vines and the sticks supporting them. Then he said to Paul: 'I want to take a photograph of you and Heinrich.'

He sat Heinrich and Paul down on a bank of grass. He posed them with Heinrich with his right arm round Paul's shoulders and his left hand on Paul's left knee, and Paul with his left arm round Heinrich's waist. Heinrich was affectionate. Paul could only laugh (a situation which fell happily into the German – *konnte nur lachen!*). As an Englishman, Paul felt flattered by the attention of these two young Germans.

After another hour's walking, when they had completed their short cut across the hills, they saw below them a stretch of the river, broadening out beyond the bend. There were strings of barges waiting to go through a narrow channel of deep water. They started running downhill towards those barges. It was very hot running. When they got to the river bank they walked along a path there and Joachim and Heinrich started singing songs. By now Paul had completely forgotten his resentment. Instead, he had the feeling almost of privilege in sharing with Joachim and Heinrich the beginnings of their friendship. He had a sense of celebration.

At midday, they left the path, which ran above the level of the river, and climbed down to the rocky shore to bathe. Heinrich said that because he came from the mountains he had never learned to swim, so he waded into the water up to his knees and watched Joachim and Paul swimming. Joachim was delighted that Heinrich could not swim, partly because he was delighted by whatever he did or did not do, and partly because he anticipated the pleasure in coming months of teaching him.

Joachim and Paul swam downstream together. Then Joachim swam upstream, while Paul walked along the shore back towards Heinrich. He waited until Joachim turned and swam level with him, and then Paul helped him ashore. As Joachim got out of the water, he said: 'Was I not saying before I came here that now I would like something great to happen to me, a *grande passion*? Well, now you see, it is happening, it is really happening.'

Paul said nothing.

'Don't you believe me, Paul?'

'I don't really understand that you can fall in love with someone because you have said that you were going to fall in love.'

'But I do love him. Already I know it.'

Still wading in the river, Heinrich was occupied in washing his shirt. This delighted Joachim more than anything he had seen him do yet. He climbed across the rocks and took a photograph of Heinrich washing his shirt. Heinrich was pleased and said he would send a copy of the photograph to his mother.

There was no doubt that Heinrich was beautiful. His limbs seemed polished like the surface of some thinly varnished, rare, light-coloured springy wood. When he had finished washing his shirt – and after Joachim had taken a second photograph – he waded out of the river and started clambering up the shore, balancing on the most narrow edges of rocks. He raised his hands above his head in order to keep his balance, and his body kept bending from side to side. In that little walk of only a few yards it presented a sequence of changes, every one of them beautiful.

Paul watched the surface of rippling muscle which sprang upwards from the thighs, across the body, to the roots of his arms. The direction, the impulse of his body was simple yet complex – a single gesture of a statue's eloquent extended hand.

'He looks so pleased with himself', said Joachim, 'he is strutting like a bird, like a peacock.'

Joachim put down the camera.

'I think that I shall swim for a long way now. Will you swim also, Paul?'

Tired, he said: 'No, I think I will stay here and lie in the sun.'

'All right. I will not be long.'

Joachim walked down to the shore, and then, with long, leisurely strokes that almost seemed to lift him out of the water, he swam into the middle of the stream.

Heinrich came down off the rock on which he had been standing. He sat down beside Paul. He looked at him in silence. Then he said, with great deliberation, in a rather childish voice: 'You – spik – English?'

'Yes, I am an Englishman.'

Heinrich laughed again. Then he put his arm round Paul and drew himself close to him, more, as it seemed, to make himself understood clearly (with lips pressed against Paul's ear) than for any other reason. With his free hand, he pointed first to himself and then at Paul: 'I learn – from you – to spik English?'

Paul smiled, nodding assent.

He laughed again. Then, quite suddenly, he kissed Paul and then, as suddenly, turned away again. He said, ponderously, in German, while he held his arm: 'I am so happy that you and Joachim and I are all three here together. You will not go away because I am here, no?'

'No.'

'I am so glad. Then we are all three happy. Joachim and I are very fond of you.'

Before noon, each morning, when they were walking, Joachim and Paul would talk in English together. Joachim would report to Paul what he thought to be wonderful remarks, or stories told by Heinrich the previous night. On the third or fourth morning of their journey, he said to Paul: 'I read some poems when I was at school – Schiller's "The Bell" and Goethe's "The Bride of Corinth" – and enjoyed them. But I never understand the point of writing poetry. Why are you a poet?'

Paul felt totally incapable of answering this, but thinking it would be insulting to Joachim for him not to make the attempt, he said: 'I try to make images in words out of what I feel about experiences, poems which live beyond the experiences themselves.'

'How? How is that?' asked Joachim, looking puzzled. 'Surely living is what you are while you are doing it. We are experiencing our lives now in this walk down the Rhine. Isn't that enough? That we are doing this now? Tomorrow we will be experiencing something different.'

'Well, the point is to make the experience alive for someone else, who can enter into it. Someone who is perhaps not yet born.'

'Why? Why?'

'I don't know why. I just want to do that.'

'If, while I am doing something pleasant, I start thinking about some other meaning than that which I have while I am doing it, then I am not living in that moment, I am somewhere else. With half my mind I'm already in some kind of future or other place. I would not like that. I want to be to the fullest extent what I am, here and now. Besides, it is I who am here in my own world, not someone else whom I can make share what only I can be.'

'In that case you are living just for yourself and just for the moment.'

'Well, what else can I do, if I am truthful about it? I can't be living my life for someone else or for something that happens after I am dead.'

'But you should live for something more than the moment.'

'Well, I suppose already I do that,' said Joachim. 'I live for a whole chain of moments which just now add up to our walking for a few days down the Rhine. That is more than one moment, I guess. But I can only live for myself, I can't do so for anyone else now living, and still less can I for someone who is not yet born. What I want is to have completely lived each of those moments while I am here.'

'What do you mean by "live"?'

'Well, I suppose I mean that with all my mind and all my body, with every atom that is or that I call my own self, I embrace what is outside myself, and make it my experience, my life. I can only do that in the present, I cannot do it in the past that has gone away or in the future which is not yet here. I like to take photographs partly because in a photograph the past is the past and does not pretend to be the future. Nor does it become the life of someone looking at it. It belongs to the past, and the picture remains outside the person who looks at it.'

Paul began to feel that everything he most cared about in his work – his life – was being challenged. He had a sensation of choking. He remembered listening to Mozart's Clarinet Quintet at Castor Alerich's house. He said, with a passion that caused Joachim to gape at him with amused amazement: 'When you hear, say, a quartet by Mozart, or Beethoven, or Schubert, there is something in the arrangement of sounds played by the instruments which is unique to each composer. Each composer is uniquely himself in the music and however much he tried to, he could not be either of the others. There is a voice which is his and only his and is enduring and which after more than a hundred years within the music is Mozart or Beethoven or Schubert.'

'Maybe,' said Joachim, 'but I would not care for being a voice for other people, if I myself had to sacrifice my own capacity for living whatever it is I most want to experience, in order to do that. I think that maybe people who live disembodied lives after their deaths also lived disembodied lives during their lives. They sacrificed their lives to the dream of their immortality. I would only want to exist as Beethoven after my death if I was also prepared to be Beethoven during his life. And I would HATE to be Beethoven, from all I've ever heard about him.' He laughed and glowed with emphasis of the word 'HATE'.

Paul said: 'Well, I hope I would be prepared to be whatever was demanded of me if I could be great in my poetry.'

Joachim stared at him with enormous eyes of total incredulity.

'Well, why are you here then with us?'

Then he roared with laughter, and rushed away downhill to join Heinrich who was standing by the river, undressing. For now it was midday, the time when, with much fooling around, Joachim would give Heinrich his swimming lesson. After that was finished, they would eat a picnic lunch which they had bought from the previous night's hotel. They ate very little during the day. Thus the evening meal, when they ate a lot and drank Rhine wine, formed the climax of the day. They would sleep early because they were tired after the day outdoors.

The weather presented all that week the same immaculate aspect, so that they seemed to move through days that stretched out perfect to the horizon and pulsing beyond that, quietly through the world. Each morning when they awoke in a different village inn, there would be a coolness of the late summer air, and a mist would hang over the river. But the mist would evaporate early and the sun would drive a burning wedge through the upper layers of fleecy cloud. Then at early morning, while they walked, its rays would fall diagonally on the river, throwing reflected lights within the shadows of over-arching shelves of its rocky banks. After Joachim and Paul had finished talking together, Joachim and Heinrich would start singing their songs, until it was time to bathe. Then, at midday, just when it was getting too hot to lie in the sun, the upper sky would be faintly veiled with clouds whose shadows were like an infinite number of moth wings.

On the sixth day of their trip they climbed a hill on top of which was the famous statue of Germania. This colossal bronze-cast figure of a strapping maiden clad in armour and eternally occupied in looking, with a thunderous expression, across the Rhine towards France, was an immense landmark. Parties of Germans gathered together at its base and listened reverently to a guide who explained how narrowly the Emperor, the statue and, indeed, the whole mountainside escaped being blown up at the moment of its unveiling, by a bomb hidden by a terrorist nearby. Luckily the bomb failed to explode.

Heinrich was very quiet that morning, obviously moved by what the guide had said. They walked from the hilltop to the river in a changed mood, due partly to his seriousness, and partly because the landscape through which they were now walking was changed. They had been walking through country where on either side of the Rhine there were steep hills, terraced and with vineyards and where copses seemed little more than green mould on rocks. Near here the Rhine flowed past the rock called the Lorelei, seat of the Rhine Maidens, the golden horde of German song and poetry. But now they were approaching an entirely different landscape where, to the east, the hills fled inland, and the country was undulating. They clambered down from Germania to the river. When they reached the river bank, Heinrich said earnestly, speaking the words with difficulty: 'I am a Communist. All that old patriotic stuff' – and he pointed back uphill in the direction of Germania – 'is nonsense. It is rot – sentimental – old – outdated – and it must go!' He spoke with surprising vehemence. There was rage in his voice.

'A Communist from a Bavarian village!' exclaimed Joachim. 'Well, that is really funny!'

Paul was moved, for he had not imagined that Heinrich could speak sincerely – and with apparent disregard of the effect he was producing on his companions – about any subject. Seeing Germania and hearing the patriotic speech of the guide had clearly produced a conflict in Heinrich, resulting in this outburst.

But Joachim was irritated at the idea of Heinrich holding an opinion seriously. Laughing, but a bit contemptuous also, he lifted him up and threw him down on to the grass.

'You a Communist!' he shouted. 'What will you be saying that you are next, I wonder? Who told you you were a Communist?'

While Heinrich remained crouching on the grass, Paul caught sight of the furious look of resentment which he directed towards Joachim. It was the only sign he saw on their trip of Heinrich having an independent personality, a driven-down, oppressed, rebellious will of his own. Then Heinrich laughed in his soft, childishly irresponsible way that so charmed Joachim. He got up, and, brushing grass and dust from his shoulders, said: 'I heard a speaker who came to our village and talked to the peasants about Communism. He said that if we all become Communists we shall all have plenty of money and that there will be no more wars, and my mother will be cared for and everything wonderful will happen.' He was watching Joachim intently through his narrow eyes as he went on: 'I suppose what he said was nonsense, but I stupidly believed him.' The bemused, enchanted look returned to Joachim's face. The wheels of that summer started rolling again.

Joachim and Heinrich undressed for their midday bathe. As he was pulling off his shirt, Joachim exclaimed: 'A Communist orator in your Bavarian village! That's funny! I thought the great orator in Munich was that nationalistic man my friends tell me about who is such a hypnotic speaker that they go to hear him just like you go to the theatre. They say that while he is speaking, he seems completely convincing, you believe everything he says. But as soon as you have left the hall you realize that it is all complete nonsense, and that you have been listening to a madman.'

'Yes, it was him I heard speaking,' said Heinrich. 'Everyone in our village was convinced, including myself. Now I see it was all nonsense. But I thought he was a Communist.'

Joachim turned away, with a shrug, and Paul saw Heinrich look at him, while Joachim's back was turned, with the same expression as when Joachim had thrown him down on the grass.

Somehow this look, so visible to Paul but ignored by Joachim, had the effect on Paul of showing Joachim as insensitive and obtuse. For the first time Paul felt satirical about the outfit Joachim had bought in Cologne for this trip: the corduroy shorts, the khaki flannel shirt, the beret, the light-brown, thick-soled leather walking shoes. Paul despised berets – unless worn by Frenchmen – more than any other form of headgear. Now he noticed how this beret, worn at a rakish angle, gave Joachim, if only at this moment, a look of loutish self-assertiveness, a note reiterated below the line of the shorts by the bare knees. Paul, for his part, wore old grey flannel trousers of the kind called 'Oxford bags', held up by tape, and a cheap green-striped shirt. But he was thinking about Joachim, not how slovenly in appearance he himself was. Paul realized that the near contempt he felt for Joachim's appearance was the momentary physical expression of a feeling he had that was less easy to define about Joachim and Heinrich. All that Joachim saw in Heinrich's confused declaration about politics was that Heinrich was stupid. What he failed to see was that, for an unguarded instant, Heinrich was being serious. This was, for Joachim, simply a glimpse of a reality which he refused to accept about Heinrich, and which he responded to by throwing him to the ground. If he loves Heinrich, Paul thought, he ought to love what is real about him, even if it seems unacceptable.

He noticed how great the contrast of Joachim's sneering profile was with the generous, humorously perceptive and sympathetic impression he had of him, seen full-face. In profile, he was the Aztec with deriding mouth, arrogant nose, a hard stare: cruel, obtuse, stubborn, lazy, slouching, self-willed. Paul could understand Heinrich's look of loathing.

Paul had got into the habit of treating Heinrich in a manner partly playful, partly affectionate, stroking him like a cat, not serious. That evening after their visit to the statue of Germania, Paul thought that Joachim was beginning to show signs of resenting his partly playful, partly affectionate attitude to Heinrich. Or it may have been that Paul himself felt guilty at having witnessed that moment of Heinrich's bitter look at Joachim. Paul now felt that he should leave as soon as possible. During their early morning conversation, he told Joachim so. At first Joachim would not hear of his leaving. Then he said: 'I hope you do not feel I have let you down over our trip together.'

Paul, from his heart, said he did not think Joachim had done so, but nevertheless that he thought Heinrich and Joachim should now be together alone for the last few days of their trip. Joachim went on protesting, but Paul could see that he agreed.

The next day they crossed the Rhine by steam ferry and reached Boppard. When they were at Cologne, Joachim, businesslike, had arranged that their luggage would be forwarded here, half-way through their trip, where they would consider plans for the second part of their journey. Joachim and Heinrich went to the hotel, where Joachim and Paul's luggage was waiting. Paul went for a walk through the town before rejoining them. Paul's luggage was sent to the railway station, Joachim's remained in the hotel. (Heinrich, of course, had no luggage.) Joachim and Heinrich arranged to stay the night at the hotel and, next day, leaving Joachim's luggage there to be forwarded again, to continue their trip down the Mosel.

Before Paul caught his train, they crossed back to the other side of the Rhine where there was a bathing place which had a seesaw. After they had swum, Heinrich jumped on to this and stood in the middle, balancing it while Joachim and Paul sat at either end. Then Paul got off and Joachim began to sway the wooden plank on which Heinrich was standing. The boy laughed uproariously, trying to keep his balance. He pressed against the board with his feet, trying to control the swaying.

The effort made the muscles of his thighs harden. They shone like mahogany. Balancing precariously, he swung his arms wildly, first in one direction then another. His hair fell down over his face and eyes, making his appearance savage. Then with an almost terrifying agility and with a howl, he leaped off the seesaw on to the ground. The howl was of rage as well as laughter, Paul thought.

Paul went to the railway station and bought his ticket for the night train. He also bought a rather elaborate camping knife with several blades – a farewell gift to Heinrich. Then he went back to the hotel where he rejoined Joachim and Heinrich. They were laughing excitedly. They had shocked the staff of the hotel and some guests by wearing shorts and shirts open at the neck. Joachim had changed his clothes and was dressed as for town. He had lent a suit to Heinrich. The suit was almost grotesquely large for him but fitted well enough for Paul to be able to imagine how completely transformed Heinrich would be in a city suit: like a villager in his Sunday best. And like a provincial youth, he had smeared his hair back with brilliantine.

Paul gave Heinrich his present. He seemed pleased. He said that as soon as he was in a position in which he need not send all his earnings back to his dear mother, he would buy Paul a present even more expensive than this. They had supper and drank wine and they toasted Paul on his journey and a happy return to England. Joachim and Heinrich were affectionate to Paul with the kind of tenderness two people show to a third of whom they are fond, but whose presence reminds them that as soon as he is gone they will rush into each other's arms. They would continue the trip Joachim had arranged for himself and Paul, without Paul. They assured Paul they were convinced that they would all three be meeting soon in London. But he could not imagine Joachim and Heinrich in London.

They went together to the station, Heinrich running in front in order to find Paul a good seat on the train. As soon as he was out of earshot, Joachim said: 'Now do you believe that I love him?'

Paul replied that he was sure he did.

Heinrich called out that he had found an empty compartment on the train. Paul kissed them both goodbye, and got into the compartment. The train moved out of the station.

It ran beside the Rhine for most of the journey until Cologne. Paul looked out of the window and watched the lights of the villages which they had walked past, and at some of which they had stayed the night, run by like a film in reverse. The train very soon, and very quickly, passed Bingen. At Cologne, he changed on to the express for Hamburg where he collected his belongings, paid for his room and went to the boat train. Now the country was completely flat. He was alone in the compartment. He did not draw the blinds. He was fascinated by the night, and by the beams from lights in goods yards and stations which occasionally sloped across the compartment ceiling for a moment, and then vanished.

The rhythm of the train excited him, so that, against its basic repetitious beat he could hear, quite distinctly, the voices of Heinrich and Joachim singing their midday songs. For the most part he remembered only the tunes, but there was one inane sentimental line of one inane sentimental song which he could not stop from repeating itself in his mind: 'Es war so wunder – wunderschön.'

London and Oxford towards which he now knew himself being hurled seemed to spell out unutterable grey blankness, a permanent fog. The summer he was leaving seemed more than happiness. It was a revelation. For a moment he thought he had been insane ever to leave Joachim and Heinrich. He should have gone on walking with them down the Rhine for ever. His only aim in life now – to return to Germany as soon as possible. He would write this in his Notebook.

He fell into a doze, remembering the paths on which they had walked along the Rhine, the places where they had swum. The river itself became a stream of light flooding land and sky. He watched those radiant disks of foam floating upwards from it, melting into space. The sun of that summer, the sun! The sun! Drunk with the sun, he fell asleep.

PART TWO

TOWARDS THE DARK

1986

Paul did not manage to get back to Hamburg until the November of 1932. By then he had published a volume of verse and one of stories: the poems sold about 1,000 copies, the stories 2,000. The poems were well, the stories badly, received. He began to make a small but regular income out of reviewing and writing occasional articles; but it was not until the spring of 1932 that he was sure of being able to earn between £4 and £5 weekly. This enabled him to return to Hamburg.

His £4 or £5 weekly was the equivalent of 80 or 100 marks. The rent of the room which he took in the Pension Alster, at the end of that lake near the commercial city, was 20 marks weekly, inclusive of breakfast and luncheon. A prix fixe luncheon or dinner in a cheap restaurant cost 1 mark; in a better one, 1 mark 50 or 2 marks.

1932

The Pension Alster was a warren of rooms, opening off a corridor like intestines going through it. At the centre was a reception room dimly lit by lamps with yellow shades and with two bulging chintz-covered sofas and fleshy armchairs. On the walls, there were sepia-coloured aquatints of paintings of nymphs, sylphs, a statue of Hermes surrounded by ladies in draperies, knights in armour, and Frederick the Great. There was a framed photograph of the immense granite pepper pot statue of Bismarck in the Hamburg Park. In the winter this interior, heated by a huge cast-iron stove, smelled like the inside of a cardboard packing-case.

Paul's room had bed, chair, table, clothes cupboard (on top of which he placed his suitcase), all of the same kind of stained pine wood with many knots in it. The table top which consisted of two sections of this, glued together, put Paul in mind of a ship's deck cleared for action. Action with pen, paper and typewriter.

What made him feel claustrophobic here was not the room but the weather outside. This, indeed, had penetrated into the room as blotches and stains of damp on walls and ceiling.

From his Notebook, November 1932:

It has been raining ever since I came here a week ago. The country between Hamburg and the Baltic is flat, so that the full force of the northerly gale strikes the town. Now, in early November, gusts of torrential rain are cannonading through the streets. The rain batters against houses and soaks the walls as if stone and concrete were paper. The gale jumps from one side of avenues to the other. The lake is whipped up into thousands of spouts of water that meet the descending spikes of hail and rain like teeth gnashing in the mouth of earth and sky. The gale seems some giant that has taken over the city whose inhabitants flee before it. Sounds of traffic are reduced to a whisper.

Of course, in returning to Hamburg in November, Paul had not expected it to be like July: but neither had he anticipated anything like the ferocity of this prolonged, dark northern winter. It was so much the opposite of that brilliant summer of 1929 that, perhaps as the consequence of shock, for over a week he did not have the heart to take up the threads of the life he had shared with his young German friends that summer. Taking it for granted that they would be there, he had written to none of them announcing his arrival.

Sometimes, lying on his bed in his room, with the storm beating on roof and windows, he would have a vision of Joachim, Willy or Ernst sunlit – at swimming baths, in canoes, on lake or river, on beaches, or eating and drinking at tables on pavements. He recalled scenes at all the places where they had been one day that lasted all the summer. He had no wish to meet them now in stuffy smelly interiors.

He seemed to himself to be forever occupied in beating his head against the walls of his room and crying to the weather – STOP!

Nearly always, to save money, he had luncheon together with his fellow lodgers in the Pension dining-room at its single long table, covered with a thick green cloth that hung over the edges in triangles terminating in bobbles and tassels. The youngest, Herr Macker, a pale, steel-frame-spectacled, white-collared, dark-suited bank clerk with hair like a cap of brown felt, was at least five years older than he. Paul pretended to know less German than by now he did, in order to avoid participating in lunchtime conversation, mostly about the appalling weather. His silence had the inevitable result that the salt-and-pepper-haired, bristle-moustached Dr Schulz spent the hour telling him, in atrocious English (which sometimes Paul helped out with his rather better German), that the only way to learn the language was for him to become affianced to a German *Braut*. Fräulein Weber, who always wore a knitted dress of mulberry-coloured wool – and who, she said, had once been governess in a laird's family in Peebleshire – recounted to him in her Scots English the plots of Wagner's *Ring* cycle – very difficult to follow, Paul found. In the evenings he nearly always went out, often to eat alone at some restaurant, listening to the conversation at the table next to his, something for his Notebook.

In the summer of 1929 Paul had never gone into the town alone – he was always with Ernst or Joachim or Willy – but now he made a point of exploring the city by himself, weather permitting – that is to say, between storms. He never went by public transport but always walked very rapidly in long strides through the streets. Sometimes, in order to fight the bitter cold of the streets, he ran. He went bare-headed and he wore a greatcoat buttoned up from neck to knees, a coat like a hussar's, given him by his grandmother, quite new when she gave it, but dating in fact from 1916, when she had bought it for her favourite son, Edgar Schoner, on leave in London from the Western Front. Killed in France a month later, Lieutenant Schoner had only twice, when on leave, worn the greatcoat, and, after his death, Mrs Schoner had locked it away in a cupboard with others of his things she could not bear to look at, until one day Paul told her he was going to winter in Germany. Then, by some illogical association of ideas, she thought that her favourite grandson should wear in Germany the coat worn by her favourite son who wore it twice in London and then was killed, not wearing it, in France.

One afternoon, Paul walked to the Sankt Pauli area, wanting to see it by daylight and to take photographs. Knowing Joachim, and seeing Russian films, had given him ideas about black and white photography which he wanted to try out with his Voigtländer camera. In fact, he did not, on this first visit, see anything to photograph. He came back with a memory of Sankt Pauli not as the brilliantly lit pleasure garden of his nights out there with Joachim, Willy and Ernst, but as a desolate area of grey, wet streets and quaysides where young men who had absolutely nothing to do stood around staring at dismantled docks. Something for his Notebook: how the cloth-capped, unemployed workers leaned against railings overlooking the harbour for endless empty days, or lay down, awake or sleeping, on benches; or spent what few groschen they had on cigarettes. Lifting a hand to a mouth and inhaling and expelling the smoke was a drowsy, drugged something-to-do. They had absolutely no resources, like those which filled up Paul's own life of reading and writing. The lack of connection between his occupations and their idleness seemed to him like a gap between wires which ought to be joined, powering action with imagination. Without that connection the inactivity of these made his imaginings void. These workless workers were born and brought up solely in order to provide their employers with their labour. And now that those employers had no use for their bodies, they were derelict machines: only, unlike machines, they happened to have thoughts and feelings, and would starve.

After a week had gone by, Paul telephoned to Willy, now no longer living with Joachim, but with a tiny flat of his own. His name was listed in the telephone directory. Willy was surprised, delighted and comically indignant to hear Paul's voice: 'Paul – why didn't you let us know when you were coming to Hamburg? I would have gone to the station to meet you! You should have written! Your friends here would have given you a party . . . ,' etc., etc. Paul did not think he could ask Willy to his room in the Pension Alster, so they met in the Café Europa, in the centre of the town, facing the commercial end of the lake.

From his side of the marble table on which their coffee and cream and cakes were placed, Paul studied Willy's face. The lines on the forehead and round the mouth were pale, like skeletal veins on an autumnal leaf. Paul remembered his first meeting with Willy and Joachim, when Ernst had taken him to the *Schwimmbad*. On that brilliantly fine day, as Ernst and he approached them, Willy was throwing a multi-coloured rubber ball at Joachim who, with eyes gazing heavenward like those of a saint in a Renaissance triptych, stood waiting for it to descend into his outstretched hands . . . And after that there was the party at Joachim's studio . . . and the conversation with the little Zeppelin commander Fedi who, in 1916, had been shot down in the Baltic . . . and then dancing with Irmi (later, Irmi at Altamunde!) . . . Paul went on inwardly reminiscing and turning the memories into fantasies, until he was brought back to the present and the café by the expression on Willy's face, scrutinizing, from his side of the table, Paul's own three-years-later November face.

Willy smiled at him and said, 'Do you realize that you have become quite famous in Hamburg?'

'Famous? Famous for what?' Paul asked, flushing in authorial anticipation. 'My poems or stories?'

Willy laughed, harder this time. 'Oh no, not for them! I am afraid your publications have not got much further in Hamburg than Ernst Stockmann. For something quite different – '

'What?'

'As the mysterious English poet who went on the walk down the Rhine with Joachim Lenz when Joachim first met Heinrich. Tell me – what happened exactly?'

Paul described the first evening of their tour, at Bingen, when they saw Heinrich looking out over the Rhine, and Joachim offered him a cigarette, and they went to the restaurant above the little town for supper, and Heinrich talked about his mother. He did not mention the note which Joachim left on the door of their – Joachim and his – room.

'Oh, that was how it happened! How simple! And what did you think? Did you like Heinrich?'

Now the scene was superimposed like images flickering on a screen across the café's gilt interior. 'Not when I first saw him at Bingen. But later I became interested.'

'Interested?'

'Well, I saw that he was more complicated than I had first thought. I saw that underneath his charm Heinrich was an angry person.'

'Did you think that he was good for Joachim?'

'I don't think Joachim wanted someone who was good for him. He told me when we were in Cologne, before he met Heinrich, that he wanted someone with whom he could form a passionate attachment, and that this person might well be wicked – not good or good for him. You were good for him, I think, Willy.'

'I wasn't thinking, really, about us – about him and me. I was thinking how very clever Joachim is, and how he needs a friend who helps him develop his gifts. Everyone ought to know about his photographs. He should be famous all over Germany.'

'I doubt whether Heinrich helps him in that way.'

'Why not?'

'He is incapable of appreciating art.'

'Oh, but that is a terrible pity, Paul! Joachim needs to be appreciated. Surely, he is a genius!'

The word 'genius' annoyed Paul. He thought he knew an English poet, Simon Wilmot, who was a genius. One genius was enough. He changed the subject by ordering another coffee. Then he asked Willy what he had been doing since they met two years ago.

'Well, during that summer, when you were with Joachim and met Heinrich on your famous journey down the Rhine, I was going all that while to a small village in the Austrian Tyrol. It was called Medes. I studied there all the summer for my examinations in order to become a school teacher, for which I think I have already told you two years ago I was studying to become.'

'Did you feel lonely in Medes?'

'For the first few weeks I was perhaps a little solitary – I missed Joachim so much – but after that I got to know the villagers. What was funny is that because I carried a lot of books with me for my studies, which I was sometimes reading in the sun outdoors – but not swimming very much (I was oh so serious!) – I got a reputation in the village for knowing things I didn't really in the least know – not at all, really! The villagers came to me, especially the young people, boys, but not only boys, also many girls! – with their problems. I was always being asked silly questions – well, sometimes not so silly.'

'So you were happy?'

'Oh yes, indeed I was. It was really wonderful. I would like always to live in such a village, and be admired and consulted by the villagers – famous – as, Ernst tells me, you have become, Paul. Besides, it is so quiet in Medes, one need never worry about anything.'

'Did you meet anyone else in the village?'

'Well, I met lots of people, as I have been explaining to you. Who else would I meet?'

'I mean anyone who meant as much to you as Joachim?'

Willy put on gold-rimmed spectacles (Paul had never before seen him wear glasses) and stared at him rather hard across the table perhaps to discover how, over the past three years, Paul had changed. The lenses slightly magnified his candid blue eyes which, in their soft cushions of pink flesh, seemed to have acquired the total innocence of some benevolent school-marm, someone whose satisfaction and self-fulfilment consisted entirely in improving the lot of others. His bubbling-over, light-hearted sexuality of two years ago was evaporated entirely. For a moment Paul felt chilled by this newly acquired Quaker-oatish personality, but the next moment he felt touched by Willy's fundamental goodness, his simplicity, as he saw it.

'No, I did not meet anyone who was like Joachim to me. All that is not necessary, you see. That is what I learned in the village. I used to think that I could not live at all without Joachim. But, you know, I've learned that one can be happy alone. It is not necessary to have someone.'

'Perhaps not for a month or two. But for always?'

141

He shrugged his shoulders. He did not seem interested: 'Perhaps for others. Not for me. I do not know.' He seemed on the verge of saying something more, but fell silent.

Paul asked him whether he had seen Ernst recently.

'Oh yes, I meet him quite often. I like Ernst very much now. I think perhaps he is much nicer than we all thought he was. Three years ago, when you were with us, all of us were against Ernst, and that was unfair, and perhaps made him act suspiciously to us. He became too self-conscious, always acting . . .' He paused, then he added, 'Surely you must have heard that Hanny, Ernst's mother, died?'

Paul's first reaction to this news was to feel snubbed at not having been informed of it by Ernst. He said in a detached kind of voice: 'Was Ernst very upset?'

'For six weeks, he shut himself up in that big big house on the Alster, and he would not see anyone. Then, when he emerged, he seemed changed. For one thing, he had taken over the family business, which was his reason for seeing no one. There was so much to arrange, and his father had become senile – unable to work. But at last he did give a party for his old friends at his house and he seemed much easier and friendlier and more open than he had ever been before. At this party where there were many people, some of whom I had never seen, the great surprise for Joachim and me was that there was lots and lots to eat and drink. We all got terribly drunk – especially Ernst, who was very jolly! Also, he did something he would not have done before – he invited a young friend of his who plays the violin at a newly opened bar at Sankt Pauli (you must go there) – a Lithuanian violinist called Janos Soloweitschik. He would never have done that when Hanny was alive, you know. And, lately, Ernst has been very generous, I mean really really generous! He has even given me some money to help me with my fees to become a teacher of English. You will say my English is not very good for someone who is to teach it.' He had quite recovered his old laughing, gossipy manner. But now he got up from the table. 'Well, I must be leaving you,' he said. 'I have to learn to teach English.'

Paul remained at the table for a few moments to settle the bill. While he was doing this Willy came back, looking worried.

'After all, I am early for my lesson,' he said sitting down again.

'Paul, there is something which I have not told you.'

'What?'

'I did not tell you all the truth. I thought you might be upset to hear it. That made me nervous.'

'What is it?'

'The fact is, I have a *Braut*. She is called Gertrud. Gertrud and I are to get married.'

All memory of the past was instantly wiped out. The pictures in Paul's mind of Willy at the first party in Joachim's studio, and of Willy throwing a ball to Joachim at the *Schwimmbad*, had vanished. Paul looked across the table at Willy who was now smiling back at him with a shy, slightly apprehensive, almost girlish expression. Paul asked: 'Is her hair blonde and done in plaits, and does she have blue eyes?'

Willy roared with laughter. 'Yes, she has both those things, but the plaits are twisted round and round like a loaf at the back of her head, so you do not quite see they are plaits.'

'She has blue eyes like yours?'

'Yes! Yes! How clever you are, Paul! How would you know that?'

'Does she wear spectacles, as you are doing nowadays?'

'She has them, but she does not wear them more than is necessary. She is a little vain, I guess, but not as much as me! I do not like to see glasses hiding her eyes. She knows that, so she does not wear them.'

'How did you meet Gertrud?'

'In Medes. She is not from there, though. She was on holiday, with other friends, from Vienna. She is so good and kind, Paul. She does wonderful work for the Party.'

'The Communists?'

'Oh no! Not in Vienna. It is ridiculous. The Nazi Party,' he said, laughing very hard.

Paul felt he was in a lift which had crashed down from the top storey of a building to the basement – would perhaps crash through the concrete foundations – bury itself and him with it deep under earth. He said in a stifled voice, 'Then you are a Nazi?'

'Oh no. Not at all. I told Gertrud that I never could be.'

'Why not?'

'I do not like all their policies and I cannot quite agree with what they say about the Jews. Knowing Ernst so well I cannot agree. But at Medes I came to see the Party does wonderful work among the young, especially those who are unemployed. They offer hope when no one else does – especially not the old, not Chancellor Brüning and that old senile dodderer President Hindenburg. Do you know what they tell about Hindenburg?'

'No.'

'They say that a secretary at the President's reception office told a visitor who was carrying a packet of sandwiches in his hand not to leave behind the sandwich papers, as if he did so, the President would be sure to sign them.' He laughed harder than ever, his white teeth showing under his petal-pink lips.

'Oh. Have you ever seen any of the Nazi leaders? Have you ever heard any of them speak?'

'Oh yes, in Hamburg once, I heard Goebbels. I went simply out of curiosity, just to see what he would be like. I did not take in the sense of what he said. But I saw he was a cripple. That he is in pain always. You can see in his face how he always fights down this pain with his faith. There was such a light in his face when he talked about Germany's future, such a radiant smile. Whatever he was talking, nonsense perhaps, his smile was like a saint, *ein Heiliger*.'

Paul got up, abruptly. 'I have to make some phone calls,' he said, and left Willy alone at the table. He felt stupefying fury. He hated the Nazis because every thoughtful person he knew hated them. But he did not know why he hated them. Perhaps Willy was right, and yet he could not believe that he was. What he had witnessed was the stupidity of Willy compounding Paul's own ignorance.

When he got back to the Pension Alster that evening, he found a letter there for him. Registered and expressed, it was from William Bradshaw. Written on the back in William's very small, crystal-clear handwriting was his name and address in Berlin, where Bradshaw was now living. This, and several stamps on the front, together with the Registration mark and number, made Paul imagine William handing the letter over a Berlin Post

Office counter and, as he would certainly have put it, asking the assistant to 'give it the works', William wrote:

> My novel is proceeding slowly. Meanwhile I am earning money by prostituting myself to the Film Industry. Don't be surprised if very soon after you get this, Otto and I descend on you unannounced. Owing to my work on a film I am making with Georg Fischl, I can't bind myself to any certain date. Everything happens here when it happens, unannounced. I haven't told Fischl yet but I have a plan to write a peculiarly nauseating scene to be shot in Hamburg. Otto wants to accompany me as his father was a pilot at Cuxhaven before Otto was born. The moment there is a break in the clouds we'll almost certainly make a dash to the north. Otto is going through a very interesting period of returning to his roots.

Otto, Paul knew, was 'Karl' in a story by Bradshaw about Berlin.

This letter gave Paul an elated sense of belonging to a family outside either his own or William's families. Their writing was the blood and spirit of their friendship. Each wrote in his separate circumstances, his separate life, yet each was a member of one body of literature, common to them all. He rejoiced in their successes, and whereas he felt discouraged if his own work received adverse criticism, when he read attacks on their work, or on all of them as a 'group', he felt that the critics were imbeciles and these friends spirits of light fighting the forces of darkness.

The immediate result of reading William Bradshaw's letter was for a name to come into Paul's head of someone he had not thought of since that evening three years ago when Joachim, Willy, Ernst and he had spent most of a night at Sankt Pauli. The name was 'Lothar', the boy who at the end of the evening had accompanied them for part of the way on the last train from the Freiheit, back to the station near the Stockmann residence. At the *Lokal*, The Three Stars, Lothar had told Paul that he worked in the amusement arcade where there were pornographic peep-show films. He had asked Paul to come to look at these. Paul now urgently wished to see Lothar himself, whose face he remembered very clearly. Thrusting William's letter between the leaves of his Notebook, he put on his immense greatcoat, ran out into the street and ran all the way to Sankt Pauli.

At night, in the still falling rain, with the lights from yellow, red and blue lamps splashed on pavements and the bonnets of cars, and with brightly lit plate glass windows in which there were crude notices and photographs inviting clients inside, Paul felt as though his hands were on levers of a machine fabricating happiness. The amusement arcade was easy to find. It extended along a considerable length of the Freiheit. Almost as soon as he had passed its glowing, roaring entrance, he saw Lothar, with his hands on the levers of a Try-Your-Strength machine. Lothar recognized him at once, exclaiming, *'Ach, du, Paul, der Engländer,'* and grasping his hand, as soon as he came in.

Lothar left him in order to go on instructing a bald-headed client, with a bulging chest and hairs bristling above his vermilion-striped jersey, in the use of the Try-Your-Strength machine. Lothar, looking all the time at Paul and away from his client, gripped the handles each side of the machine, tugging at and squeezing them, while his features clenched like his hands. In three years, his face had become bonier, squarer, like the sculpture of a Roman head hewn out of stone, into which eyes of some other mineral – onyx or crystal – had been screwed. Face and hands and his whole body getting ever tenser as he wrestled with the machine, Lothar continued looking at Paul with an expression in which agony and a radiant smile seemed the same. Above the machine a needle rotated on a disk, 20–30–40–50–60–70–80–90, and then, suddenly reversed, returned to o. Lothar gasped and sprang away from it with a shout, leaving the customer in the striped vest to try his strength.

'Do you remember?' Paul asked, reminding Lothar of that night three years ago when he, Ernst, Willy and Joachim had met him in The Three Stars. Lothar said, *'Ach so!'* He had seen the Herr Doktor several times since then and been to his wonderful home on the lake. Paul reminded Lothar of his promise to show him the pornographic peep-shows. Lothar laughed.

Walking away from the Try-Your-Strength machine, Lothar looked circumspectly all round the interior of the amusement arcade, as though to avoid the inquisitiveness of some overseer, then he beckoned Paul into a side room where there stood the machines with their binocular eyeholes. Standing there in his 1916 greatcoat, Paul felt as though he were looking through some periscope above the parapet of a trench that spied on no man's land; but instead of seeing German enemies in trenches there he saw what perhaps all soldiers and sailors of enemy sides would most like to see through periscopes – dirty pictures. Smudged and brown and with white blotches at the edges they were crude variants of the pictures in the magnificently bound and printed *Encyclopaedia of Pornographic Art* which Ernst had shown Paul three years ago. Instead of ranging over the whole of human history and geography for their rich harvest, the subject matter of these photographs seemed exclusively German – patriotic perhaps in the selection. These nudes seemed to be of German bankers, Prussian officers and Berlin landladies whose bodies, far from exciting Paul, seemed casts of the clothes they had stepped out of.

While Paul was looking through these binoculars, he glimpsed – quite literally out of the corner of one eye – Lothar standing like a Roman centurion on guard beside him. As soon as Paul stood away from the machine, Lothar went to attend to another client of the Try-Your-Strength machine. Paul walked over and thrust into his hand payment for the show, saying as he did so: 'Lothar, I want to take your photograph.' 'But where?' asked Lothar, the expression in his eyes dissolving into pleasure.

'Come to my room, number 17, in the Pension Alster,' said Paul, glad to think that he had found one friend whom he could receive as guest there.

'But my work at the arcade doesn't finish until midnight.'

'Well, come at midnight. Go up to the top floor of the building and knock very gently at the front door. At 12.15 I shall be the other side of the door, waiting for you. Here is money for a taxi.'

Preceding Lothar, Paul himself took a taxi to the Pension. Back in his room, he screwed his Voigtländer Reflex camera on to its tripod. He moved chair and bed and table around so that he could take the photograph at the distance the space permitted, experimentally putting the chair (to stand for Lothar) on top of the table so that he could get it in focus from the door.

While Paul was fixing this apparatus and after he had finished doing so he was thinking feverishly about Lothar. He had invited him solely for the purpose of taking the photograph and, quite obviously, Lothar was delighted at the idea of being photographed. Lothar doubtless would have thought, however, that part of the deal was that he had been invited for sex. The idea that Lothar would think that the basis of their relationship was a commercial arrangement – selling his body – was repulsive to Paul, who recognized, though, that there was hypocrisy in this repugnance. Still, he told himself he was perfectly sincere in not wanting Lothar to feel that he had been brought here just for sex.

Paul remembered, at this point, the expression in Lothar's eyes three years ago, at The Three Stars, when Ernst touched Lothar's jacket. Lothar had made no protest but he had looked away towards the far end of the room with an expression of shining detachment from Ernst touching and fingering his jacket. Paul had never forgotten this look. And when he had gone to the amusement arcade earlier and Lothar had said, *'Du, der Engländer,'* it had surely been the greeting of a friend.

These thoughts arose partly from Lothar's physical appearance. It would be absurd of course to see him as 'innocent' in the way that Marston, for instance, certainly was, yet, Paul thought, he had that beauty of noble flesh out of which eyes gaze shining which has the consistency of innocence. At this point he remembered Wilmot saying about Marson: 'You want to be rejected because you are afraid of physical relationships.'

At ten minutes after midnight he waited in the corridor. At twenty minutes past, there was a very faint knock at the door, which Paul opened. Lothar came in.

Paul grasped Lothar by the shoulder and thrust him into his room, number 17, three doors along the corridor. As soon as they were inside, he locked the door and said: 'Undress!' With smiling alacrity, Lothar did so. 'Now stand on that table.' Arranging the camera, screwed to its tripod beside the bed, and squinting through the opened back section on to its ground glass screen he focused the image of Lothar standing on the table. On the screen, Lothar showed upside down and reversed. He was like the reflection of a marble statue in a lake. Now Paul mentally corrected this image and saw Lothar standing straight up on the pediment of the table-top. The musculature was pearly cloud layers, horizontal along the shoulders, round on chest, stomach, buttocks and thighs. Above the neck his body was capped and crested by the helmet of the hair, below which, in profile, were the eye, like a comma, the L of the straight nose, and the curve of the lips.

Paul took the photograph from the same angle as that from which Joachim had taken the nude youth standing by the lake – that photograph which had obsessed Paul ever since he saw it three years ago in Joachim's studio and which he had called 'The Temple'. He used up the whole of his film – twelve shots – and all his flash bulbs. In the black box of the camera he had trapped Lothar's image exactly as it was an hour after he had seen him standing by the Try-Your-Strength machine, and as it would remain, unrelated to whatever either he or Lothar would, during the rest of their lives, become, the moment of vision, heroic, ever receding into the past.

Nevertheless, there was the self-evident fact that whatever else Lothar had come for, it was for money. And now Paul thought that what he would like to do was produce the fee (20 marks) for sex and then say: 'Here is the money, I require nothing for it. Whatever we do or do not do I shall give it to you because we are friends, and whatever in future we do together it will be because we are friends. If you need money and I am in the position to give it to you, that will be an entirely unrelated matter.'

Thinking this, Paul experienced a sensation of freedom which excited him. This was succeeded by a realization of his hypocrisy.

Before dressing, Lothar asked: 'Is that all?'

'Yes, for tonight,' said Paul, and gave him 20 marks. 'Let us meet tomorrow.'

'*Du bist mein englischer Freund,*' said Lothar.

Written by Paul when waiting for Joachim Lenz in the vegetarian restaurant in Hamburg on 11 November (Armistice Day) on a sheet of paper intended to be pasted in his Notebook later:

149

The friend whom you expect to arrive late always arrives even later than you anticipated. He overdraws on the credit of time you have conceded him. However, just when your patience has run out, and you are about to leave the place of your appointment with him, he will appear – and your sense of joy and relief at seeing him will cancel out his overdraft as you embrace.

Joachim arrived three-quarters of an hour after Paul had written this, giving Paul time to recall waiting for him three years ago, outside the hotel in Cologne, into which Joachim had gone to look up possible addresses for Kurt Groote, the boy whom they had met at the *Schwimmbad*.

Joachim took Paul's hand in his, greeting him so warmly that the interval of waiting (not an hour, but the three years between September 1929 and November 1932) seemed spanned on the instant. Joachim said: 'Paul! You seem a little paler, but that is the winter, surely.' Then, looking at him intently: 'Perhaps you are a little fuller in the face. Have you been eating such a terrible lot?'

His own face seemed not in the least altered, though perhaps with lines a bit more thickly indented. Joachim's complexion was as bronzed as it had been in summer but that might be due to sun-tan powder.

The vegetarian restaurant, with its wooden tables, had a pleasant lightness and airiness and a look of being dedicated to higher food. Joachim ordered nut cutlets and fresh fruit dessert, Paul an omelette and salad.

'I am late', said Joachim without, however, apologizing, 'because I have spent the entire morning in the most stupid way possible. Sheer imbecility!'

'Doing what?'

'Well, there is an election today here in Germany, and I am supposed to vote, so, as I know nothing of politics, I have spent the entire morning reading the programmes of fifteen different political parties.'

'Are there fifteen?'

'Far more – thirty-seven in all, I think.'

'Why?'

'That's because of the wonderful system which we have under the Weimar Republic.'

'What system?'

'I don't know exactly what it's called, but the result of it is that anyone who forms a political party which in the whole of Germany can obtain as many votes as are 1-500th (or whatever the total of parliamentary seats in the Reichstag amounts to) of all votes of voters in Germany can elect a member to the Reichstag. I believe there is a dachshund-lovers' party.'

'So how will you vote?'

'I won't vote.'

'Why not?'

'Well, after reading the manifestos of all the parties, I decided that the only one that made any sense was the Communist.'

'In that case, why don't you vote Communist?'

'I am a merchant. Voting Communist would mean voting myself out of existence. Besides, the Communists could not tolerate a person like me who lives for things that have nothing to do with politics. They regard everything and everyone as political, in being either for them or against them. I don't want to live in a world where whatever I do is judged as being either for or against politics. Even if I agreed with the Communists about everything else, I couldn't agree about that.'

'I wrote a poem about our trip down the Rhine,' Paul said.

'A poem? About our trip down the Rhine? I knew you had published a book of stories – Ernst had been telling me – but I did not know you were writing poems now.'

They ordered coffee. 'Here it is,' said Paul and, fishing it out of his pocket, he handed the typescript across the table to Joachim, who, holding it in front of him, at once started reading it. Paul watched his eyes move from side to side as he read the lines – the first, the second, the third. Paul, who knew the poem by heart, could follow each line that Joachim was reading as though he could read it looking-glass from the back through transparent paper. The opening lines were:

A whim of Time, the general arbiter,
Proclaims the love, instead of death, of friends.
Under the domed sky and athletic sun

Three stand naked: the new, bronzed German,
The Communist clerk, and myself, being English.

Paul wanted Joachim not to be distracted. He felt like shouting to the people in the restaurant to stop talking and making so much noise with the rattling of their knives and forks on plates, the crunching of nuts and crackling of lettuce leaves between their omelette-yellow teeth. He himself provided a model of absolute silence and attention, watching Joachim watch his lines.

It troubled him that the first two lines of the poem were obscure. He half-expected Joachim to question him about them. But, although Joachim's eyes seemed to hesitate before moving to the third line (and again, at several other places), he read through the poem right to the end. Then he raised his eyes and looked seriously into Paul's eyes without saying a word. He took the poem up again and read it right through, more rapidly at the second reading. Then he read the first two lines out loud.

'"A whim of Time, the general arbiter, / Proclaims the love, instead of death, of friends." I do not understand.'

Paul, trembling and very red, making a tremendous effort, said:

'The poem takes place in the summer of 1929 when you and I and – later on – Heinrich were going on our walk down the Rhine, with the sun always shining. If it had been twelve years earlier, we couldn't have done so because in 1918 young Germans and young English were killing one another in war. In the poem I say:

Yet to unwind the travelled sphere twelve years
Then two take arms, spring to a soldier's posture.

After that the poem goes on to prophesy that in another ten years, in 1939, there will be a new war, this time a world revolution:

Or else roll on the thing a further ten,
The third – this clerk with world-offended eyes –
Builds with red hands his heaven: makes our bones
The necessary scaffolding to peace.

The "whim of time" in the poem is not really a whim, it is human history, "the general arbiter", which may seem whimsical, though, in deciding that in 1917 young Germans like you and young English like me must be occupied in killing each other: whereas in 1929, it permitted us to be friends. Perhaps in 1929 we loved each other all the more, because in doing so, we unconsciously felt ourselves to be the resurrected bodies, the fleshly ghosts of those killed in 1917 or perhaps as they will be killed in 1939.'

Joachim was staring at him across the table, with that widening of his eyes Paul remembered from the time when they had talked about poetry in 1929, the day that Joachim knocked Heinrich down. Paul felt compelled to go on. He said in a lecturing voice that seemed to fill the restaurant: 'An English poet who was an officer in France in the Great War (his name was Wilfred Owen and he was killed in November 1918) wrote a poem called "Strange Meeting" in which a conversation between an English and a German soldier – each of whom has killed the other – takes place moments after they are both dead. They talk about the life each might have led, which they have been prevented by the war from leading, the love which should have existed between them made hatred, the further wars which will result from so much accumulated pressure of hatred. The poem ends with the line, "I am the enemy you killed, my friend"; bringing together the idea of their being enemies, conscripted by mechanized killing, and that of their being friends, and loving each other had there been peace, making love to each other perhaps.'

Paul was sweating, trying to explain his poetry to Joachim. His voice did seem to be having the effect of silencing, with his penetrating English, the German spoken at neighbouring tables.

Joachim said: 'So you mean that, ten years from now, in 1939, we Germans might be killing you English and the Communist clerk with "world-offended eyes" might be murdering both of us in the name of World Revolution? And that in 1929 we were friends, standing naked under the sun and swimming and enjoying ourselves together, instead of killing each other.' He took the poem up again and repeated: ' "Three stand naked: the new, bronzed German, The Communist clerk, and myself, being English." That's me, the new bronzed German, and you are "myself, being English". But who is the Communist clerk ... Communist,' he went on, holding up the poem, and reading from it, '"Who builds with red hands his heaven," and has "world-offended eyes"? Why?'

'I suppose I was thinking of Heinrich, though it isn't really about him. The point is that the poem requires, for what it says, a character who kills the other two in revolutionary war in 1939 –a completely new situation – and something Heinrich said on our trip suggested this.'

'Still, if the Communist who kills his German and his English friend in world war or revolution isn't Heinrich, the poem can't really be about us three during our trip up the Rhine,' Joachim said, relapsing, Paul felt, into a kind of willed refusal to understand.

To Paul it became desperately important to defend his poetry as being about Joachim and Heinrich and himself. 'But don't you remember, that day when we walked down the hill after seeing the statue of Germania, and Heinrich said he was a Communist? Don't you remember knocking him down?'

This was an incident they had never spoken about.

Joachim looked at Paul very hard, and slowly shook his head. 'No, I don't remember Heinrich ever saying that he was a Communist. Not any more than he ever said he was a clerk with "world-offended eyes". That is just to do with your poem. Heinrich a Communist! It is an absurd idea! And surely I could never have knocked him down except in fun, in play. Not then! Not on our walk along the Rhine! Perhaps later, in Hamburg.'

'Well, then the poem is not about us. It is just a poem,' said Paul, giving up.

Joachim handed the poem back to Paul, as though finishing off the whole subject of poetry. He said slowly and very deliberately, refusing to think, refusing to understand: 'But with Heinrich this could not be because he was a Communist. He never was one.'

'What was he? What is he?'

'He is a Nazi,' said Joachim. This brought the conversation to a halt.

'Was he always one?' asked Paul.

'Oh no, not always. Only in the past few weeks.' To this he added dubious, 'I think. So he says.'

'Then what was he when we first met?'

'Nothing. Nothing. Absolutely nothing. He was just himself, Heinrich, a wicked person perhaps but Heinrich, a person. He was beautiful.'

To change the subject, Paul asked: 'What was it like during the last week of our trip? – not "ours", yours and Heinrich's – I mean, after I had left?'

Joachim looked happy. He glowed. He escaped into that past. His eyes looked as though they saw it all. 'It was wonderful! Wonderful!'

'You continued the walk, along the Mosel?'

'It was always the same. The weather held out until our very last day. I know you thought you ought to go and leave Heinrich and me alone – that was nice of you – but we missed you. Also Heinrich did. But I missed you more perhaps, because I missed our morning talks together when you and I were alone and SERIOUS, almost as much as we are being now, not quite as much perhaps.'

'What happened when you had finished the trip?'

'I had more business to do for my father's firm, in Berlin. So while I went there Heinrich was going to visit his mother in his Bavarian village. I gave him a little money to give her, since he'd said he gave her his "earnings" which were all made in order to support her! Don't you remember his saying that? He went to Munich for three days of that time. I don't know what he did there, but he seems to have lost the new suit I gave him. Perhaps he sold it and gave the money to his mother as earnings! But whatever happened I was very glad really because it meant that a few days later when I went to meet him at Hamburg station, he was wearing his Lederhosen and shirt and braces – exactly the same clothes as when we first met him at Bingen. It was so wonderful seeing him dressed like that on the platform among the crowd of business people and tourists!'

'Did he go on wearing his Lederhosen?'

'Oh no, I bought him at least five different suits, for autumn and winter and spring and summer, even one very English one with pinstripes on jacket and trousers. And he had his hair trimmed and fixed in one wave, and he wore brown, highly polished leather shoes. He looked so elegant and so soon became quite the young man about Hamburg, though always with something provincial about him that made him seem, to some of my friends, so INNOCENT. He kept his Lederhosen for fancy dress parties. They were very popular. He was a great success with many of my friends and a lot of other people who were not such friends – though never with Ernst, who did not like him.'

'Did you mind that?'

'Mind Ernst? No, I was glad for someone who did not love him. I was very jealous often. I used to make TERRIBLE scenes. We both cried. But, under it all, I did not mind because I thought that, even if he was a terrible liar, in being so, as in all his other cheating, he was being true to his own self. I never thought of him as being GOOD. I liked him for being sly and telling all those lies about his village, like he did when we first met him. It was so funny, I didn't mind his being wicked.'

'You mean, you wanted him to stay always the same?'

'Yes, as he looked when you told me you did not like him.'

'That was only a first impression.'

'He was a lynx or a fox, some small animal, cunning, a liar.'

Paul shifted uncomfortably in his chair: 'What did he do all day in Hamburg?'

'Well, for many months, he either stayed in my studio or went out, sometimes with my friends, other times I don't know where. Perhaps he was earning money to send to his mother! But anyway it was difficult to get a job. There is so much unemployment – *Arbeitslosigkeit*. But finally I realized he must do SOMETHING. Then I remembered I knew a man called Erich Hanussen who owned a shop for selling English fashion. Interior decoration, not clothes – fabrics and tables and chairs and lamps and pottery, everything looking handmade and hand-painted – and very STUPID, I always thought. I imagined them being done by English old ladies living in country cottages with their cats. You know how people in Hamburg adore EVERYTHING English. It was called House Beautiful, and you can imagine the jokes when Heinrich started working there – because Hanussen offered him a job the moment he set eyes on him. "Is the most beautiful object in House Beautiful for sale?"'

Joachim lit a cigarette. It was getting late and the restaurant was gradually emptying. 'Erich Hanussen is known as "Erich the Swede". Not that he is Swedish, but his name Hanussen is, and it sounds VERY, VERY Nordic. Erich comes from Lübeck and he has blond hair and blue eyes which are very, very pale, and orange freckles.' Cigarette in hand, Joachim looked as though he was blowing Hanussen away, very contemptuously, through smoke rings. He went on: 'Erich has a house on the Baltic, not far from Altamunde where you once spent a very happy weekend with Ernst, do you remember?'

'It is one of the most vivid memories of my life! I remember every second of it! Every second seemed a century.'

'Well, Heinrich spends nearly every weekend with Hanussen and his family at Altamunde.'

'Are they lovers?'

'Oh no – not at all. Erich has a blonde wife and two blond sons and two blonde daughters, all exactly the same – like him. He and Heinrich do not make love. Never.' He seemed to be appraising this assertion, then he repeated, expertly, 'Never.'

'Then why does Heinrich go there?'

'Because he knows that Hanussen stands for everything I HATE.' This brought the conversation to a halt again.

Paul asked Joachim for a cigarette. 'Do you really think that Heinrich hates you?'

Joachim went on in his manner of not giving answers to direct questions. 'After he began staying weekends with Hanussen, Heinrich changed his attitude towards me. This happened very slowly of course. He seemed to grow superior in his manner, disdainful, condescending. At first I was amused when he started saying that everything in my studio which I had got from the Bauhaus was bourgeois and that all the great artists who taught there – Gropius and Moholy Nagy and Paul Klee – it amazed me that he knew and could pronounce their names – after all, he's not so stupid – were Jews and culturally decadent. Hearing him talk all this jargon about decadence and the bourgeoisie was rather FUNNY at first. Until I began to realize who taught him it all. That was when he started saying that I was incapable of understanding a new generation of patriotic, pure-blooded Germans, because I was a decadent, aesthete individualist who thought that art and beauty and his individual self-expression mattered more than the German nation. Then he started talking about the Nordic race and how every other nation was inferior to Germany. It was as though he had ceased to be the person I knew and had become one anonymous unit of Youth all wearing uniforms and strutting around and with no views except those which came from their leaders. Then I discovered that during those weekends at Erich Hanussen's he was one of a group of Hanussen's followers who go on military exercises in the woods, doing firing practice, learning to murder their political opponents – Communists and Socialists and Liberals – and people like you and me.'

'All the same, nothing that you've said shows that Heinrich hates you. It may show that Hanussen does. And Heinrich is under Hanussen's influence. But it might show only that he bitterly resents you. It may be just because he loves you that he resents you.'

Joachim looked tired. He asked with what seemed flagging interest: 'How could that be?'

'He may resent your loving him for what you consider him to be – that is, wicked. He may think that your way of loving him shows you look down on him.'

'In that case, he resents me for loving him as he really is – or was. He has made himself no one, nothing, now, with Hanussen. You're not suggesting that he is not a liar, are you?'

'He well may be as you say. What I am suggesting is that if he feels that you insist on loving him for that, he may feel that you are tying him down to your view of him. Perhaps there is some side of him which wants to be different, and he would like you to love that side of him.'

Joachim said with a rather heavy irony, which Paul found discouraging: 'So he shows his resentment of me by becoming worse, even than I ever thought him to be? To change from being the person I love, to making himself to be not a person at all, no one, nothing, not a human being. Just a cypher in a political programme of violence.'

'You really feel that?'

'Yes, I will tell you why. Most of last week, including the weekend, Heinrich was away from the studio – on the Baltic,

I suppose. He did not tell me he was going away. At last I decided that I must find out what was going on, so I searched through all his things, which were in a cupboard. What I found, which finally decided me that we would have to separate, was the uniform of a Nazi storm-trooper – a very smart one, his best which, I suppose, he keeps for special occasions, or he would have taken it with him.'

'What did you do when you found it?'

'What did I do? Well, I suppose you will think me very idiotic. But what could I possibly do? I tell you what I did. I spat on it, not once, not twice, but at least a hundred times. I covered it with gobs of spit. When Heinrich finds it, he will wonder what has happened to his beautiful uniform. The spit will have dried by then – I guess he will think snails have been leaving their trail all over it. Then I telephoned him to say we have to part.'

'Will he have found the uniform by now?'

'No, he has been away till today with Hanussen. But he will find it tonight surely, when he goes back to the studio, if he does that, as I am sure he will do to fetch his things in order to leave me without having to say goodbye, which he is terrified of doing. He knows that tonight I am with my mother and won't be there.'

Waiters were clearing away the remains of luncheon and preparing for the evening meal.

Joachim stood up, suddenly seized with an idea. 'Let us go and see them!'

'See whom?'

'Let us go to House Beautiful. I shall be late for the office, but never mind that. I want you to see Erich Hanussen then tell me what you think. You will doubtless be glad also to see Heinrich. You have not done so for so long. You will see how he has changed. House Beautiful is only ten minutes' walk from here. You will love to see it if you are homesick for England.'

They left the vegetarian restaurant and walked to a street of brilliantly lit shops, across which they saw House Beautiful. It was in one of the earliest examples of modern architecture in Hamburg, a grey stone building with lines that looked beautifully ruled as though on a drawing board, dating from 1912. The showroom was brightly lit, its walls papered with a material resembling satiny cedar. There were tables and chairs, pink curtains, embroidered cushions, wicker wastepaper baskets, wooden cots, lamps, lampshades, hand-enamelled plates painted with English wild flowers, cash-boxes, match boxes, cigarette trays, small busts of Shakespeare.

The first person Paul saw was Heinrich, saying goodbye to a lady who was carrying in her arms a pomaded miniature poodle. There was no doubt at all that Heinrich was trans-formed, another person. The single wave of his hair brushed back from the forehead was no longer the result of winds blowing in the Bavarian Alps (if it ever had been that). It was the effect of shampoos, blowers, sprays and dryers. He was wearing a charcoal-grey linen suit with a pale pink shirt and a flowing blue tie. As soon as he saw Paul he glided across the shop floor to greet him. With a quick turn of his head he gave Joachim a disdainful glance as he seized both Paul's hands in his, exclaiming in English, which had a slight, rather pretty accent: 'What a wonderful surprise, Paul! We haven't met since we said goodbye on the station at Boppard – that must be three years ago – how happy, really happy, I am for us to meet again now in Hamburg! Excuse me, I have a client I must attend to,' and he turned round and walked rapidly away.

Paul stood there, trying to reconcile the image of this effete Heinrich with Joachim's description of a Nazi storm-trooper doing military exercises near Altamunde on the Baltic coast. But it was not really difficult to do so. All a matter of dress. Heinrich just now was wearing his 'House Beautiful' uniform. In Nazi uniform, he would simply be another person. There were soft-looking, soft-spoken Nazis. That was what made them so popular with old ladies. Just as he was thinking this, Erich Hanussen – it could be none other – appeared from behind a partition that screened the main showroom from an inner office where clients could discuss problems of English good taste either with Hanussen himself or an authoritative-looking, grey-haired lady colleague who looked like a schoolmistress.

Erich Hanussen seemed smaller than his actual height, which was medium. Under the surface of his healthy brown skin, skull and skeleton seemed to be slanted forward – energetic, ingratiating, aggressive, sinister. His skin seemed to have a high polish. A bit too mahogany perhaps. In strategic places, there was hair – clustering on his head in golden ringlets silvering at the edges, thrusting in wiry bristles from his nostrils, protruding in tufts from his ears. His mouth seemed a slightly small fit for his teeth, very white under his lips. His eyes were cornflower blue and, like everything else about him, shiny. He seemed a walking advertisement for ideals aggressively pure.

He clasped Paul's hand too closely in both of his, and exclaimed: 'I am so glad that you visit me. I have heard so much about you from Heinrich. I was always so wanting to meet you. Come into my little "den", as I suppose an Enn-glisch would call it, sit down awhile and have some coffee while we have a little chat. *Fräulein Gulp, Kaffee bitte für uns!*' he barked out to an assistant. Paul glanced back at Joachim who remained outside the office, looking disdainfully at a wooden dog kennel.

Hanussen thrust Paul into a chair in front of the desk behind which he himself sat. 'How long have you been here in Hamburg, *ach*, only a week, *ach*, but you know Hamburg from a previous visit I have hert, I see you learnt ex-zel-lent Cherman from our dear friend Joachim Lenz, who has also been such a friend for Heinrich during summer 1929 – swimming, boating, sailing – *wunderschön!* And Heinrich tells me you three went a walk tour down the Rhine where he met you! *Ex-zel-lent!*'

There was a pause now, while Fräulein Gulp brought in the coffee. This seemed the sign for Erich Hanussen to become earnest. As soon as she was gone, he cleared his throat and said, as though Paul were a meeting that he was addressing:

'Mr Paul Schoner! I understand that you are a writer, very gifted, very valuable to Enng-land. I am delighted you are in Chermany, and hope we perhaps go together in a great work of politics, perhaps even more important today than poetry, much as I value Rilke. I have met some Enn-glisch already and am very glad always to meet new Enn-glisch, because I think just now, we Chermans and you Enn-glisch have many *Interessen* in common. In Hamburg here I am not only a shopkeeper: that is only for window-dressing, you might call it: more importantly, I am Direktor of a Committee for bringing together some Chermans, some Enn-glisch and some *Skandinävier*, even some *Holländer*. The purpose of this is to make ties between members of these nations – most importantly, of course, Chermans and Enn-glisch – which are racially superior to lower races. There are many such committees spreading now through Chermany – the first thing we must combine for is to undo the impositions on Chermany of the Treaty of Versailles – not – I say, not – that Chermany become above Enng-land – but so that she may share with her to be superior in the world to all other nations.'

Paul felt the strongest aversion to Hanussen, not made less by the fact that he was memorizing his sentences in order to repeat them word by word to Bradshaw, when they next met. They would roar with laughter over them. The fact that he agreed with Hanussen about the injustice of the Treaty of Versailles only increased his revulsion. It was terrible to see real grievances being exploited to justify evil ends.

There came now a moment when he no longer listened to Hanussen's sentences. Beyond the grotesque phraseology there blazed the searing apocalyptic vision like a furnace that shrivelled up Hanussen's words. This prophesied final war between forces of darkness and light – the golden-haired and the olive-skinned: those whose veins flowed with Aryan blood and the Jews. Hanussen showed with prophetic eyes the gathering together of the armies of the blond warriors speeding across the Eastern plains in their chariots of fire and with, in the heavens above, their winged machines letting fall metal and fire to destroy cities and populations that obstructed their advance. He saw the conquest of vast Eastern territories where such survivors as there were in the conquered lands would be slaves of the pure-blooded victors. These would build cities which were vast concrete fortresses made to resist any invader for the next thousand years.

By one merciless act of purification the Aryans would cast in dark valleys and tunnels beneath the earth all the impure lives that had fouled German blood since the stabbing in the back of the nation by aliens and traitors in 1918: Jews and Bolsheviks, decadents, expressionists, homosexuals – all that was not Nordic would be destroyed.

Paul no longer listened to Hanussen's words. What he saw was that the grotesque, little, mentally crippled athlete was a sapphire-eyed, golden-haired force, a demonic flame of pure revenge, the scourge of all the world that did not belong to his kingdom of self-righteous indignation.

'Mr Hanussen,' he said at last, getting up from his chair, 'I neglected to tell you when we met that by any definition of yours, I am a Jew.' But although in retrospect this gesture seemed courageous – or at least it would make a good story to tell William and Simon – at the time he knew that it made no more sense than spitting into the wind. Being English, he had indeed nothing to lose by this, something of which he was intensely aware as, joining Joachim in the showroom, he left Hanussen's 'den'. Heinrich, who was standing at the street door, said to him with ironic politeness, taking his hand and shaking it warmly, 'Goodbye, let us meet soon.' Heinrich seemed not to have seen Joachim.

Outside, Joachim and Paul walked together in silence. Then Joachim asked: 'What do you think?'

'Horrible, monstrous, stupid, terrifying.'

'Well, that is Germany's future, and that is what Heinrich has joined to be on the winning side. Perhaps my father is right, I should become only a coffee merchant.' Then he added: 'Already in Germany it would not be a very good idea for me, as a German, to tell Erich Hanussen that by his definition I am probably Jewish. It is all right for you – you are English – but my grandmother . . .'

'It's like a monk's cell,' said Ernst, standing in the middle of Paul's room. He was in a black pin-stripe suit, held a light grey raincoat over one arm, and in his left hand a trilby hat. He looked plumper but somehow bonier. He smiled with faint patronizing amusement as he looked discreetly round Paul's room. That morning his secretary had telephoned to announce that the Herr Doktor would fetch Paul from the Pension Alster at seven and drive him back to his house for dinner. Ernst now had his own car.

'Are you really satisfied to be here?' Ernst went on, looking up at the weather-stained ceiling. 'Because should you want to come to my house, I am alone now. If you wanted to work all day in a larger room at my house, you would not be disturbed.'

'That is very kind of you, Ernst, but I work better when I am alone.'

'So this is where you write your poems,' said Ernst, looking at the pine wood table which had Paul's Notebook placed rather prominently on it (Paul had forgotten to hide it away). 'But you can hardly entertain your friends here. I assure you that if you ... now that ...' He had embarrassed himself, and did not finish what he was going to say.

'Only one friend has been here,' said Paul, producing the photographs – much influenced by Joachim Lenz – of Lothar.

Ernst put on his glasses and scrutinized them. 'I seem to recognize that – er – face,' he said, with a return of his coyly suggestive way. 'It is Lothar, isn't it? The boy we met all that time ago – three years, was it? – at The Three Stars? I haven't seen him since then.'

'Yes, Lothar.'

'So he has been your guest here? I see this room has its advantages!'

'I brought Lothar here to take those photographs.'

'Oh! You have been taking lessons in photography from Joachim? My impression when we met him that night is that Lothar is a particularly nice boy, but what at Cambridge we used to call thick. Do you see Lothar often?'

'I might have done so. He just about fits into this room, as you can judge from the photographs. And he is very nice, as you say. But stupid. Anyhow, he turned up yesterday to say he has lost his job at the amusement arcade and that he is going to relatives in Stuttgart who say that they can find him another job.'

'Did he want his fare?'

'He did not exactly ask for it, but I gave it to him.'

'How strange! I saw him at The Three Stars last night. He also asked me for his fare to Stuttgart. And I also gave it to him.'

'I thought you said you hadn't seen him.'

'Not until last night.'

'Perhaps he is going to Stuttgart today or tomorrow.'

'Perhaps!' – a discreet smile from Ernst.

Moving towards the door, Ernst said: 'Well, at least you have agreed to come back to my house for dinner. Perhaps we should be wending our way there now.'

They went downstairs to the street where there was Ernst's smart Bugatti two-seater. Paul remembered last driving with him in Altamunde. But then Ernst was driving a hired car. Now he was in command, the Bugatti's proud owner.

They got into the car. As they moved off, Paul apologized for not having written when Ernst's mother died. He explained that he had only heard the news the previous week, from Willy.

Ernst's eyes were on the road.

'Didn't my secretary send you the announcement of my mother's death?'

'If she did, it never reached me.'

'I must speak to Miss Boom about that.'

They reached the Stockmann residence with, beyond it, through the darkness, the black boughs of willow trees like twisted iron rods against the metallic waters of the lake.

Ernst opened the great oak door with his keys, and they passed through the lobby into the central hall. Everything seemed exactly as it had been when Paul first arrived there three and a half years ago: on the walls, the early Matisse nude, the Van Gogh *Still Life with Irises*, the self-portrait by the youthfully grinning Desnos, the heavy oak table at one side of the room, the brocade-covered armchairs and sofa, the staircase leading up to the first floor. The fact that nothing had been moved or altered had the effect of giving this room, weighed-down though it was with expensive objects, a feeling of desolateness. The void was, of course, the absence of Ernst's mother with her solemn black eyes and her strident voice. Paul looked in vain for a new picture, a chair missing, even a table moved, as some kind of pivot around which the new life of Ernst might turn.

Perhaps, like the odour of dust, there was some faint deterioration though. Surely the oak banisters of the staircase were not quite so highly polished as three years ago, evidence of the servants taking less trouble, now that Hanny was gone.

When they had finished drinking sherry, Ernst got up from his chair and indicated that they should go into the dining-room. As he stood there, in his black pin-stripe business suit, bowing slightly, the malicious thought occurred to Paul that the undertaker at his mother's funeral must have looked like Ernst.

Over the soup, Ernst said: 'I miss my mother very much. She

and I depended so much on one another. I feel rather alone now, because my father, I am afraid, has become quite helpless and unable to look after himself, and is in a home where, of course, he is very well looked after. This also means that much of the family business has fallen on me. After my mother's death and when my father fell ill, there was a lot of confusion, but I think things are now sorting themselves out.'

Paul murmured sympathy. Ernst went on:

'As a matter of fact, I think that I myself am better than I was. My life seems to have more purpose than it did, now that I have so much responsibility. As long as my father was around I could take no initiative. But to return to my mother. She admired you a lot, Paul. She always said that she wished you and she could have become friends. Your writing, she said, considering that it was, after all, only the work of an undergraduate, was quite promising, even if rather immature.'

'But I thought you told me she had never read anything of mine?'

'Oh, there were one or two things. Didn't you publish a few pieces in *Isis* while you were an undergraduate?'

'Yes.'

'Well, of course, I had shown them to her. They were quite enough for her to form an opinion about your work. She had such exceptional connoisseur's taste. She always said that you were a promising journalist. Certain passages in your Notebook seemed to show talent.'

Paul felt remorse. Ernst changed the subject with a conscious air of letting Paul off: 'And how is dear old England?'

'Just the same.'

'That is what I like about it. It is always the same. That is its charm. I wish one could say "just the same" about this country.'

'Do you have difficulties in Germany?'

He smiled, faintly superior: 'Well, you remember the Sharp-shooters whom we heard from the depths of the forest near Altamunde that weekend we were together quite alone – you do recall that weekend, I hope? – they've come a lot closer now. As a businessman in a firm with Jewish connections, I myself hear quite a lot from them.'

'How?'

'Well ... I get insulting letters every week because I am, technically, partly a Jew.'

After a pause, Paul asked: 'Does that mean that you may have to leave Germany?'

Ernst puffed out his cheeks as if to blow away metaphorical thistledown: 'Not in the least. Nothing of the sort. These letters are sent by stupid fanatics who do not understand our situation.'

'Your situation?'

'I think my mother told you once, three years ago. It is that the Stockmanns are Germans who lived here for centuries. An uncle of mine was killed in the War, fighting for Germany.'

'So did one of mine fighting for England,' said Paul irrelevantly. 'I have his greatcoat. He, too, was technically a Jew.'

'My uncle was just as much a German patriot as Joachim's uncle, General Lenz. Joachim also, through the Brazilian side of his mother's family, has Jewish blood, though he does not talk about it very much, I understand.'

'Then why are you being persecuted?'

'Hooligans! Like those Sharpshooters we heard at Alta-munde. Not a serious political factor, there are always plenty of those around in this country. You are lucky not to have their like in England.'

'Why do you have them?'

'There was an influx – or should I say inflow – of Jews into Germany from Lithuania and Poland between 1918 and 1920 after the War – extremely poor people – my mother told you – didn't she? – how she helped some of them – who got blamed for many of Germany's misfortunes. But though, through the perhaps too liberal policies of the Weimar Republic, many of them became German citizens, they were, I suppose, an alien population and resented by many Germans as such. But the Stockmanns are quite different. We are Germans. Moreover we are an essential part of the German economy. My firm brings in a lot of currency from abroad. The leaders of the Nationalist parties realize this. Anti-Semitism is only their propaganda. If the Nazis come to power there will perhaps be a few victims among the Eastern European immigrants. That is very much to be regretted, of course, but it cannot be helped. My mother worried about our firm's Jewish employees on her death-bed. But things could be worse for them as well as for us.'

Paul felt a perverse desire to challenge so much complacency. 'Joachim told me that Heinrich has become a Nazi. He discovered, hidden away in his studio, Heinrich's storm-trooper uniform. And then he found out that Heinrich goes on military exercises over weekends near Erich Hanussen's house at Altamunde where, three years ago, we heard the Sharp-shooters.'

'I don't think that the activities of Heinrich are of any significance.'

'And Willy is engaged to a girl with plaits who is some kind of Nazi Girl Guide, he told me.'

'Willy! Heinrich! Do you mean to say that you see them while you are here? I should have thought you would have grown out of that. And as for Erich Hanussen, he has no weight at all. He is simply a fanatic stuffed with racial theories and other nonsense. Joachim, of course, is a serious person, a different matter. But if I may say so, all that sounds typical of Joachim and shows his irresponsibility. As he himself admits, he knows nothing about politics. He doesn't even bother to vote, so I don't think his opinions carry any great weight. He judges the condition of Germany by Heinrich and Erich Hanussen. There are lunatics like that Hanussen around, it is true, and some of them even write books and some of the books even get published, but they do not count. Supposing that the Nazis did get into power, people like that would quickly vanish from the scene. The conservatives and business-men and certain aristocrats might just conceivably at some point in the future put Hitler in power. But they would know what they were doing. They are people who bear great responsibilities, and Hitler could only attain power on their terms. They would make him get rid of the fanatics and extremists. He would be their prisoner. It is very unfortunate that Joachim gets his ideas from the behaviour of Heinrich and the activities of Erich Hanussen.'

Paul was not listening. He fixed his attention on the Courbet *Still Life* with its emerald and vermilion apples on a grey tablecloth against a coral background.

Ernst said brightly: 'If you'd come here eighteen months ago, you wouldn't have seen that picture. It wasn't there.'

'Where was it?'

'My mother lent it to an exhibition of French art being held in Munich. While it was there an art critic called Holthausen, who was no friend of our family, wrote an article declaring that it was a fake. My dear mother was very upset, not just on account of the value of the picture which would in that case have been worthless, and which, for a time we had to take down from that wall, but because one of her little foibles was that she prided herself on her shrewd judgement in having bought an authentic masterpiece in Paris, when she was scarcely more than a girl.'

'How did it get back on the wall then?'

'As a matter of fact everything worked out rather well. Eighteen months ago my mother and I took the Courbet to an expert in Paris, and he provided a certificate authenticating that it was by Courbet. So my mother was very happy on what proved to be our last excursion together. So whenever I look at the Courbet now it brings back beautiful memories.'

Paul said he was glad.

'There is a new *Lokal* I think we might go to,' said Ernst at the end of dinner. 'It is called The Modern. A friend of mine, whom I would like you to meet, plays the violin there. He is a Lithuanian and a gifted ... well, amateur. But the violin is not his real interest. His name is Janos Soloweitschik.'

The Modern Bar was quite small, bright and new, decorated in what seemed to be the futuristic style. Crimson walls had painted on them rectangles of blue and yellow overlapping like playing cards. There were bright black polka dots painted just below the ceiling. The tables were placed so close together that it was difficult for Paul to find room for his legs.

The orchestra, a trio only, was on a low platform at one end of the room. A bald pianist in a greasy morning coat sat at the piano, which was an upright. A statuesque lady who looked like a sofa stood on end played the trumpet. Ernst's friend Janos, the violinist, aged nineteen or twenty, certainly stood out from his companions. He had long black hair which, when he was playing *appassionato*, as he did most of the time, flopped down over his forehead, almost covering his eyes. He had an air of energetic gaiety. He seemed to be treating the whole thing as a joke.

Ernst ordered champagne at their table and also sent up drinks to the 'orchestra', which received them with bows, and then expressed their thanks by playing a florid *prosit!* directed to Ernst. Responding to this, Ernst, without standing up, smiled and raised his glass to them. The public here seemed respectable if *louche*, a better class of citizen than the habitués of The Three Stars. Ernst was in his element at The Modern Bar. This was his apotheosis. Ernst was happy.

During a very long interval, Janos came over to their table. When he talked, he had a way of holding his head down, shyly almost, and looking up at his interlocutor with eyes smiling as though over the brim of a toastmaster's cup. His large, well-formed lips reminded Paul of those melon-slice lips of the young Desnos hung on a wall of the Stockmann house. Janos seemed frivolous, but offered surprisingly serious opinions with light irony, as though they could be taken as jokes. 'I am a terribly bad violinist,' he boasted – almost – to Paul the moment they had been introduced. 'I trust that Ernst provided you with ear-plugs when he brought you here.'

'You certainly play very temperamentally.'

'You mean all those scrapes and squeaks? Well, I'll try and reduce them in the second half. I'll just play trills.'

'I enjoy watching you.'

'But not listening to me? Never mind, I have no intention to remain a violinist.'

'What will you become then?'

'Oh, I am studying to be something quite different – the opposite, you might say. I am afraid you will not like it. It is so disgustingly down-to-earth. The last thing for a violinist!'

'What is it then?'

'Oh, you will laugh! My real interest is studying agriculture.'

'Why are you doing that?'

'It may seem strange to you, but my absurd ambition, to fulfil which I am milking pennies out of this bordel, is to go to Palestine and live on a kibbutz, sowing and reaping the land.'

'Why Palestine?'

170

'I think there is no future for our people in Europe. I cannot fight here for a future. I cannot be a Communist or a Socialist, which is what I am nearest to being, because I do not like the idea of Socialism on an enormous scale, that is to say, running a whole country. There would be too many forms to fill in! I think that Socialism, if it is to make people happy by letting them remain individuals, can only work in small communities where everyone knows everyone else by name and is working for himself – but not just for himself, also for family and friends, those he has supper with at the end of the day's work. That is like a family, a real family of brothers and sisters, and as few fathers and mothers as possible, I hope. To talk about a family that is the State is hypocritical, because everyone in the State does not know everyone else, so it all becomes simply a matter of regulations for the masses. To impose the family idea on people who do not all know each other is repression. Or that is my idea. I expect you will think I am being absurd.'

He laughed, as though he really were not serious about all this. Paul laughed: 'I prefer listening to you talk, to you playing the violin.'

'You come with me!' Janos said impulsively, leaning forward, and suddenly intense, half-mocking but perhaps half-serious.

'I don't think I can do that. But, anyway, where are you going? Where would I be going?' asked Paul thrilled, suddenly thinking, I might go – to be with him!

'Weren't you listening, my dear fellow? Surely I made that clear: I want to go to Palestine and join a kibbutz. There I would be with my people but as one of a family. You must think that crazy! Will you become my brother?'

The trumpeter let off a tremendous blast on her instrument. With a dazzling farewell smile, Janos ran to the platform, took up his violin, tucked it against his chin, lifted his head and embarked upon a dynamic trill, the opening phrase of some piece to do with Mephistopheles.

Ernst asked: 'What do you think of my friend Janos?'

'Wonderful! Will he really go to Palestine?'

'Well,' Ernst gave a patronizing smile, 'I think at the moment he believes he will. The important thing, however, is that he is seriously studying agriculture.'

171

'Do you want him to go to Palestine?'

'If he proves to be really serious about it, yes, I do. Who knows, I might even join him there.' He looked mysterious.

'You mean you would give up everything you have here?'

'Not quite everything perhaps. I have responsibilities here. Besides, my interests are not confined to Germany. Not entirely.' He seemed to be revelling in the multiplicity of his interests. He said: 'Perhaps – partly on account of my mother's death – I am going through a phase when I am rather uncertain as to what nation I adhere.'

'But, surely, it was your mother who always insisted that your family was German?'

He put his head on one side, calculating, considering: 'It depends on what "being German" means. It seems to mean different things at different times in history. There were moments when even Goethe felt himself a foreigner in Germany – felt himself French – and hated the Germans. So did Hölderlin, thinking himself an Athenian of the fifth century BC. So did Nietzsche. So did Rilke, insisting he was Czech. When the vast majority of Germans are feeling very German, the minority may begin to feel themselves a little foreign.'

'What kind of national do you feel yourself to be, then?'

'As you know, I am bilingual – trilingual, really, with French. Sometimes I think that, through the language, I am more English than I am German. Though I do have perhaps French sensitivity. I am *nuancé*. More and more, recently, I seem to think in English.'

'And French?'

'No, not really, though I am sometimes a bit *rive gauche*.'

'And do you ever feel Jewish?'

'Only sometimes, though perhaps a little bit all the time. I think there are two ways of being Jewish. One way is the result of things your gentile neighbours do to you. Another way is the distinction you make between yourself and your gentile neighbours. In Germany today, their gentile neighbours are doing a lot to the Jews; and some Jews are beginning to see ever greater distinctions between themselves and their gentile neighbours.'

Janos was playing a solo, very Hungarian, very gypsy, very poignant. Ernst said: 'Janos makes me think there is a third way of being Jewish – to go to a kibbutz in Palestine. If he goes, I might go some day too. That is possible, just possible. But to go there by myself – no, I would prefer England. One reason why I am so fond of Janos is because I think my mother would have liked him. She was quite proud of her Lithuanian blood and fond of her Lithuanian relations, particularly one grand-nephew, who looked rather like Janos. It may seem fanciful to you, but there are times when I am with Janos that I feel my mother smiling down on us, and once I even heard her whispering to me: "Ernst, why don't you adopt Janos? Then I would have a grandson!"'

4 December 1931. From Paul's Notebook:

Lothar appeared at 7.00 last night. He explained that after I gave him money for his ticket to Stuttgart last week, he went directly to the railway station. The train was not due to leave till midnight. So, as it was only 9.00, he lay down on a bench, putting his head on an improvised pillow consisting of his jacket folded up and his cap. When he woke up at 11.30 p.m. his cap lay on the floor, torn from under his head, ticket and money vanished. He now had no job, no money and no ticket. Would I give him the money again for his fare? Only the money for his ticket, he said. He would walk to the station and eat nothing all night. He only wanted the fare, he repeated, just the fare.

I said I did not believe what he told me because I had met Ernst the day after I had given him money for his ticket and Ernst had told me that he had seen Lothar in The Three Stars that very evening.

'*Das ist eine Lüge, es ist nicht wahr,*' said Lothar.

'What do you mean – it is a lie?'

'I never saw Herr Doktor Stockmann at The Three Stars that night.'

'When did you see him then?'

Lothar appeared to be making a rapid calculation on his fingers. Then he said: 'The night before that.'

'Did he also give you money for your rail ticket?'

'*Das ist auch eine Lüge,*' said Lothar. Then he added: 'Everyone at The Three Stars knows that Ernst Stockmann never gives anyone anything.'

173

I did not care to go into the matter of Ernst's much-altered personality. I said: 'Well, I find it very difficult to believe that the ticket I paid for and the money I gave you were stolen from your cap.'

For two minutes Lothar was impressively silent. Then he said: 'I thought you were my best friend, different from all the others.'

'I still am your friend. But I find your story hard to believe . . .'

He walked from the writing table to the bedstead and stood very still and upright again as if on guard over it, just as he had stood beside me when I was looking through the pornographic peep-show machine with the staring stillness I find so strangely moving. For some reason I remembered how, raising or letting fall a hand, his conversation was largely confined to his saying in his North German dialect, Platt-Deutsch, *Ja* or *Nay* (not *Nein*), like the biblical Yea or Nay.

Then he said: 'Do you have those photographs you took of me which you said you would give me prints of?'

'Yes.' I went over to the writing table, putting my hand on his shoulder as I passed him. I took them out of the drawer and gave them to him. As I did so I glanced at them, suddenly feeling they were beautiful, because Lothar himself was beautiful. How can a statue be petty and calculating?

I handed the photographs to him. He held them in front of his chest, looking at each of them in turn. One by one, he tore them up, scattering the pieces on the floor. Then he made the longest speech I have ever heard from him: 'If you do not believe my word, I do not want you to have any pictures of me.' He said this very seriously, adding: 'All I ask now is that you destroy the negatives,' as if this was his last will and testament.

Paul saw now that for Lothar, Truth and the question of whether he had been lying about the rail ticket and the money, were entirely different matters. Truth was bound up with Friendship and his belief that Paul was his Best Friend, *der*

174

Engländer. These concepts were like medals, Sword of Honour, things pertaining to an entirely different order from petty concerns about a railway ticket and a little cash. Truth was the photographs of him which now lay in pieces on the floor. Paul had ruined everything by forcing into the open the contradiction between Truth and an unimportant lie, dictated by half-necessity.

Paul said: 'I won't give you the negatives. I'll have new copies made which I'll send you when you get to Stuttgart.'

Lothar, who had been looking down at the floor, raised his head about half an inch.

'Not if you don't trust me.'

'I do trust you,' said Paul. Then he added: 'This time I'll go with you to the station myself, put you on the train and give you a little money as well as your ticket. While we are waiting for the train, we can eat sandwiches at the station bar and have a farewell drink.'

Three hours later, Paul saw the end of the train vanishing like the tail of a dragon into darkness as it went round the curve beyond the end of the platform.

He went towards the ticket barrier where, three years ago, he had seen Ernst Stockmann waiting for him when he first arrived at Hamburg, then out of the station into the street. No more need ever to pay Danegeld to Lothar! But then suddenly, quite unexpectedly, like a violent attack of giddiness, he felt terribly lonely, as though he might fall to the ground.

He could not go back to his room, that he knew. He had to walk, go on walking. This was the madness of the young English poet: solitary walker across barren heaths and wild shores, muttering to himself, shouting obscenities into the wind, hearing the voices of angelic choirs singing from storm clouds. Sometimes when he walked a tune would start up in Paul's ears, which he would hum, improvising variations on it, slow and fast, sad and frenzied.

Walking, he tried to work out problems for his novel.

The one that had kept nagging at him ever since his conversation with Joachim in the vegetarian restaurant (No! ever since the day Joachim knocked Heinrich down on their walk along the Rhine) was: Why had he found himself secretly

175

siding with Heinrich against Joachim when Heinrich was not only being stupid but expressing views which Paul abhorred? Suddenly now, he knew the answer. It was that Joachim was obstinately dumb about himself. He wanted Heinrich to mirror the wicked, sensual, animal existence which was the shrouded image of himself in Joachim's heart. Paying for Heinrich he subsidized the mirror image of his darkest self. Yet while wanting Heinrich to be wicked, he wanted him to be so as an individual, as he himself was individual – beautiful fox or lynx. Intolerable to Joachim that Heinrich should sink down into the anonymous mass of his fellow evil-doers – the storm-troopers. Yet it was Joachim who had driven him into the position where he had made that choice.

Paul reached the footpath alongside the road by the lake. Beyond railings, through glittering darkness, he saw waves like white teeth gnashing at perpendicular reflections from distant towers.

Paul crossed the road and went down a side road leading through obscurer roads towards the Pension Alster, where his room was, scale diminishing as the streets grew narrower.

'Fool! Idiot! Hypocrite!' he turned upon himself. 'You know that however Joachim behaved to him, Heinrich would be exactly the same. Given their existence, he would have joined the Nazis. The truth is that their existence has defined for him his level. He has joined the mass of those as nothing as himself, to which he already belonged – except that they were not there three years ago. Certainly he and his similars are victims: victims of the Peace Treaty, victims of Reparations, victims of the Inflation, victims of their starved and battered childhoods; but they would have been what they are without all these, most of them, most of them (perhaps there are exceptions) because already they were that. Injustices only serve to provide them with excuses for being what they already were, excuses for them, the sludge at the bottom of the world, to rise to the top and cover the surface with brown slime.'

And on the scale of the whole nation, was not this true of Germany herself? All those things Erich Hanussen said about the Peace Treaty – concerning whose injustice Paul himself was agreed – excuses, excuses for the emergence of a uniformed caricature of righteous indignation – Erich Hanussen swaggering and his storm-troopers.

Rhetoric poured its filth through Paul's mind, vulgar, public, detestable as its targets. He might as well himself be a public man making speeches, writing letters to the newspapers, always enraged, always self-righteous.

His friends were not like this. Wilmot and Bradshaw despised everything public, political and journalistic.

Wilmot spoke and wrote as an individual, without the pomposity of rhetoric. He saw that although the society, since it was made up of individuals, could only be healed by healing each individual, this was a grotesque proposition. He could laugh at the absurdity and at himself for being absurd. Absurd now that there was no cure for the storm-troopers of Altamunde except healing each one of them individually. Paul stopped in the street and laughed hysterically, imagining, quite in the manner of a poem by Wilmot, teams of healers dressed in white hospital overalls parachuted into the forest (some of them dangling in the branches of pine trees) near Erich Hanussen's house at Altamunde, and curing Heinrich and his fellows by dredging the oppressive childhood out of each subconscious, liberating each into surrealist love-play. There went Erich Hanussen, dressed up as leader in a game of blind-man's-buff, blowing whistles on orgies of the liberated storm-troopers, all their hatred transformed to love. He saw them fucking on the beach where he had lain with Irmi.

He came to an open space where the street down which he was now running, crossed a wide avenue. He had to cross this to reach the narrow street that contained the Pension Alster. A brilliant street lamp suspended from a cross of converging wires shone like the star of Bethlehem above the centre of this crossroads. Then he saw dark figures like phantoms running along the edge of the wide road, opposite where he now stood still watching them. There were two groups: the foremost, in Nazi uniform, was being chased by the Reds who wore caps with badges on them, jackets or coarse woollen sweaters, and trousers that looked as though they were dark blue or grey. All had a creased and leathery glint. Both groups were shouting slogans, of which he recognized the familiar *'Deutschland erwach!'* smashing against the *'Rote Front!'* of the second group. The Reds, who were trailing the Brown Shirts, caught up with and started throwing themselves upon them. Paul saw a knife flash. One of the group not in uniform and for that reason looking almost pathetically unmilitary, fell to the ground. The group of Brown Shirts went on running. The Reds stopped to help their comrade who had fallen. They raised him up and seemed to be dragging him away into the darkness. Both groups were now invisible to Paul. Some moments later, from the distance, he heard a shot fired.

He reached the Pension Alster, went to his room, undressed and went to bed. Ten minutes later he heard the sounds of ambulance and police cars screaming through the street and then stop. He knew now he would not sleep. He saw Joachim's eyes as he had seen them across the table at the vegetarian restaurant when he was describing his life with Heinrich: the eyes of a movie director who stands behind a camera controlling the actors in their scene. This scene was bands of youths chasing one another through the darkness. The street light shining down above the crossroads now seemed more spidery than the star of Bethlehem, dropping filaments of light that clung to the boys and entangled them in a sinister grey web. The houses at street ends now seemed armies massed and drawn up in the darkness. Again and again Paul saw the mob of boys in uniform being pursued by the mob of boys in jackets or sweaters and cloth caps and what seemed like armbands. Then there was the flash of a knife, and the boy struck down and the pack of Nazis running away, while the Reds lifted their comrade from the ground.

If he had not heard for certain the shrill police cars and ambulance he might have thought he had dreamed what he had certainly seen.

The first light shining on the wall above his bed was like a friend gently laying a hand on his shoulder, a friend who pushed him into sleep instead of waking him. Paul slept till midday. When he got up, he read through a poem he had written the previous week. Everything seemed a weariness. What he had written was no good. He took up his Notebook and wrote in it the entry describing his farewell scene with

Lothar. Outside, the weather was finer than it had been for weeks. The room filled with light. He decided that taking advantage of it, he would photograph himself – 'Portrait of the Young Poet Writing At His Work Table'. His camera had a delayed-action release for self-portraiture.

He screwed the camera on to its tripod, focusing it through the ground glass at the back on work table and chair and Notebook. He set the delaying mechanism, went over to the table, sat down on the chair, took up his pen and wrote in his Notebook. He tried to concentrate on what he was writing so that his face would assume an inspired expression. He could hear the camera giving out a buzzing sound. At this very moment, just when the lens clicked and the photograph was taken there was an insistent banging at his door and he heard his landlady's loud and angry voice: '*Sie haben Besucher, Herr Schoner!* – You have visitors' – then a hand not hers flung open the door, accompanying the gesture with a roar of laughter. William Bradshaw entered. He said: 'Well! Exactly what I would have expected! Taking his own photograph!'

Bradshaw was wearing a tweed jacket, a grey knitted jersey and grey flannels. He carried a heavy, dark blue overcoat over one arm. Accompanying him was a young man with puffy features, snub nose, full lips, piggy eyes. His hair was plastered back and he wore a sensationally new suit, every crease of which seemed narrowed to a point like the apex of a solid triangle. He also wore shoes polished to look like brown mirrors. 'Allow me to introduce Otto!' said Bradshaw in a voice which indicated that Otto was strongly under his protection. Paul shook Otto's hand enthusiastically. Otto produced his one phrase of English: 'How you do?'

'How did you get here? Why didn't you let me know you were coming? When did you arrive?' Paul asked.

'We came last night. We telephoned the moment we arrived, but you were out. We decided quite suddenly to come yesterday.'

'Why so suddenly?'

'To tell you the absolute truth, the night before last we had the most appalling row. You see, Otto and I share a room in the house of Otto's parents at Hallesches Tor, the East End of

179

Berlin. When I say "a room", I mean really a very narrow bed with a space of about twelve inches all round it. This room seems absolutely palatial compared with it,' he said, looking up at the ceiling and walls of Paul's room with smiling, intent eyes. 'So a row like the one we had two nights ago tends to wake up the whole of Hallesches Tor, which doesn't make one exactly beloved by the neighbours. I thought it best to make a quick, if only temporary, getaway. At this moment in history the Berlin police are not exactly friendly with foreigners and if my permit to stay in Germany were revoked, then we'd really be sunk. So we got Otto this brand new outfit and then we took the train to Hamburg to pay you a visit. I warned you, didn't I, that we might appear unannounced. We have a room, if it can be called that, in the station hotel. I hope we haven't arrived too early.'

William stood in the centre of the room. Grinning, he lifted up his arms in a gesture of mock helplessness and then let them fall again with a little spurt of laughter. He embraced Paul.

Paul said: 'It's wonderful to see you. How long are you able to stay?'

'That's what's so unforgivable, Paul. We can only stay a couple of nights. But the point of this visit is to persuade you to come to Berlin.'

'Do you really have to go tomorrow?'

'Yes, I'm afraid this visit is minimal. Herr Fischl not only wants me to write scenes for him, he also insists on my giving him English lessons. The fact is, I have to give English lessons to that rich movie director all this week. It's a kind of crash course, as he has to go to Hollywood the week after next. We can't afford to miss a single lesson, either of us, least of all me, after getting Otto's new suit. Besides, I may have to go to Hollywood myself in a few months' time, who knows? Of course, it goes without saying I absolutely refuse to move unless Otto comes with me. That's the deal as far as I'm concerned, and Fischl has to take it or manage without me.' He looked at Otto who, in turn, grinned at Paul, giving him a friendly punch in the ribs and saying '*Du*'.

William sat down on Paul's bed, gave a laugh which was like a magnified chuckle, and again he said 'Hmm!'

Although William had told him that his room in the Berlin

slum was smaller than this in Hamburg, Paul felt that, in terms of where the action was going on, his room had dwindled to a pin-point.

'Paul,' said Bradshaw, 'I'm afraid it has to be admitted that there's a price that has to be paid for this visit. I think I told you in my letter that Otto's father was a pilot in Hamburg harbour. Well, in order to persuade Otto to come here, I promised that we would do a tour of the harbour and see what I suppose Hamlet might have recognized as his dad's ghost's old haunts. I also promised Fischl that I'd write a scene with shots of the harbour.'

'Sankt Pauli,' said Paul. 'I'll be glad to go there myself. I'll get hold of some friends of mine, and we'll show you and Otto round.'

'By all means, we'd be delighted to do that too. I've heard so much about the Red Light District from Wilmot when he first opened up Hamburg in 1927. However, when I said the harbour, I wasn't thinking of Sankt Pauli, but of the port itself – tar, ships, dry docks, wharves, derricks, cranes, water, oil, fish, sailors, the whole shoot.'

In the taxi on their way to the harbour, Paul said: 'Last night, or rather very early this morning, I had rather a shock. I saw a gang of Nazis murder one of a group of Reds in the street outside, below my room at the Pension.'

This was not an exact account of what had happened but Paul felt that in order to gain William's attention he had to pack information into the smallest space possible.

'What happened?' asked William. And then Paul told the whole story. 'Well, I must say, that's terrible. Devils! Swine! But of course with us in Berlin that sort of thing happens the whole time. It's like daily bread to us. Only last week in the Uhlandplatz I saw a boy shot dead in front of my eyes. The murderers were in a car and they drove on so fast I could not even see which side they were on. And of course there were no police, no arrests, nothing. I suppose he was a Communist, but one can't be absolutely certain that it wasn't the other way round – I mean, the Communists shooting a Nazi. They're not so different and they change sides all the time.'

He looked into the distance, his forehead furrowed and under eyebrows like thatching, the eyes bright and fixed, his mouth wide as though he were tasting a very bitter medicine. 'It's all leading up to an unspeakable catastrophe,' he said as though he relished with horror the taste of the future. 'The breakdown of everything as we now know it. *Das Ende!*'

When they got to the harbour, the quayside seemed deserted of all but some unemployed, a few merchant seamen and strollers and a few men busy carrying packages and on errands. There were no tourists and no advertisements for trips round the harbour. For some time they walked rather aimlessly along the quayside, Paul experiencing that sense of emptiness, the every-day despair of being with guests specially arrived for a purpose he had failed to satisfy. Otto looked sullen and William looked as though he was on the point of returning to Berlin. Then Paul saw approaching them a man whose face he seemed vaguely to recognize from three years back. Suddenly he remembered who it was: the Mussolini-jawed owner of The Fochsel, the bar where he had gone with Ernst, Joachim and Willy the first night he ever visited Sankt Pauli. He remembered the crowded bar with its grotesque objects: the great bats nailed like escutcheons to the walls, the stuffed alligator, the fence of dried pampas grass at the end of the bar. He remembered being struck by the complete indifference of this old rogue to the laughter which the objects with which he had surrounded himself provoked. The publican now strolled, with his rolling gait, to the quay's edge and stared down proprietorially at a motor launch which was tied to rusted concrete steps leading down to the water.

'Is that yours?' asked Paul.

The publican, crossing his arms in front of his chest, stared silently at Paul, without a flicker of recognition.

'Is that yours?' Paul asked the Old Salt again.

The tavern-keeper growled in the affirmative.

William Bradshaw, who had come forward, asked with exag-gerated politeness, easier for him in German than in English, whether for a consideration the gracious gentleman would con-sent to take the little group of two English students and their young German friend who had come from Berlin where he himself was living – for a *Rundfahrt* of the harbour on his so exceptionally beautiful ship.

'*Nein. Das will ich nicht,*' said the tavern-keeper.

But perhaps the kind gentleman had been acquainted in time long past with the father of this young German friend (dragging Otto forward at this point) who was accompanying them and who particularly wished a tour of the scene of his father's so important activities as a pilot in Hamburg and Cuxhaven twenty years ago, suggested William.

'*Nein.*'

William produced a bank note for 50 marks and held it up in his hand.

The tavern-keeper said: 'Wait here for ten minutes.' Then he walked back across the quayside, entered the side door of a small house which Paul recognized as The Fochsel bar and, ten minutes later, returned with a can of petrol under his arm. Without saying a word to William and Paul, he nodded to Otto who then followed him down the concrete steps, along a plank, and down into the cabin of the launch. There was a swishing sound from the entrails of the launch. Then Otto and the man emerged, Otto carrying with him a glass and a bottle. Meanwhile William and Paul had climbed aboard and walked on deck past the hatch of the cabin to the bows of the ship. There was a roar and the launch moved into the harbour, steered by the tavern-keeper who was standing in the stern of the craft at the tiller. Otto, carrying the bottle and his glass, had disappeared again downstairs into the cabin.

'I suspect that Otto wants to have this experience alone,' said William. 'He's better off without us jabbering at him.' A rusty anchor lay on the yellow painted triangle of deck in front of a winch. As the boat moved off from the quayside into the port William stood facing the sea, a frown on his forehead, his eyes strained, looking into the distance. His profile, with the jutting nose below the eyebrows was like the beak of an albatross suspended in the air a few feet above the deck of a whaler. There was a tension of the lines around his mouth. The ship seemed directed by his will. Paul said, laughing, 'William, you look as if you were steering the ship by pure will-power.'

William laughed. 'If I didn't concentrate my entire will on keeping the ship afloat it would sink to the bottom like a stone INSTANTLY.' He said this in a voice like Wilmot's, isolating the word 'instantly' from the rest. Then he barked out in a voice all his own:

DA
Damyata: The boat responded
Gaily, to the hand expert with sail and oar

'Hmm,' he concluded, then barked out again: 'DA! *Damyata,'* and in deliberately ill-pronounced Italian, *'Poi s'ascose nel foco che gli affina.'* This was followed by, 'Hmm! "The awful daring of a moment's surrender" – what millions of those I've had. Surrender! Don't I know how!'

Although some cranes seemed rusted, the panes in the windows of some buildings broken, some docks deserted, there was much activity in the port. Looking intently at a tanker moving and a ship from Caracas unloading bales at a quayside, William said: 'Well, I see the point of Hamburg. As usual, Wilmot was right.'

'Hamburg can't be as exciting as Berlin, from all you've written to me.'

'Nothing, absolutely nothing else on this earth can compare with the excitement of a great port with all its fixtures – cranes and fuel tanks and dry docks like guns pointed at the sea. "The ports have names for the sea"! Hmm,' he said, looking round him at the objects in question. 'All that equipment! I loved your poem "The Port". The port that spews out and sucks in the ships bursting with cargoes. Like a great hooting, howling, steaming cunt into which the foreign-language spermatozoa from all over the world SHOOT; and an arsehole which expels all its trash and garbage back into the ocean,' he added.

He said words, yelling them out, with the comic exaggeration of his clique consisting of Wilmot, himself and at most two others.

Paul insisted, 'But the Berliners surely are more exciting than the people in Hamburg.'

'People! That's it! Yes, but the people reduce it to their human dimensions, whereas the port is on the scale of – oh, the moon. Hamburg's a place of stony wharves and giant cranes – hmm! Birds of steel! Berlin's an enormous sluice, a drain.' He gave his explosive bark, followed again by, 'Hmm!' He went on: 'Everyone in Berlin is equal, really equal as an individual, not as some kind of social unit or common denominator. There are

Nazi gangs and Communist gangs. But the truth is, no Berliner cares. They're beyond politics, like being beyond good and evil. In Berlin, everyone speaks to everyone else, even if not out loud. But everyone knows everything about everyone else at a glance. Rich and poor, professors and students, intellectuals and bartenders all share a common vulgarity. It all comes down to sex. It is a city with no virgins. Not even the kittens and puppies are virgins. The temple of Berlin where all meet and worship is the boarding house, the priestess is the landlady who knows the dirt about all her lodgers. How true that remark some ancient Greek made – Homer or Aeschylus or Plato or someone – that *Panta rhei*: everything flows. He must have been thinking of Berlin. And Goethe, of course, saw it all. How terrific: *"Und was uns alle bindet, das Gemeine"*. He must have been thinking of Berlin.'

'What does that mean?'

'How the hell should I know what it means? I'm not a professor!' He crowed with laughter, ending again with a 'Hmm!' and flapped his arms against his sides, hugging himself.

'Well, give a rough translation!'

'*Ja!* A very very very rough translation, so rough you will know even less in English what it means than you don't know what it means in German! As I said, I haven't the slightest idea what it means. I'm not a professor! I heard Wilmot say that once and I thought it sounded cute, so I got stuck with it.'

'Well, roughly, very roughly then.'

'Well, all I know is my idea of what it means, which may be entirely false. This is what it means to me: "That's what makes all one – we're all vulgar"!' He pronounced the English words as a parody of the way they sounded when he said them in German. 'Vulgar! Irremediably, irretrievably vulgar! Hmm! Common! Base!'

The boat had returned to the quayside at the place where they had boarded it. They fished up Otto from the cabin. He seemed rather dazed. William said: 'Evidently Otto's had some great illumination here. He doesn't want to tell us about it, and I won't ask. *Le retour à Hamburg* for him. It's like Proust. Recapturing his father's lost days before he was born. From this dead end his new beginning.'

185

They took a taxi to the hotel near the station where William and Otto were staying. William ran up to their room, from which he fetched the opening section of his novel, *The North-West Passage*. He handed it to Paul, who took six poems in typescript from his pocket which he gave to William.

They arranged that Paul should meet William alone in the hotel café at 6.00 p.m. when they would discuss their work. Otto, who required a great deal of rest, would go on sleeping until their supper.

Paul rushed back to his room, buying a sandwich *en route* so as to avoid losing an hour of reading *The North-West Passage* by sitting through the Pension lunch. He lay down on his bed, tore open the envelope which contained the manuscript of the novel and started reading it in ecstasy. William's handwriting was minute, clear as print, though it was not script. It had eyes that spoke to Paul reading it. The narrative was clear as the handwriting. The novel laid bare the inmost behaviour of his Berlin characters, with a cruelly loving scalpel.

Two hours later, sitting in the café, Paul told William how excited he was about *The North-West Passage*. With equal excitement, William praised and criticized lines in Paul's poems. Then they both talked about Wilmot's poetry.

This was the exultation of young writers in sympathy with one another who feel that their work, though separate, meets in expressing the response to life of their generation. Although aware of how much they differed in their writing as in their lives, yet they identified with each other in their ambitions, their failures and their triumphs. Each felt the success of one as intensely as if it were his own. To Paul the poetry of Wilmot, the fiction of Bradshaw, was like his own blood flowing through his veins. The novel he was writing in his head about his life in Hamburg was a letter from him to Wilmot and Bradshaw.

William insisted that they eat at a very inexpensive restaurant near the station. He was going through his austere phase: living as Karl, the character in his novel based on Otto, lived – that is, near starvation: though it is true that the real Otto lived according to the standard that he exacted from William. William chose the cheapest dish on the menu. This was called *Lungensuppe* – lung soup. William had a further motive for this diet: to demonstrate to Otto that he was denying himself through silent example – a kind of dumb crambo – proper sustenance in order to sacrificially pay for the suit and the shoes. The next demand from Otto, his behaviour indicated, would mean, for William, death. Otto, who ordered *Schweinkotelette*, seemed impervious to this kind of theatre. Partly to sustain him and partly to draw Otto's attention to William's plight by underlining it, Paul pressed upon William half the portion of conger eel which he himself had ordered. William, with a look of Christ on the cross, refused, saying, *'Was ich gegessen habe, habe ich gegessen.'* He could act funny and tragic at the same moment.

After this appalling meal, they went to The Three Stars *Lokal* where Paul had arranged that they meet Joachim and Ernst, whom they found already seated there. Joachim shook William's hand warmly: 'I am very glad to meet you. Paul has told me so much about you.' When he took Otto's outstretched hand, he stared at Otto with unconcealed amazement, taking in the pointed brilliance of the suit and shoes. William froze. Ernst, following the unobtrusive style of manners which he had acquired at Cambridge, did not shake hands with anyone, but smiled demurely at William and Otto. As a compliment to William, he was wearing his Downing College blazer.

William looked round the chapel-like hall filled with bourgeois citizens of both sexes seated at many tables, and with its orchestra one end and its long bar and bar stools the other, with displeasure. There was a silence, during which William stared unresponsively across the room at a blank wall, without meeting the eyes of anyone at their table. Then Ernst said to William: 'I understand that you studied at Cambridge. I wonder whether the dates of our being at the Varsity coincided?'

'When were you at Cambridge, Herr Doktor Stockmann?' William asked with a politeness like the thinnest trickle of water over a glacier.

'Well, I am afraid I was only there for one year – in 1927, after I had completed my studies at Heidelberg.'

'Oh, 1927. That was the year I was sent down from Cambridge. I am afraid it is most improbable that our paths crossed.'

'You were sent down? Surely that must have been the result of some misunderstanding?'

'Not at all, it was the perfectly logical consequence of the most conscious provocation on my part.'

'It must have been some undergraduate lark, some practical joke? Sometimes they laughed at me in a not altogether kind way, I found. So I can sympathize with you.'

'Well, I suppose you might call it a joke.'

Ernst was so disconcerted that in the next sentence his English faltered, he fell into German usage, *Wenn ich fragen darf*: 'What was it, if I may be so bold as to ask?'

'I wrote the History Paper in the first part of my Tripos in limericks.'

Ernst sat up bright-eyed, the collector in him revived: 'How very, very interesting! What has happened to the original manuscript? Is it obtainable?'

'I am told that it is in the "Forbidden, Only for Research Specialist" book section of the University Library, together with a lock of my hair.'

There was a silence. Then, with ever greater politeness, William asked: 'And you yourself, Herr Doktor Stockmann – how did you like the University *wenn ich fragen darf* – if I may presume to ask?'

'The happiest year of my life was at Downing College.'

'Well, I really do congratulate you. Perhaps if you had stayed more than a year, you might have felt differently. It was certainly the most unspeakably miserable in mine.'

Ernst sat very upright, very solemn and very pale.

Joachim had been an onlooker during this exchange, delighted with its progress. Now he said, 'Well, I myself loathed all the institutions to which I was sent to be educated. Most of all the University. I HATED all those students fighting duels and getting scars on their faces to prove to themselves that they were men.'

William instantly forgave Joachim for the sceptical manner in which he had regarded Otto's suit. 'Have you enjoyed your life since you left the University?'

'Well, I do not very much like my work as a merchant of coffee. But I enjoy most other things, especially things we do in Hamburg during the summer. And I enjoy Sankt Pauli and The Three Stars where we are now. How does this compare with bars where you go to, in Berlin?'

'It all seems on so much grander a scale than the bars which I go to in Berlin. They are quite small places really, and very casual. This seems rather like a beer hall to which a lot of people go from all over the place. Without putting too fine an edge on the matter, where are the boys?'

'The boys?' laughed Joachim, his eyes widening. 'Well, I think they are everywhere, if you will look. There are some over there standing round the bar at the end of the room.'

'I think you know one of them,' said Ernst to Paul, as a young man wearing a new dark blue jersey entered the far end of the room. 'Isn't that Lothar?'

Lothar joined the group of sailors and other young men at the bar. He did not appear to have seen Paul. 'I am furious,' said Paul.

'Why are you furious, Paul?' Joachim asked, teasing. 'I have never seen you angry before. It is not like you to be angry, Paul.'

'Well, isn't that Lothar standing over there? Yesterday, I took him to the station, bought him a ticket to go to Stuttgart, and put him on the train.'

'Are you sure the train left the station, Paul? Are you absolutely certain, Paul?' Joachim asked, still teasing.

'Yes, I saw it do so, with him in it.'

'Well, there's another stop for passengers from Hamburg a bit further down the line. Perhaps he got out there,' said Ernst, who had his own reasons for being sore with Lothar. 'A week ago, I also gave Lothar his fare to Stuttgart.'

'Why always Stuttgart?' asked Joachim. 'Doesn't he know the names of any other German towns? Perhaps we should give him a map of Germany.'

'Tell me, which one is Lothar?' William asked Paul, avoiding Otto's eye. Paul pointed him out. 'Stuttgart or no Stuttgart, ticket or no ticket, he looks the starriest of the whole galaxy. He's where the lights go on,' declared William.

Paul felt exhilarated at William's approval of Lothar.

Ernst said primly: 'I must admit that I am a little disappointed with Lothar. Three years ago when we first met him here (I have only seen him twice since then), I thought he was particularly nice. I would not have suspected him of being dishonest, if only in a small way.'

Meanwhile, William was translating the conversation into German for Otto. Otto, who had been rather somnolent, now woke up with a start. '*Unerhört*,' he exclaimed in a loud voice that reached as far as Lothar. 'Shameless! What a swindler! What a swine! And with someone so nice as Paul, a first-class fellow.' He put on his hat, squared his shoulders, glared in the direction of Lothar and started to get up from the table.

William said: 'Otto always gets like this if he feels that some friend of mine has been cheated, or even slighted. He has taken a great liking to you, Paul.' Then in rapid German, he pointed out to Otto that, if he attacked Lothar, he would be taken as champion of Berlin youth by all those standing round the bar, and as challenging Hamburg. Grumbling loudly, Otto sat down again.

Joachim put his arm round Paul and said affectionately: 'Paul would believe any story anyone told him. In fact, it is all your fault, Paul. You lay Lothar open to temptation, so he should not be blamed for taking advantage of you.'

'I do not agree,' said Ernst.

William who, without ever having spoken to him, found Lothar, seen from a distance, attractive said: 'Well, I don't agree that Paul has been cheated. After all, quite apart from the fact that one day Lothar probably really will go to Stuttgart, his saying he will go there is only a polite formula, like characters in a Chekhov play saying they will go to Moscow. It's only his abject admiration for the landed gentry that prevents Chekhov admitting that the girls in *Three Sisters* are always trying to borrow the fares for a ticket to Moscow from their brother.'

Joachim said: 'Lothar gives all the money he borrows to whores. I happen to know that.'

'Well, what could be more chivalrous? He does not spend it on himself. He gives it to the ladies. After all, I myself am financially dependent on my uncle William, whose boring first name my mother christened me with in order to suck up to him so that I might inherit. Uncle William is as skinflint as a weasel. So I am always in the position of having to write to him asking for what might be called the fare to Stuttgart. Come to think of it, if I wrote to him to say that I needed money in order to pay Lothar his fare to Stuttgart my uncle William might receive that

190

request quite sympathetically. It would be less boring to him and to me than having to pretend to us both that my landlady's put up the rent,' he said, glancing at Otto's new suit. 'Excuses like "my rail ticket to Stuttgart" are really formulas of *politesse* and only show that Lothar doesn't want to make gross and obvious demands on Paul. They show that Lothar loves Paul.' He was drunk.

Paul, who had also drunk a good deal, felt so moved by this speech that he went over to Lothar and shook him warmly by the hand. Lothar simply said, '*Gruss*,' without offering any explanation for his presence in Hamburg. But after all, it was none of Paul's business.

Paul said: 'I am with friends. We can't talk here. Come to the Pension Alster in two hours' time, as you did when I photographed you.' He produced the money for a taxi.

'No.'

'Why not?'

'You don't trust me.' Lothar handed back the taxi fare to Paul. 'I don't want to take any money from you.'

'You have to take a taxi to get there. Please take it.'

'I'll only come to the Pension Alster on one condition.'

'What is it?'

'That you don't ever again give me any money for anything.'

'This isn't giving you money, it's for your expenses. I'll agree then, only to pay your expenses – fares and things like that.'

Lothar pocketed the taxi fare and said, '*Einverstanden.* Agreed.' He shook Paul's hand, sealing the bargain. 'We meet at the Pension Alster two hours from now.'

When Paul let Lothar out of the street door off the Pension at 1.00 a.m., he felt mysteriously thrilled that he had persuaded Lothar, after much argument, to accept 20 marks as expenses.

Next morning, Paul rose early and went to the station hotel where William and Otto were staying, to have a farewell breakfast and then put them on the Berlin train. He found William already in the dining-room sitting at a bare greasy table on which there was rusty cutlery, china mugs and plates. The coffee was terrible, the rolls stale and the jam a thin blood-red liquid. William sat there like the figure of a Saint in the Desert in a Flemish painting, surrounded by the knife, the nails, the rods – all the accoutrements of his martyrdom. He played it as comedy. Unfortunately, Otto was not there to take in the drama of the sacrifices made by William for his suit, for he was snoring in bed.

'Take this cup from me!' said William, pressing his lips to the rim of the mug, taking one sip of the bitter coffee and pushing it disgustedly aside. And then with a glance at the stale rolls, he added: 'Unthinkable, uneatable, indescribable.' He cut a roll in half, covered the halves with jam, and with the sombrely enacted air of one eating the bread of the Man of Sorrow said in a lively voice between munches: 'I was thinking all night about your coming to Berlin. I see it all now very clearly! I am sure you agree that we should not be on top of one another, yet be close enough to meet whenever we want. I intend to leave the Hallesches Tor fairly soon, as Otto's mother does not seem altogether to approve of my relationship with her son – not that she really cares a damn. It's just her formula for putting up the rent. My idea is to take a room near the West End of Berlin. I know of a pension on the Nollendorfplatz with a marvellous storm-free landlady. After that, we could find you a bedsitter in a street nearby.

'If we arrange this, each of us can work separately all the morning, then have lunch together in my pension, and after lunch take a train to the Grünewald and go for a walk there, talking about the work we'd shown each other the previous day. In the evenings we could either go our separate ways or be together. If together, we could eat in an Aschinger restaurant – which corresponds to a Lyons Corner House – and then go to the movies or the theatre. There are terrific Russian movies by the producers of films like *Ten Days That Shook The World*, *Potemkin*, *Earth*, *Mother*, *Menschenarsenal*, *Turksib*. There are also marvellous German movies by directors such as Pabst. *M* is hair-raising and *Kameradschaft* stupendous. Apart from movies there is the theatre. As you know, I don't care much for concerts (I don't like the rapt expressions on the faces of German music-lovers) so you'll probably have to go to them yourself, if you want to, and the same applies to art galleries, but my friends tell me they are terrific – ancient, middling and modern – the whole shoot! Then in the Kurfürstendamm, there is a bookshop you'd love – Wittenborn's. And there are cafés where you can sit and write if you got bored with working in your room.'

William poured out before Paul's eyes the envisioned cornucopia of Berlin. It made his Hamburg life seem to dwindle into the past as they sat there talking in the squalid dining-room.

'I've promised Joachim that I'd see him at his studio this day week.'

'Naturally,' said William, in a voice with a distinct chill in it. 'I absolutely see the magnetism of Joachim and that you can't let him down. He is most remarkable and I very much want to see his photographs. I didn't appreciate the extraordinary merit of Dr Stockmann, though.'

'Oh, I won't be seeing Ernst – not ever again I hope.'

'What about Lothar, then?'

'Oh, Lothar! Well, he really will go to Stuttgart some day. Or maybe he'll discover in a week's time that I have my Stuttgart too – and it's called Berlin.'

'You see, Paul, what I feel is that although I greatly prefer Berlin to London, and although, of course, I am utterly and finally committed to Otto, and although I have some very intelligent friends in Berlin, what I lack there and what I tremendously need is a friend who is a colleague, a fellow writer, writing in the same language.'

'That's exactly what I need too. I'll come to Berlin in a week or ten days. I'll send you a telegram.'

'Bear in mind though,' said William as they parted, 'Otto and I will definitely be going to London for Christmas so that I may introduce Otto to my mother.'

A week later, the night before he was to leave for Berlin, Paul rang the doorbell of Joachim's studio. After what seemed an unusually long time, Joachim opened the door. The first thing Paul noticed was the large patch of plaster on his left cheek.

'What has happened, Joachim?'

The door was not fully open.

'Oh, that!' Joachim touched the plaster with his finger: 'Just a little cut. My farewell present from a friend of Heinrich.' The plaster was at least two inches wide.

Joachim opened the door to its full extent, entered the little foyer, a platform beyond which three steps led down into the main body of the studio. He leaned against the wall, surveying the damage spread before them.

The studio, lit only by four light bulbs from which the enclosing covers of white glass cubes had been torn, looked like the wreck of the interior of a ship, deeply quiet on the sea floor under stormy waves of a dark day.

Paul stood without going down into the studio: 'What has happened? Why didn't you let me know, Joachim?'

Joachim walked into the studio. He said: 'It happened two days ago. I didn't ring you because I guess I thought you would see what had happened well enough when you got here without my having to talk about it on the telephone. Besides, I thought if I told you all that perhaps you would not want to come and have supper with me. My studio is not so nice as it was three years ago. Also I am beginning to think that now in Germany maybe one should be careful what one tells on the telephone. Things are changing today in Germany, as you may have noticed.'

The four lamps in which there were bulbs were the only ones of which the sockets had not been ripped out. Wires hung down from walls and ceiling. The mattresses of the tubular metal chairs had been bent and twisted. Some books had been placed on top of the exposed coiled springs of the divan. Several had their covers ripped off.

'It would have all looked much worse if you'd come yesterday. The books were scattered all over the room, some of them trampled on. Very kindly, Willy came this morning and tidied up for me. His *Braut*, Gertrud, offered to come and help, too. But I thought that would make her very very content so I said no.'

In the centre of the studio a table and two chairs either side of it had been put out. There were bottles of wine, glasses, plates of bread and ham, rollmops and Westphalian cheese.

Joachim walked over to the table. 'I think we need this,' pouring out for them each a glass of wine. 'I got Rhine wine as a souvenir of our walk along the Rhine three years ago.'

'When we first saw Heinrich?'

'When we first saw Heinrich!'

'You still haven't told me. Are you badly hurt?'

He touched the plaster again with his finger: 'No, not badly. I guess that for the rest of my life I'll have one of those scars that duelling students have, that I was telling your friend Bradshaw about the other night when we were at The Three Stars. I said how I HATED them. People will think I got it in a duel when I was at Marburg University. I think it will make a very good impression on my uncle General Lenz.'

'You still haven't said what happened.'

Joachim spread out his hands and looked round the room, with something of a showman's smile: 'Can't you see what happened? Do you have to be told? Heinrich said goodbye, that's what happened. He's left for good, I guess. He could hardly come back and make friends with me again in all this mess. Or perhaps he could. You never quite know with Heinrich.'

'Did he do this?'

'I think we had better eat now. Sit down, and I will tell you everything.'

He refilled their glasses and cut some bread. They started eating rollmops. Lifting their glasses to each other they said: 'Prosit!'

'Do you remember me telling you when we had lunch at the vegetarian restaurant that I expected Heinrich would take his things away from here on that night because he knew I was having dinner with my mother then and since he would not wish to do so when I was here, as he would want to avoid having to say goodbye to me?'

'Yes, I do remember.'

'Well, I was wrong. He did come here that night when I was away, using his key to the studio, but he did not take his things. I know he must have come because he saw what I had done to his beautiful storm-trooper uniform.'

'That you had spat all over it?'

'Exactly. He must have seen the uniform. Without telling me he had done so. Next day he telephoned and said, in a very friendly way, that he would like to come and fetch his things on a night when I would be there, so that we would be saying goodbye to each other. He also said that a friend of his called Horst would be coming a bit later – after we had finished saying goodbye – in order to help him carry his things which were too burdensome for him to carry alone. He said he particularly wanted us to say goodbye to each other alone before Horst arrived. That is all he said.

'I told Heinrich that I would meet him at the studio at ten. I said that if he arrived before I did he could let himself in with his key, before giving it back to me when he finally left to go to Altamunde and stay with Erich Hanussen – for good, I guess.

'When I got to the studio about half an hour after then, he had already arrived, which surprised me, as I took it for granted he would be late, for he was always even later than I always am when you and I meet. When I arrived he was very angry, accusing me of being late, though we'd fixed no definite time for my being here. He said he was upset because he had been wanting to say goodbye to me alone, and how he was afraid that Horst might appear and prevent us saying goodbye. It was really quite mad considering what he had arranged with Horst for them to do when he arrived. Perhaps he still had some feeling of fondness for me, perhaps he was ashamed of what they had planned. I do not know. Anyway he wished for a touching farewell scene.'

'Did you have time to say goodbye then?'

'The first thing I said to him when he had got over being angry was, "Whatever happens in the future I shall never forget that first evening when we met at Bingen on our walk on the Rhine."'

'What did he say to that?'

'He took it as though I was accusing him of something.'

'Of what? Ingratitude perhaps?'

'How should I know? He said I was being sentimental. He started haranguing me in that way he has been learning from Hanussen. He said I had always tried to avoid facing reality. He said Hanussen said I was an "escapist" – one of those words he'd learned from his new friend.'

'What did you say?'

'Well, I said I realized that we were separating now but that this made the past very present to me because I was being quite realistic in adding up the happy times in our relationship, which would go on existing into the future and in trying to forget the later unhappy ones.'

'Nothing could be truer than that. How did he take it?'

'He was so hysterical, he didn't make sense really. He said that I was the one who had decided that we must part, and that he hadn't come here thinking this was the last time we would meet. It was typical of me, he said, that I should have made this decision for him and pretended it was his decision. He even started talking about plans we had made for the future. He said we had planned to visit you in London.'

'Well, we did talk about that at Boppard before we said good-bye but I never imagined that it was serious, though.'

'He said that I had promised to take him to Venice and to Africa. The craziest thing of all was that, after a few drinks, he started talking as though we might go out to a bar or to see friends that very evening. He looked out of the window and complained about the weather. "We shall never be able to get a taxi," he said.'

'Probably there's a side of him that doesn't want to leave you. After all, he had a much easier life with you than he will have with Hanussen.'

'Most of the time, of course, he was complaining about how I'd ruined his life. He said Hanussen had told him that, until he was ruined by me, he was an innocent, healthy, young only-beer-drinking Bavarian. Then I'd met him and perverted him, prevented him from developing normally, made him spend too much money, so that he had none to send to his mother. I'd taught him to drink wine and spirits and raised his standards of living above those of his class. He said a lot about belonging to his class: how he was a simple peasant, and proud of it, though I'd probably corrupted him so that he would never be able to return to his innocent state before he met me. At the same time he boasted that now he had become a respectable citizen he intended to marry one of Hanussen's daughters – Helmgrin or Grinhelm – called after Wagner's Valkyries, of course.'

They went on drinking the Rhine wine. Paul said: 'But I don't altogether follow. Was it Heinrich's idea that Horst, his friend who was going to help with carrying the luggage, would go out on the town when he arrived, with the two of you?'

'Horst? The friend? Impossible! You should have seen him. Heinrich had probably forgotten all about Horst coming when he said those crazy things.' He got up from the table and walked to

197

the door. Then, turning back and taking in with his glance the whole room, he said: 'The friend wasn't the kind of person you'd take out to a bar or night club and have a good time with.'

'What was he like then?'

'Oh, he was WONDERFUL! He was like a dark angel of destruction. Look around this room and you will see what he was like.' Joachim was standing on the little platform of the studio entrance. He raised his arm in half parody of the Nazi salute. He looked all round him, his eyes glowing – a producer, a showman.

'You mean, he smashed up all this?'

'Yes. This is what I have to tell you about. While Heinrich and I were talking, the door bell rang. I got up to open the door, but Heinrich had already opened it before I could. Whoever was there seemed in an enormous hurry to get past the doorway, as though he thought I might slam the door in his face, to keep him out, I suppose. Before I could see who he was, he was standing in the middle of the studio.' Joachim walked to the middle of the room and stood where Horst had stood that night. 'Just where I am now.'

'What was he like?'

'WONDERFUL!' he said again. His eyes were open very wide as though he could see Horst standing in front of him.

'He was dressed in black leather and he had black hair and a very pale complexion, like ivory. He looked like a pen drawing of a knight in armour, done by Dürer. When he came into the studio he said nothing to his friend Heinrich at first, did not seem to look at him even. Then he said "*Heil!*" to him, and they lifted their arms to each other in the Nazi salute. Imagine that happening in my studio! Even at the time I could not help thinking it terribly FUNNY when I remembered the beautiful parties and people I had here. Then he marched very stiffly up to Heinrich, and said: "Fetch the damaged uniform!" Heinrich ran to the alcove cupboard where he kept his clothes and produced the uniform which I had spat on. Of course, they could not see what had happened to it except that it looked rather soiled. Heinrich had really only guessed what I had done to it, he did not know. Perhaps it was slimy in one or two places, as though a snail had walked over it. I could not see. I do hope so. This was the first time Horst appeared to have noticed me. He turned his head, in a single military parade movement, and glared in my direction, but without any expression in his eyes really. It was as though he looked at me but did not actually see anything. Then he shouted in an official impersonal voice as though I was a crowd or rather, perhaps an abstraction, a concept – "You are charged with PARTEIUNIFORMSCHÄN-DUNG!" I thought what a wonderful language German is, for someone to be able to say a word like that.'

'Bringing disgrace on the Party uniform. I suppose it is an offence. How did you respond to the charge?'

'I didn't answer at all at first. I could not think of what to answer. Perhaps I was too busy looking at Horst. His uniform was too black to look like any Nazi uniform I had seen. It went with his hair and eyes and the little straight moustache as though he had it specially designed by himself to match them. Also I kept on wondering whether I was attracted by Horst, and whether now that Heinrich had gone, it would not be fascinating to get to know him. Anyway, it would be an amusing vengeance on Heinrich. Heinrich had brought the soiled uniform to Horst and was holding it under his nose as though it was some obscenely desecrated altar cloth. Horst looked down at it and then, looking ferociously at me, asked: "Did you do this?"

'It occurred to me that Horst had no authority to ask me courtroom questions, and I should not answer them. After all, I was not even certain that he and Heinrich were members of the Nazi Party. They might be just acting a role that they had invented for themselves or that mad fanatic Hanussen had invented for them. Horst might simply be a lunatic dressed up in a uniform which he had designed for himself. I thought perhaps I ought to ask to see their Party cards. Then I also thought – even if they had real Party cards, they still had no authority. The Nazis are not the government or the police – not quite yet. I said: "I do not choose to answer your questions. Leave my premises, or I shall call the police."

'Now Heinrich said something for the first time since Horst had arrived. He said: "It is my uniform which you have desecrated, and I have the right to an answer."

'Well, I did think that perhaps Heinrich was entitled to know why I had desecrated his beautiful uniform. I said to him, trying to make clear as I did so that I was answering HIM and not answering Horst: "That uniform is obscene and evil. If you do not remove it from here, I shall destroy it."

'Horst took my answer as being addressed to him, the representative of "The Party". He said: "Since you have desecrated the Party uniform, now we shall desecrate your studio." He rushed to the kitchen and took a hammer out of a drawer and he gave Heinrich a clasp knife – perhaps the same one you gave him as a farewell present once. Then Horst rushed around like a dervish, smashing the glass of all the lamps in this studio and the mirror in the bathroom and the bookshelves. Then he started wrenching the chairs out of shape. He must be WONDERFULLY strong. He shouted obscenities about decadent Jewish art. Heinrich followed him round, using his knife to slash the covers of the bed and divan. But he did not shout very much. In fact, I thought how quiet he was being. Finally he threw himself down on a rug and started whimpering like an animal.'

'What were you thinking all this time?'

'I did not think anything really. That is what was so funny. Well, perhaps at first I just watched them like watching a play or making a movie. I felt removed from it all. I did not think, "Those are my things they are destroying." I had almost no feeling that these were my things they were destroying,' he repeated. 'I only felt relieved that I happen to have taken my photographs to my room in my parents' house a few days ago so they could not destroy them. Those beautiful photographs of Heinrich I took on the Rhine! What changed everything was that when Heinrich collapsed on the floor, Horst took up the knife that he had, and started slashing at the books, ripping off the covers, slashing at the pages and tearing out illustrations. Until then all my possessions seemed like stage properties in a film I have to make one day. I had no sense that these things belonged to me until Horst attacked the books. And even then at first I only felt indignant because Horst seemed a vandal out of some terrible past time, destroying Literature – I was surprised how much I cared about Literature, but I still didn't think, "Those are my books". It was only when he started carving up with his knife a wonderful edition of Grimms' *Fairy Tales* which had very beautiful old woodcuts as illustrations, and which I had read as a child and even now read sometimes when I come home late at night after a party, and take it down from the bookshelf – that I had the feeling that he was MURDERING my soul. Until then I had simply been watching him. But now I ran across the room and tore the book out of his hands. I didn't feel the least bit afraid, in fact I felt as though I had tremendous power and could do anything my mind or, rather, my anger, willed me to do. I did manage to get the book out of his hands – there it is, on the divan, with only the cover torn off and the woodcuts not damaged.'

'What did he do then?'

'He went for my face with the blade of the clasp knife.'

'Well, you must have been terrified then!'

'I was still not being frightened like I had been a little bit when I was just passively watching him destroy my things. When he attacked me with the knife blade I was more curious than frightened. I was interested like a scientist, a surgeon doing an operation, though the surgeon was my murderer and the operation was on my face. I was very curious – hypnotized with wonder – waiting to see what would happen.'

'After he'd slashed your face, did he go on attacking you? How did you manage to stop him?'

'As a matter of fact,' said Joachim slowly, 'Heinrich stopped him. If it hadn't been for Heinrich he might have gone on slashing at me. So you might say that Heinrich saved my life, though I don't really love him any the better for that.'

'How did he save your life?'

'I really didn't notice him doing anything except crouching on the floor and whimpering. My attention was all on Horst. But when Heinrich saw blood streaming down my face, he got up from the floor. He was terrified. He didn't shout. All he did was to say in a very frightened whisper, "Horst, stop!" And Horst did stop. It was absurd and MARVELLOUS!'

'And then?'

'They both seemed to remember what they'd come for. They went to Heinrich's alcove and fetched his suitcases, full of my things I expect. I haven't bothered to look yet. They went out of the door like burglars, dragging sacks of loot. Heinrich was carrying the uniform, which of course he hadn't packed – because he needed it as "evidence" – over his shoulder. Then, as he went past me, he suddenly seemed to want to get rid of it – I suppose because it had been ruined for him and was disgusting – for which I was responsible. Anyway, he THREW it at me, at the blood pouring from my face, which discoloured it even more than it was slimed already. It wasn't a very friendly thing to do, right after he'd saved my life. Perhaps it showed he didn't wish to save my life.'

'Did he say anything when he threw it at you?'

'Yes, I've been wondering about what he said ever since.'

'What did he say?'

'He said one word – "SHIT".'

'And did you say anything to that?'

For the first time that evening, Joachim really laughed. 'I was wondering whether he was thinking I had shat over his beautiful uniform, so I answered: "Not shit, SPIT"!'

'Or perhaps he meant you were the shit?' roared Paul.

They both went on laughing. Their laughter was succeeded by a mood that seemed worse than depression: a vision of despair waiting beyond and behind everything – a vision of the world.

'By the way, did you send for the police?'

'No. It was better not to. The police, if they caught up with Heinrich would believe everything Hanussen told him to say against me. The police are Erich Hanussen with legal arms instead of illegal ones.'

'So what did you do?'

'What did I do? Well, I went to my doctor. He is a very good doctor. He is a Jew.'

Then Joachim put his head in his hands and stayed like that for perhaps five minutes. When he took his hands away again, he stared all round the studio, taking in the wreckage. Paul remembered with what pride he used to survey it. 'Well, Paul, I think that the party which began three years ago, when Ernst brought you here that first night in 1929, is over.'

'You can replace all the things that are broken. You can have other parties. You have many friends. After all, Willy, the first friend of yours I met in Hamburg, has just been helping you clear up, as he was helping you clear up after that first party.'

'Haven't I told you Willy is getting married? Besides, as you know, Willy is too nice for me. I think I would find it more interesting to be with, well, Horst. I like to think of his dark world.'

'Willy himself told me he was marrying. His *Braut* is a Nazi. Do you think Willy will become one?'

'No, never. Not in the least. There is nothing of the Nazi about Willy, even if he joins the Party. It is what you are in your own being that counts. The terrible thing is that there are so many people today who are Nazis in their hearts even without belonging as yet to the Party.'

'At any rate another friend of yours, Ernst, will never belong to the Nazi Party.'

'Ernst no longer wishes to speak to me. He is too IMPORTANT. He is up there in the sky' – Joachim raised a hand heavenwards.' He is circling round and round, wondering where to come down to earth. Not in Germany much longer, I think. Perhaps he will land in England. Then you will be able to visit him every day and look at his collection, brought from Hamburg.'

They each drank another glass, after which Joachim said, raising his glass: 'Well, here's to your stay in Berlin to visit your friend William Bradshaw, whom I liked very much. He is so clever, so amusing. I did not like his friend so much.' Then he asked: 'Do you come back to Hamburg? How long do you stay in Berlin?'

'I don't know. William and I want to discuss our work with each other. We plan to meet every day.'

'Oh! – your poetry! Will you be doing that with him for ever?'

'Oh no. William and I will be friends all our lives, that I know. We will not be together always.'

There was a long pause, at the end of which Joachim said: 'Do you remember those long talks about life and poetry and photography and LOVE that you and I had together while Heinrich was sunbathing on the rocks when we were SERIOUS?'

'My memory for facts is very bad, but yes, I remember everything we talked about then.'

'Did you ever wish that it could always be like that? Do you feel that you and I were like two people who will always be alone and who, just because we have that essential loneliness in common, we can talk with one another in a way that we can talk with no one else, however close to us?'

'In the train going back to England, after I'd left you and Heinrich at Boppard, I imagined a conversation between us and our walking together going on for ever.'

'Well, couldn't we step out of that door now, and go to Athens, and Rio de Janeiro (where I was last year representing my father's firm and which I could show you) and Mexico and Peru and every day be talking for an hour or more together?'

'How would we earn our living?'

Joachim saw it all quite seriously: 'I would take better photographs than I have ever taken yet and you would write travel books which my photographs would illustrate.'

'And that would go on for ever? What would happen when we got old?'

'In comparison with what we were when we were young we would, like everyone else, be grotesque when we are old, but we would go on talking and taking photographs and writing. We would be a famous collaboration. Our fame would cancel out our ugliness. Beautiful young people would still make love to us.'

Paul filled himself another glass of Rhine wine, drank it down completely, put down the glass, and said in a different voice: 'By the way, what happened to Irmi?'

'Well, I guess she got married. She has two children. Her husband is a doctor. They live somewhere in the suburbs. They are very, very boring. I never see her now.'

'At Altamunde when I was on that trip with Ernst, I got up early one morning and made love to her on the beach.'

'Oh.' Joachim was not listening.

'I made – never mind. There is someone else I want to ask about – people Ernst and I visited on that absurd trip we took to Altamunde – Castor and Lisa Alerich I think they were called.'

'Oh, he left her, after they had a baby. He could not bear to be a father. He is a terrible fellow anyway and probably very soon he will be planning our lives as Gauleiter of this district.'

'I only saw Lisa when she was standing on a balcony, looking down at a bonfire which Castor had made Ernst and me build in the garden. It was very beautiful.'

'The bonfire?' He was tired.

'Lisa standing on a balcony and looking down at the sparks drifting all round her. She was pregnant.'

'All my friends will change,' said Joachim, drinking more wine. He held up his glass, swaying as he had done, addressing his friends, one night three years ago at The Three Stars in Sankt Pauli. 'But I will stay the same. I will always be alone because the people I like, people like Horst (I am afraid I am going to hunt for Horst), are not people I can talk with. But I no longer want to be a coffee merchant. I no longer want to live in this studio and give parties to Heinrich's, or Horst's, lovers. I no longer want to live in this city and this country. I know now what I will do. I will go to Potsdam and visit my uncle.'

'The fire-breathing dragon, General Lenz?'

'He is the one person I am certain really hates what is going on now. He hates the Nazis. I shall take my photographs with me. I shall please him and I shall ask him to use his influence so that I may become a photographer attached to the German army. I do not want to be an artistic photographer in a city taking artistic photographs for artistic magazines. I shall photograph the soldiers on manoeuvres, in their tanks and carrying machine guns: and, sometimes, swimming naked in lakes or the sea or rivers. I think my uncle will be glad to see my photographs. I think I shall travel a lot. I have a strong conviction just now that the German army will do a lot of travelling to a great many foreign places in the next few years. But, then, I am TERRIBLY drunk, drunker than I have ever been before in my life. So are you, Paul. You are TERRIBLY drunk also.'

1929–1931
1986–1987

205

EPILOGUE

In 1929

I

A whim of Time, the general arbiter,
Proclaims the love, instead of death, of friends.
Under the domed sky and athletic sun
Three stand naked: the new, bronzed German
The Communist clerk, and myself, being English.

Yet to unwind the travelled sphere twelve years
Then two take arms, spring to a soldier's posture:
Or else roll on the thing a further ten,
The third – this clerk with world-offended eyes –
Builds with red hands his heaven: makes our bones
The necessary scaffolding to peace.

II

Now, I suppose, the once-envious dead
Have learned a strict philosophy of clay
After long centuries, to haunt us no longer
In the churchyard or at the end of the lane
Or howling at the edge of the city
Beyond the last bean rows, near the new factory.

Our fathers killed. And yet there lives no feud
Like Hamlet's, prompted on the castle stair:
There falls no shadow on our blank of peace,
We three together, struck across our path,
No warning finger threatening each alone.

III

Our fathers' misery, their spirits' mystery,
The cynic's cruelty, weave this philosophy:
That the history of man, traced purely from dust,
Is lipping skulls on the revolving rim
Or war, us three each other's murderers –

Lives, risen a moment, joined or separate,
Fall heavily, then are ever separate,
Sod lifted, turned, slapped back again with spade.